THE NIGHTMARE COLLECTOR

David Berardelli

THE NIGHTMARE COLLECTOR

GRAVESTONE PRESS

PART ONE
"THE PACT"

CHAPTER ONE

The darkness of the night covered the city in heavy bleakness.

Dressed in his lightweight tan windbreaker, frayed jeans and tennis shoes, Aaron Grill passed the shattered streetlamp and used the soft orange glow from the lamp at the end of the next block as his guide.

Darkness no longer bothered him. It had become his constant companion. He'd spent the last twelve months of his existence alone in his two-room apartment, the blinds closed in both windows, the curtains pulled. He kept the TV on constantly, but with the sound muted. He kept it on to remind himself that life went on elsewhere. However, the mute button did its job to keep things quiet and mellow.

Although the haze from the lamp farther down the street guided him, he knew exactly where he was going. Frank's Liquors sat halfway down the next block. He'd run out of bourbon and needed a bottle or two to get him through the weekend. Bourbon had become his best friend. Along with the comforting darkness, bourbon was the only thing he cared about nowadays. It warmed him and kept the demons at arm's length. And when he'd consumed enough, he simply fell into the deep stupor that had been his only refuge for the last year. It permitted the darkness to settle over him but also prevented him from dreaming. This was good. He didn't *want* to dream. When he dreamed, the nightmares came back.

He kept up his pace, his eyes fixed on the haze of the distant streetlamp. He could already distinguish the familiar faint square orange glow in the middle of the sidewalk made by the reflection of the light coming from inside the liquor store.

His heart sputtered when he saw it. The light meant the store was open. He already knew it was open; he'd committed their hours to memory long ago. But the square orange light made him rejoice anyway.

If the light coming from the local liquor store makes your heart do the happy dance, your life must really and truly suck...

He didn't want to think of that right now. Getting philosophical at this point in his life made him nauseous.

Just as he stepped down from the curb, he heard hysterical yelling. The alley directly to his left was too dark to make anything out, but he could tell by the sharp slaps and thumps echoing off the brick walls of the surrounding buildings that a fight was going on.

He'd wanted to keep on walking, but something inside him interfered, preventing him from moving away. Before he'd realized it, he'd stopped cold.

You really don't want to stand here like this...
Frank's, remember? The bourbon?

His inner self tried reasoning with him. He knew damned well that what he was doing was foolish and potentially dangerous, yet he remained standing there, staring into the solid darkness while the sharp slaps, thumps, and grunts of pain jumped off the walls, escaping out into the street.

He couldn't help wondering what was happening—if this was a fight club thing. Or was it some private matter?

A fight over a woman? A money matter gone sour?

Were drugs involved?

This didn't sound like some bare-knuckle, fight-club-type situation. He couldn't hear evidence of a crowd—not even a small one. He heard no voices and no cheers. It was probably a private matter. In today's world, such behavior could most likely be the result of a drug burn or money lost from a bad investment.

Time had stopped. All the while, his inner self continued its frustrated efforts to coax him away. As he listened, he struggled to determine what he should do. Rushing in to help was out of the question. Getting involved would not be very bright. This was a frightening world. Society had progressed by leaps and bounds technologically while people grew colder and more distant toward one another. In this modern civilized world, the killer instinct remained alive and well.

Should he call 911?

Again, he saw no reason to stick his neck out. He had no idea what was going on or who these people were. He didn't know if they were armed or if they were felons. He hadn't heard a gunshot, but that didn't mean much. A gun could be lying on the ground close by. This might be drug-related after all. It would be stupid for him or anyone else to put themselves between two stoners fighting over drugs.

His inner voice finally won its argument. He began moving away.

Just as he took the first step, all sounds of the scuffle stopped. Silence followed. He took another step. In the very next moment, a flurry of heavy footsteps rushed toward him. His heart skipped a beat. He realized right then that he'd stayed there a couple of seconds too long. Nevertheless, he continued moving away.

The footsteps quickly grew louder and closer.

Instinct told him to run, but he knew that would only make the situation worse. Keeping calm might work better. If he acted clueless and nonchalant, he might not be considered a threat.

Before he was able to take another step, the footsteps grew deafening. An instant later, they stopped dangerously close. Something grabbed him by the collar of his jacket and pulled, and he was nearly knocked off his feet. Before he had the chance to regain his footing, he was spun around.

He found himself gazing stupidly at a man's jacket collar. His heart was thumping, and he was shaking, but he somehow found the courage to raise his eyes. The man facing him was about his own age, with thick black hair, cold eyes and a ruggedly handsome face. His cheeks were clean-shaven. Judging by the tie, lapels and cut of the jacket, his clothes were expensive. In other circumstances, such an individual would be considered bright, motivated and successful. But the man's glistening eyes and furious manner revealed a feral spirit emanating from within.

An unpleasant mix of cologne and sweat clung uncomfortably close.

Was it the smell of fear? The killer instinct?

It no longer mattered. The only thing that really mattered was getting away safely.

"What'd you see back there, asshole?" The man's voice was a raspy whisper. Aaron found himself engulfed in the miasma of stale whiskey. He wanted to gag.

The man held on to the collar of Aaron's windbreaker and began shaking him. Aaron gasped as the pins in his knees and hip from his car accident two years earlier ground into his flesh. He gritted his teeth as the jagged waves of fire sliced through him.

"I asked you a fucking question!" The man let go and stood tensely, his clenched fists at his sides.

Once the dizziness subsided and the searing pain in his knees and hip had eased to a low simmer, Aaron found that he was able to focus again. He'd wanted to kick the man in the testicles and finish him off with an elbow to the jaw, but the simmering pain in his old wounds had settled down to an uncomfortable hum and he saw no reason to antagonize them again. Besides, he didn't want to get into a major battle—especially one in which he could not possibly win. This man was at least six-four, obviously very strong, and pumped up with adrenaline from his recent victory. Aaron guessed that the man had probably killed the other man in the alley.

Before he could give this any further thought, he heard himself say, "It was too dark…to see much…"

"You didn't see *anything*!"

Aaron knew better than reply.

"Did you hear me? You didn't see *anything*!"

Another whiskey-soaked haze rubbed his face. Fighting the nausea, Aaron thought once again about kicking the man in the balls and running away.

"Did you hear me?" the man asked.

Aaron wanted to point to the alley to show the man how dark it was but knew that would do no good. This man was much too geared up to listen to logic. Reason simply wouldn't work here.

"Yes…"

The man reached out again. This time, Aaron backed up. He didn't care how big, strong or angry the man was; one assault was more than enough for anyone.

The man took another step and jabbed an index finger into Aaron's chest, forcing him against the building. "Nothing. Get it? You saw *nothing*!"

Gasping, Aaron pulled away and gently massaged his tingling torso.

"*Say* it, asshole…"

Say it and he'll go away and leave you alone…

Once again, his inner voice tried reasoning with him, but he realized it was unnecessary. He'd had enough and decided to walk away.

Before he could turn around, the man grabbed him by the collar again. Aaron tried pulling to the side, but two enormous, bruised fists had grabbed

10

his shirt collar and held him fast. Aaron wrapped his hands around the man's large wrists and tried pulling them away, but the other man had yanked him upward. Aaron no longer felt the sidewalk beneath his feet. He was being shaken again.

Then he was slammed into the building again, this time much harder. A sheet of bright pain danced up his spine. He lashed out, his right shoe connecting with something soft. Gasping, his attacker let go of Aaron's collar. The arms holding him up vanished and Aaron felt the bottoms of his feet slap the sidewalk. A moment later, a huge fist came back out of the darkness and slammed into his midsection. The breath was knocked out of him, and he felt his back smack into the building again. Another sheet of blinding hot pain cracked through him. He caught a glimpse of the black sky and a cluster of twinkling stars. The pain in his gut had become a massive ball of numbness that reached his legs and spread down to his feet. He felt himself falling to the sidewalk. His forehead whacked the concrete.

The blackness enveloping him turned the growing numbness into comforting warmth.

CHAPTER TWO

When Aaron awoke, he discovered that he was lying on a hard rocklike floor in the darkness.

His head hurt, and his legs and back felt as if he'd been run over by a truck. He tried to get up but quickly realized that it hurt much less if he just lay still. He took a deep breath and began coughing. A heavy foulness had drifted into the area and was so strong that it made his eyes water. He wiped them. When his vision cleared, he scanned his surroundings. It was much too dark to see anything, but the darkness, dampness and foulness in the air strongly suggested some sort of cave, or tunnel. The only evidence of light was a faint dimness coming from an oval opening about twenty feet to his right. He wondered if it led to the outside world. It was difficult to tell.

What the hell happened? Where was this place?

More importantly, how did he get here?

The last thing he remembered was the scuffle in the street. Someone grabbed him, picked him up and shook him, and when he'd lashed out and broke loose, his assailant slammed him to the pavement.

Was he dead? If so, what strange, dark place was this?

Was it Heaven? He certainly hoped not. From what he'd learned in Catechism class as a child, as well as from books and the Internet, Heaven's appearance seemed consistent—pearly gates, bright skies, harp music, a large choir, and angels.

This place was dark and musty. There were no pearly gates, no choir and no angels. And that horrible foulness certainly didn't help.

My God...I'm dead, and have gone to Hell...

"Not exactly," a low-pitched female voice said somewhere behind him.

Aaron sat up sharply.

A tall, slender figure approached, carrying a candle. It stopped a few feet from Aaron and placed the candle on a protruding rock. The orange haze enabled him to see that he was indeed in some sort of cavern. The rock floor was uneven and sloped, leading to another tunnel, where the figure had obviously come from.

The figure moved closer. The candlelight revealed a woman in a long white robe, with long, flowing black hair and a beautiful face.

"Who are *you*?" Aaron's first impression was that she was indeed an angel, but her dark, penetrating gaze suggested otherwise.

"A friend."

"Do I know you?"

"Not yet..."

"Then how can you be my friend?"

The woman smiled. "You shall see." Her large, deep-blue eyes sparkled in the candlelight. "Very shortly, Aaron, we're going to be the very *best* of friends."

"H-How do you know my name?"

"I know much about you."

"Am I dead?"

"Not actually."

13

Aaron stiffened. It wasn't the sort of reply he'd wanted to hear. "Care to explain that?"

"Well, you *were* dead for a short while."

"A *short* while?"

"In mortal terms, a few seconds. Here, on the other side, time is measured differently." She took a step closer and tilted her head, and her hair slid down her shoulder. She studied his face and scowled. "That sure is a nasty clunk. That guy really pounded you, didn't he?"

The side of his head thumped the moment she'd mentioned it. He reached up and gently massaged it. He could feel a gash over a noticeable swelling about an inch above his right eyebrow. "Yeah, he wasn't what you'd call a gentle sort of guy." He felt his anger coming back. "You said I was dead for a couple of seconds?"

"In mortal time? Four, maybe five. It was hard to tell exactly, but it wasn't long enough for your spirit to completely leave your body."

"So I'm alive, then?"

"In a manner of speaking..."

He sure didn't like this babe's answers. They were vague and raised more questions. "What other manner *is* there?"

"You haven't actually gone back. Not completely."

"I don't understand."

"Would it help if I showed you what's going on right now?"

"Going on where?"

"The place where you fell into unconsciousness."

14

"You mean where I was *knocked* unconscious?"

"That's the place."

"You're actually gonna take me back?"

"It'll be necessary—if you really want to see what's going on…"

"I think I need to."

"Then we'll go back. Close your eyes."

"Why?"

"Trust me."

"Why should I?"

"If you want to see what's happened, you'll have to."

"This isn't a trick, is it? You're not gonna do something nasty to me when I close my eyes, are you?"

"If I wanted to do something nasty, I would've already done it."

"How do I know you're telling me the truth?"

"Would you really like to see a sample of what I can actually do?"

The flicker of darkness drifting past her eyes made him uneasy, but he knew he had to find out what was going on. "Please…"

She held out her hand, palm up. "Now watch closely."

"I'm watching…"

Long, slithering tongues of flame suddenly appeared from her palm, climbing upward, toward the rock ceiling.

Ignoring his aching back and knees, Aaron backed away.

15

The woman closed her hand. The flames vanished.

His heart fluttered. "H-How the hell...did you *do* that?"

"What you really need to understand is that if I can do something like that, what else can I do? More importantly, what could I have already done to you?"

Aaron didn't reply. His feeling of helplessness had grown by leaps and bounds. He didn't want to anger her, so he nodded.

"All right... *Now* will you let me show you what is going on?"

He nodded once again.

"Now—as I said before—close your eyes."

Aaron closed his eyes.

Something cold touched the top of his head. Darkness filled his mind and he sensed that he was actually flying.

Just a few moments later, she said, "You can now open your eyes."

The darkness cleared, and he discovered that he was standing in the street, staring at a figure lying quite still on the sidewalk. Several people were standing over him but were also not moving. An ambulance sat nearby, its lights on, but not blinking. Two EMT attendants hunkered over the motionless figure and were just as still as the rest of the crowd.

The scene looked like a 3-D photograph.

It took him several seconds to find his voice. "What the hell?"

"Time has stopped for you." The woman stood beside him, watching him.

16

"How can that happen?"

"It happens quite often between worlds."

He stiffened. "Between worlds?"

"There are several, as a matter of fact. Right now, you're stuck between two of them. It's not exactly a pleasant place to be. I highly recommend that you make a decision very shortly."

"And what do *you* have to do with all this?"

"I live in this one."

"What I mean is, what do you have to do with *me*? How did you find me in the first place?"

"I had a strong sense that you'd need me, so I stuck around until it was time to come to your aid."

"My *aid*?"

"You need help. I'm sure you know this already."

He wondered what she meant by that. "You're…gonna *help* me?"

"If you let me…"

"How can you help me?"

"By relieving you of your burden. It is your burden that has brought you here. You can't go back unless you get rid of it."

Her reply confused him and raised more questions. "What burden?"

The woman smiled. "Come now, Aaron. You mean to say you don't want to tell me about it?"

"What do you know about my burden?"

"I know that if you didn't have it, you wouldn't be right here, stuck between life and death. You wouldn't be living where you are now and wouldn't need all that booze to keep you from dreaming. Most of all, you wouldn't have all those nightmares

17

that have been slowly killing you for the last year or so."

Aaron froze. He found that he couldn't speak. This was too weird, too fantastic. This whole thing—his "dying," the cavern, this woman, the flame shooting up from her palm, the street scene... Everything seemed as if it had come out of some weird fantasy tale.

It took him precious moments to find his voice. "What do you know...about my nightmares?"

"As I just said, they're killing you. They're doing it slowly, and if they persist, you'll soon be dead."

"How do you know about this?"

"That's what nightmares do—especially the kind you've been having."

He was growing even more uneasy. This had gone far beyond the weird and was now venturing into the terrifying. "H-how do you *know* about this? About me?"

"I *have* to know. Nightmares are my business."

"Your *business*?"

The woman's eyes shimmered like rare gems. "You see, I collect them."

He wondered if he'd heard her correctly. "You collect *nightmares*?"

"I've been doing it for centuries."

He struggled to understand what was going on. His mind went back to what happened before he'd woken up in the dark, cavern-like tunnel. The scuffle in the alley. The struggle with the big, enraged psycho. Then he realized what had really happened.

I was slammed to the pavement and knocked out. This is a dream—a weird, ridiculous dream…

"Not a dream at all." The woman's expression was solemn. "This is real."

Aaron trembled. "W-Who'd you say you were?"

"I didn't."

"Are you gonna tell me?"

"I have several names. I prefer to be called Jessica."

Jessica. It was a name he'd heard many times before. In fact, he'd known at least two other women by that name in his life. However, this woman was nothing like the others. He strongly suspected that she was not of this world.

Once again, she'd obviously picked up on his thoughts. "I come from many places, and I've met and dealt with many people all over this world."

"I've never heard anything about someone like you."

"I know."

"How could you possibly know that?"

"If you knew about me, you wouldn't wonder how I can help you."

"How *can* you help me?"

"As I just said—I collect nightmares."

"I know what you said. I just don't believe it."

"I realize this sounds bizarre, but why would I say such a thing if I did not actually do it?"

"Why would you want to collect someone's nightmares?"

"People collect all sorts of things. In my travels, I've observed people collecting just about

19

everything. Knives. Guns. Scrimshaw. Doilies. Classic cars. Rare books. Thimbles. Baseball cards. Shoes. Typewriters. Old coins. Exotic pets. I've even come across serial killers who collect body parts, such as fingers, or ears—"

"But *nightmares*?"

"Nightmares are extremely valuable and come in handy when you least expect it. You never know when you'll actually need one to bargain with."

"You're…insane." This made no sense whatsoever.

She chuckled. "Many have said that very same thing…but if you'll consider your situation for a moment, you'll agree that I'm not the one who needs help."

"I'm all right. I just need to get back."

"Are you certain this is what you really want?"

He was getting tired of watching his form lying deathly still on the sidewalk and found the immobile crowd standing around him really creepy. "This place is freaking me out. How do I get out of here?"

She shrugged. "Just close your eyes and think of the last place you were."

"That's all?"

"That's it."

"You could've told me that before, you know…"

"I needed to try and make a deal with you first. It's what I do."

This woman was beautiful, but she was also scary, and that bit about the nightmare-collecting convinced him she was nuts. "Listen. I just want to get out of here. So, if you don't mind..." Aaron closed his eyes.

"Before you leave, just remember one thing."

Aaron opened his eyes. "What's that?"

"When you go back, nothing will have changed. You'll be back to your same miserable existence—sitting in the dark with your TV on and the sound off and drinking bourbon so you won't have to contend with those same nasty nightmares when you fall asleep."

Aaron stiffened. His panic mode jumped several notches. "How the hell do you *know* all that?"

"I do my research."

Aaron shivered as something cold climbed up his spine.

"You have nothing to fear," she said. "I am not a stalker. If you do not wish to deal with me, you'll never see or hear from me again."

Aaron closed his eyes again.

"Just remember what I said. I can relieve you of your nightmares forever."

Aaron opened one eye. "Guaranteed?"

"I guarantee that you will never have another one for the rest of your life."

"Are you saying my life will be different?"

"Very different..."

"Will I be the same person?"

"Your new situation will change in many ways, but yes, you will be the same."

"How can this be?"

"It is very simple. Your nightmares are caused by guilt. Once your guilt is gone, so are your nightmares."

"So what I'm really doing is selling you my guilt?"

"Guilt, nightmares... In your case, they are the same."

"Then all I have to do to make my life tolerable again is to agree to all this?"

"That's all it'll take."

"Then what happens?"

"Your life will immediately change."

"How?"

"That is for you to find out—but only if we close the deal."

Aaron remained staring at her. No more guilt, no more nightmares. It sounded too good to be true. Once again, he considered the fact that this was just a dream. The blow to his head could have been causing these hallucinations.

It suddenly occurred to him that he shouldn't be dreaming at all. He really should be dead.

But what if he wasn't? What if he was in a coma?

"You're not in a coma," she said.

Aaron gasped; she'd done it again. "H-How'd you...how'd you read my mind?"

A slight shrug. "One of my many talents."

"Like the flaming palm trick?"

"I have more tricks up my sleeve than you could ever imagine. But that isn't important right now. All I want to know is that we have a deal."

No nightmares. No guilt. Yes, it really did sound too good to be true. And it probably was.

"Clock's ticking," she said.

"All right, we have a deal. How much are you gonna give me? A thousand bucks? A hundred thousand?"

She smiled. "I don't deal in *money*…"

"Then what are we talking about?"

"Something much better than mere *money*…"

He watched her closely, but her expression told him nothing. "What could possibly be better than money?"

She shook her head. "Why do all mortals think money is the most important thing in life? No, this is something else…something much better than money…something money simply cannot buy."

This was beginning to sound even more unbelievable. "Can't you tell me a little about it?"

"Not yet."

"Why not? If we have a deal—"

"I don't wish to spoil the surprise."

He didn't like the sound of that. He was about to reconsider when she said, "I also guarantee you'll *love* this new arrangement."

"Really and truly?"

"Yes. So then…do we have a deal?"

Aaron sighed. "I guess we do…" He held out his hand.

"No touchy-feely. I've got my own procedure to handle this transaction properly."

"A *procedure*?"

"I'll be in touch."

"When will I expect to see you again?"

23

"Very shortly. Close your eyes, now."

"But—" Aaron was unable to finish his statement. His eyelids had grown heavier, and the darkness enveloped him again.

CHAPTER THREE

"You didn't see your assailant, sir?"

A young woman knelt beside him, gently applying a bandage to his forehead. She had long dark hair tied in a thick ponytail, a boyish face, and wore a blue EMT uniform. She also had large dark eyes, thick dark brows, and extremely long lashes. He caught a whiff of antiseptic drifting over as she applied the bandage.

"What happened?" His head was swimming the moment he opened his eyes. It took him several moments to realize where he was.

"Someone called from a cell phone as they drove by. They said they saw someone getting beaten up." She pressed the ends of the bandage lightly to his skin and finished wrapping the gauze, shoving the rest into a small white box. A small tatt showed on her left wrist, but in spite of the lights coming from the medical unit, he couldn't tell what it was. "The man who did this...did you know him?"

Someone had picked him up and slammed him against the building. He remembered pulling free, but not much else. "I...don't remember."

"You banged your head pretty hard." She applied a slender strip of tape gently to the top of the bandage and pulled away when he winced. "Sorry. Best I can do."

"How long...have I been out?"

"We're not sure. We were in the area, so I estimate no more than four minutes after the call before we found you. You're gonna have to get checked out. You might have a concussion."

"I feel okay now…"

"You need to get checked out whenever you've been unconscious. And since you can't remember much…" She shrugged.

"Maybe I'll see a doctor in the morning."

"The sooner, the better. Can you tell if you have any other injuries?"

He moved around on the cot. His knees, elbows and hip throbbed and his back ached, but everything seemed to work. "I think I'm all right."

She closed her bag and got up. She was fairly tall and extremely slender in her uniform. "Do you live very far from here? Do you need someone to get you a cab?"

"I only live a couple of blocks away."

"If you don't need us any more…"

"Thanks."

She smiled and went back to the van.

A big, burly cop walked over, scribbling busily into his notepad. He glanced briefly at Aaron. "Name?"

"Aaron Grill."

"Age?"

"Thirty-five."

"Address?"

Aaron gave it to him. "As I just told the paramedic babe, I really don't remember much."

The cop stopped scribbling. "Let me do my job if ya don't mind, okay? So what happened?"

"I just said, I don't—"

"I know what ya just said. Tell me something ya *do* remember."

He rubbed his eyes and suddenly remembered a big guy running toward him...but the instant that image flared, everything turned into a murky mix of blackness.

Then, briefly, something else came out of the dark mix: a tall, slender woman with black hair and penetrating blue eyes carrying a flickering candle.

"Sir?" The cop was waiting, his pen poised over his notepad.

A hallucination, obviously. "Everything's kind of...blurry."

The cop slammed the notepad shut and pocketed it. "Better get checked out." He pulled a card from his pocket. "Think of anything, call. Or just c'mon in to the Station. Someone'll take care of ya."

"Sorry. And thanks."

"Just get yourself checked out. And make sure ya call and let us know when it starts coming back. We'll be more than glad to haul this bastard in when we know who he is."

Bourbon. At least he was able to remember *some*thing...

Aaron shuffled unsteadily down the street and slipped into Frank's. The store was empty. He bought two large bottles of Jack Daniels.

Frank took the two bills Aaron slipped onto the counter. He opened the register and glanced at Aaron's bandage. "What happened?"

Aaron smiled sheepishly. "I cut myself shaving." He wanted to get home and didn't want to waste time talking about something he couldn't remember.

"Guess that was a stupid question." Frank dropped the change on the counter. "C'mon back and see us."

Aaron went back to his apartment, locked the door and set the bottles on the kitchen counter. He poured half a glass, plodded into the living room and collapsed on the couch. An old movie was playing—something with Orson Wells. Wells was even more enraged than usual, but it was hard to figure out what he was saying with the sound off. For one moment, Aaron considered turning the volume on. Instead, he sipped some bourbon, sat back and closed his eyes.

Once again, his mind grew hazy.

The big guy who'd attacked him filled the picture screen in his head, but the moment the man's huge, square-knuckled hands reached out to grab him, everything disappeared.

Aaron's eyes shot open; he sat bolt upright.

What the hell was going on? Why couldn't he remember what happened?

You hit your head. Everyone knows that when you hit your head, it does a serious number to your memory.

On the TV screen, Orson stopped shouting only long enough to pour a drink from a bottle. Once he downed it, he began shouting again.

That looked like a nifty idea. Not the shouting part—the drinking part. Aaron poured more bourbon, tilted the glass, and coaxed the potent liquid into his mouth. It slid slowly down his throat, soothing him. After two or three more shots, he could sack out on the couch and settle blissfully into his welcomed stupor. No dreams, no nightmares. Just a warm blackness that would surround him like a comforting blanket.

He poured more. He was about to raise the glass to his lips when someone knocked softly on the door.

He froze. *What the hell?*

No one ever came to the door but the landlord, and it wasn't time for him yet. Besides, Mel came around dinnertime, when he thought everyone was home. It was now well past midnight. Everyone knew that nothing good or wonderful ever came knocking on someone's door at that time of night.

More knocking—this time louder.

He sat stiffly, his glass in his right hand, the bourbon bottle in his left. His gaze focused on the door as he tried to visualize who could be out there.

More knocking.

"Aaron Grill?" A woman's soft, muffled voice.

"Who…is it?"

"We have an appointment."

An appointment? At this time of night?

What the hell was going on?

Why would I make an appointment this late at night? And even if I did, wouldn't I remember doing so?

"I don't know what you're talking about."

"Please open the door. I don't want to start yelling and wake up your neighbors."

"Listen…I don't know what you're—"

Just then, the door opened.

CHAPTER FOUR

A woman came in and stood in the doorway, frowning at him.

She was tall and slender, with long black hair and large piercing blue eyes. She wore a short-length black leather jacket. The collar was open, exposing her light-colored blouse. The top two buttons were undone; a portion of a tiny silver necklace winked provocatively at him. She also had on form-fitting black slacks and leather boots with three-inch heels. He figured her to be about thirty.

She was a hot-looking babe, but he couldn't help wondering why she'd knocked on his door at this time of night. She'd mentioned an "appointment." What sort of "appointment" was she talking about?

My brain really must be fried. This babe's a knockout. If I'd made an appointment with someone like her, I'd surely have remembered.

He immediately shot down the possibility that she was a hooker. You didn't make appointments with hookers; you just gave them money and they went wherever you wanted them to be.

So, what else could this be about? This neighborhood was known for drugs and prostitution; someone who looked like her and dressed like her would certainly qualify as a woman of the streets. Besides, she was alone, and hookers almost always walked the streets alone in this section at this time of night.

Somehow, that didn't wash, either. She didn't have the look of an average hooker. Her eyes were clear, and she held herself dead-steady. Lastly, she hadn't held out her palm or mentioned money. He'd only had a couple of experiences with hookers in his past and remembered that they got right down to business.

If this woman really was a working girl, she would have approached him on the street and come here with him. She wouldn't show up at midnight to remind him of an appointment he couldn't even remember making...

But aside from all this confusion and the hundred or so other questions he was dying to ask, what bothered him most of all was that she'd opened a locked door.

Had he forgotten to lock it? Hardly. He'd never forgotten before... However, he *had* been through quite an ordeal just an hour or so ago. He'd been slammed to the pavement and might have suffered a concussion; his memory could have suffered a major blip. But he had to find out for sure. "Wasn't that door locked?"

"It certainly was." Her voice was soft and low-pitched, with a soothing quality to it.

"How the hell could you open it, then?"

"I got tired of standing out there in the hall, so I decided to come right in. I didn't want to wait. You were taking much too long to invite me in."

"But—"

"I figured you wouldn't have wanted me getting loud. I might've woken up everyone on the floor."

Before he could speak, she slipped right by him, went over to the battered couch and shrugged out of her jacket.

Without taking his eyes off her, he pushed the door shut. He wanted to check the lock but didn't want to turn away from her. Someone who could open a locked door was certainly not someone to take lightly. This was totally bizarre, and he could not figure out why this was happening or even *what* was happening. He just couldn't stop wondering how she'd opened a locked door.

"Why are you here?"

She tossed her jacket on the arm of the couch. "Like I said, we've got an appointment."

"I don't remember making an appointment...and I certainly don't remember you."

She smiled. "You've obviously got something seriously wrong going on in your head."

What in heaven's name is happening? How the hell did she know?

But he just couldn't get his mind off the damned door.

"I wish you'd tell me how you opened that door..."

"It really was no big deal." She began unbuttoning her blouse.

"What are you doing?" The locked door issue had suddenly taken a back seat to something infinitely more urgent.

She wore no bra. Her breasts were perfect and did not sag. The dark tattoo of a serpent's head rested over her left tit; the rest of it ran down the center of her ribcage and over her navel, disappearing somewhere beneath her belt. She shrugged out of the blouse and tossed it beside the jacket on the arm of the sofa. "I can't do what we're about to do with my clothes on, silly..."

He didn't reply. The confusion filling his head had turned everything into a vast void. He briefly thought that he might have dozed off...

But this was much too real to be a dream.

"Well?" She began unbuckling her belt. "Aren't you gonna undress?"

"Howzat?"

"Your shirt? Pants? Some guys take off their shoes first. Personally, I really don't care, as long as you end up naked."

He watched her toss the belt onto the sofa. "I have a question."

"Go ahead and ask. I've got a little time."

"What the fuck is going on here?"

She sat down on the sofa and began unbuckling her boots. She pulled one off, dropped it on the floor then started on the other one. "You mean you don't remember *anything*?"

"About what?"

She pulled off the boot and dropped it beside its partner. Then stood and hooked her thumbs beneath the waistband of her jeans. As she pushed them down, she said, "I know you hit your head, but if you don't remember anything, nothing I say will mean much to you, right?"

"What the hell don't I remember? And would you *please* stop taking your clothes off?"

She blinked. "Does it bother you?"

"Of course it bothers me!"

She tilted her head. "I had no idea you were gay."

"I'm not gay!"

She shrugged a shoulder. "You don't want me to take my clothes off…"

"You're right. I don't."

"Then you must be gay. Would it help if I was a guy? I can do that—although I really don't like the fit. I'm much more comfortable this way."

What the hell did she mean by *that*? This was getting even weirder. "No, wait—listen…you're confusing me…"

"That's probably because your head isn't working right."

"Of course it isn't working right. Look at me." He pointed to his bandage. "I was slammed to the concrete."

"I know. That's why I'm here."

That made no sense, either. "You're here because I was slammed to the concrete?"

"And because you almost died."

"I almost *what*?"

"You honestly don't remember?"

He closed his eyes and struggled to recall the last few hours. He caught an image of what seemed to be some sort of dream. Perhaps he'd hallucinated when he'd hit his head. "I can see a flickering candle…and some sort of cave…"

"See there? You remember *some* stuff…"

"But I don't remember *you*…"

"Oh, I was there, believe me." She pushed her jeans down to her knees. She had nothing on underneath. The tapered length of the serpent tattoo

34

covered her pubis. The tattoo then wrapped itself around her left thigh and extended even farther down.

"*Please* stop undressing…and I'm *not gay*!"

She stopped what she was doing and straightened. Her pants were just a few inches from her ankles, but she made no attempt to finish undressing. She just stared at him. "You don't think I'm hot?"

"I'm not blind, dammit. Of *course* I think you're hot."

"Then what's wrong?"

"It has nothing to do with you. You're *damned* hot. I mean *sizzling*!"

She crossed her arms beneath her breasts. "Let me guess…you're shy."

"I'm not shy!"

"Good, because I can't possibly do my work effectively that way. I need to get at certain parts to make the process work."

"The *process*?" He rubbed his eyes and told himself that when he opened them again, she'd be gone. This was not happening. His head injury had somehow invoked this ridiculous fantasy. It was kind of wild, but at least it was nothing like his nightmares.

He opened his eyes.

She hadn't disappeared. Worse, she'd completely undressed. Her body was perfect. The serpent's tail reached her ankle, encircling it. As she approached him, he found that he couldn't move or even speak.

"We *do* have an appointment, you know…"

He cleared his throat. "So you keep saying. I just don't remember anything about it."

"Your head's messed up. That's why you don't remember."

He nodded.

"I'm here to fix that."

"Is that the *process* you just mentioned?"

"It'll definitely fix your head."

"Having sex with me will fix my head?"

"It's not just sex."

"Then what *is* it?"

"It's complicated."

"Why is sex necessary to fix my head?"

"For the process to work properly, you need to be in a state of total and complete submission, and you cannot be distracted for even an instant. In other words, your mind has to be totally in my hands. With a man, all a woman needs to control him is to control his body."

"That really does sound complicated. And slightly sexist."

"As I just said, it is. But it works."

Once again, he tried understanding what was going on. "Are you *sure* this isn't a dream?"

"Pinch yourself."

"What?"

"Just do it."

"Why?"

"Oh, hell..." She grabbed a chunk of his neck with her long-nailed fingers and twisted.

"Ow!" He jerked away.

"Did it hurt?"

36

He rubbed his neck and scowled. "What do *you* think?"

"Looks like it hurt."

"Of *course* it hurt!"

"Then I guess you've just figured out this is no dream."

"What *is* it, then?"

"Everything'll clear up shortly afterward."

"After what?"

"After I do my thing."

"What thing? What *is* this process you keep mentioning? And how the hell did you open a locked door? And what did you mean when you asked if I'd rather you were a guy?"

"You really talk a lot, you know."

"Only when I'm nervous and confused…and nothing makes sense."

"How do I make it where you're not nervous or confused?"

"By putting your clothes back on."

"Later, when I'm finished." She reached out and grasped his hand.

He started to protest, but she'd already begun pulling him toward the bedroom doorway.

CHAPTER FIVE

As she lay down on the bed, his blood thundered, and he began trembling. He also found that he could not move his legs.

"What are you waiting for?"

"I just…can't get over any of this…"

"You really do talk too much, you know."

"None of this is making any sense…"

"Do you want it to?"

"Of course I do."

"Then get into bed. I'll handle the rest."

As he reluctantly shed his clothes, he quickly found that his state of confusion had taken a back seat. His blood and his sex had other ideas and immediately took over. He lay down beside her. Her hand immediately reached for him, and a fire blazed around him. She pushed him down and straddled him. In the next moment, her hot palms pressed against his temples and the fire blazing around him increased.

He closed his eyes and surrendered to the flames. Bright colors filled his mind while more intense heat engulfed him. The flames grew as the fire raged inside him. The colors gradually faded into blackness, and he feared he'd pass out. Her smoldering lips mashed against his, intensifying the flames. As she began moving sensuously above him, he sensed his strength increasing to a feverish level. She moaned loudly, squirming, her hot breath saturating his chest and neck while awakening the raging fire within him.

Images swam before him. Lana. The man Lana had left him for, his face deep in shadow. The arguments and vicious words accompanying the anger they'd unleashed upon each other. The torment. The tears. His hands thrusting forward, slamming Lana into the living room wall. The side of her head slapping the corner of the table. The hospital room. The security guard standing in front of the door, blocking him.

More images flashed by. The van slamming into him, sending him plummeting into the Ford pickup parked next to the curb. Opening his eyes and finding himself lying on his back on the hot, sunbaked pavement, his legs numb, a fire blazing in his gut and lower back.

Three young faces approaching him.

A kid no more than eighteen, bending over him.

Dude, you okay?

He's all messed up. A teenage girl leaning over him, her long brown hair swaying above him like a pendulum.

Sorry, dude, we're all fucked up...didn't see ya walkin' there...

Call nine-one-one.

The girl giggling.

A third kid saying, *That adds up to eleven, man...bad number.*

Sorry, dude...this is the old man's car...he'll skin me alive, he sees what I did... Hang loose, now.

The girl reaching down and touching his pants pocket.

What the fuck ya doin', Jewel?

Maybe he's got money.

C'mon, bitch, I almost dusted this dude...can't clean out his pockets!

Help me, please...my wife's in the hospital...she needs to know what's happened to me!

Later, dude!

Blackness. A hospital bed. A nurse leaning over him.

The hospital room faded. The darkness returned, destroying the images. The colors came back not quite as bright, and when he opened his eyes, Jessica's face appeared inches away. Her hands were still pressed tightly to the sides of his head, her breasts mashed against his chest. Her lips sought his. After the kiss, she pulled him closer, until her mouth rubbed his ear. Her hot breath singed his flesh, and he felt his strength returning.

"The nightmares...they came back..." he said, his voice raspy, his breath labored.

"Yes," she replied, her hot breath heating his flesh. "It was necessary."

"Why'd they come back?"

"For you to be cleansed, I had to see them. Otherwise, they'd remain there, in your head."

"You mean—"

"They're all gone now."

"Forever?"

"As long as you wish them to be."

He closed his eyes but saw only a heavy blanket of darkness. He opened them again and discovered that he was staring directly into her eyes.

"Now everything will be yours," she whispered. "Everything you could ever want…it is yours…"

Everything I could ever want…

"Do you really want this?"

"Yes. I do. I really do, but—"

"But?"

"I still think this is a dream."

"Why is that?"

"It feels like one."

"It's real."

"All the bad in my past is gone? The nightmares? My guilt? Just like that?"

"Yes. But as I said before, there *is* a price…"

"A price?"

"Yes."

The nightmares were gone and would never come back. He'd be able to sleep soundly for the first time in more than a year. Because of this, nothing else mattered, and that included *any* price. "I really don't care."

"You're sure?"

"Absolutely."

"Then it's time to pay up."

"Pay up?"

"You must pay the price."

"I really don't see a problem. What do I owe you?"

"Your essence."

"My *what*?"

"What you are. Who you are. Your spirit. I must have it now."

He stared into her eyes and tried to decide what she was telling him. Her blank expression told him nothing. But it didn't matter because he didn't consider this much of a payment at all. His spirit for the nightmares? He wanted to laugh. His life had hit the skids more than a year ago, and his future had been reduced to living in a two-room dump, getting by with daily bourbon and an occasion meal from the fast food place down the street. He wasn't sure he even possessed a spirit anymore. If there was any order to the universe, his spirit had probably died a year ago, with the rest of him.

"That's fine with me."

"Are you ready? You don't want to think about it first?"

"The nightmares are gone. I don't have to think about it."

"Then give your essence to me."

The pressure in her palms increased against the sides of his head, and the room grew hotter. The waves of heat came more rapidly, thrashing through him. Her thighs tightened around him, and when he closed his eyes, a giant mass of hot, smothering blackness had settled over him...

CHAPTER SIX

He opened his eyes and found that he was gazing into the mouth of a cave.

The foulness in the air, thick and heavy, made his eyes water. His gut tightened and he gagged. Regaining his breath, he turned around and scanned his surroundings.

Darkness engulfed him. What was this place? He sensed his fear growing rapidly with the panic building within him.

How did he get here?

Where was Jessica?

Was this a dream? Another nightmare?

He couldn't even remember falling asleep.

A voice coming from inside the cave shattered the silence.

Sorry, dude, we're all fucked up...didn't see ya walkin' there...

It was the voice of the kid who'd nearly killed him just two years earlier, when he'd left the hospital after trying in vain to visit Lana after their first terrible fight.

Why was the kid calling him from inside the cave?

The images spun wildly. The voices faded, but another replaced them. It was also coming from within the cave.

You nearly killed me... It was Lana's voice.

It was an accident, Lana... He heard his own voice coming from the cave.

The voices faded. The eerie silence sliced into him, and he shivered. For a moment he thought death had just slipped through him. He felt like he'd just stepped inside someone's grave.

Is that where the cave led? To his death?

The silence grew heavier. This heavy emptiness made him think he was the only spirit in the universe.

He blinked and the cave vanished. In its place, a grass-covered hill went on forever, extending into the darkness, where it disappeared into the blackness of night.

Had he imagined all this? What were those images? Those voices? Why couldn't he remember them anymore? Why were his thoughts so cloudy and muddled? What had happened to his memory? Why did he have this strange feeling that the cave was hiding behind the hill?

"Do you want to leave?"

He spun around. Jessica stood behind him, smiling. Only her face was visible; the darkness had swallowed up the rest of her.

"Where are we?"

"A place you don't need to come back to."

The foulness of the air thickened. "I...don't like it here."

"You don't want to listen to your friends anymore?"

"My *friends*?"

"Those boys who almost killed you. The girl who tried picking your pocket. And, of course, your wife Lana—the woman you almost killed."

"Lana?" It took him a second to remember her name. Something was very strange…

"Don't you remember?"

"I remember some terrible things that happened a long time ago." He gazed at the grass-covered hill. Darkness hovered above it and he wondered why he thought he'd seen something else there.

"This is where everything will stay," she said.

"Why are we here?"

"I brought you here to show you that I've done what you asked me to do."

"What did I ask you to do?"

"You don't remember?"

"Most of it's a blur."

"You wanted me to help you get rid of your nightmares."

Those thoughts slowly drifted back, and for the first time since he'd opened his eyes and found himself in this creepy place, he believed he hadn't lost his mind after all.

But something just wasn't right.

"I have this strange feeling I just had one."

"Yes, but only briefly."

"What happened here?"

"I brought you here to get rid of them."

"Why here?"

"This is where I keep my collection."

"Your…collection?"

"The nightmares."

"You…keep them *here*?"

She shrugged. "I've got to keep them *some*where…"

"Why here?"

45

"It's as good a place as any. Nightmares take up a lot of room. But I'm able to keep them all here. It's my personal storage place."

He waited for more of an explanation, but she didn't elaborate. He decided that was all right; he really didn't need to know. Besides, he found that he didn't *want* to know. "So they're really gone?"

"Yes."

"You're sure?"

"You can't remember anything, can you?"

"I...don't know..."

"Try."

He closed his eyes, but the darkness clouding his mind prevented anything from seeping through. "I can't."

"Try harder."

He did as she said. The same darkness filled his head. It frightened him, but at least nothing came back. "I can't see anything."

"You never told me why Lana left you."

"Lana?" The name had a familiar ring, but...

"Your ex-wife."

Her image drifted back. It was hazy, but at least he could make it out. "I think she...found someone else."

"What happened?"

He struggled to remember. It was difficult—the memories had somehow become so blurry, he couldn't distinguish them in the darkness. "We had an argument. I can't remember what it was about. One day I came home from work and found the house empty. I guess that was the end of it."

"There was nothing else you can remember?"

46

He sensed something stirring, but the emptiness came right back. He guessed there was more to it than that, but nothing else would come. "Nothing else I can think of..."

Jessica smiled.

"There *was* something else, wasn't there? I'm sure of it. But I just can't remember..."

"It must not be important, then."

He suspected it was important but decided he wouldn't be able to wrap his mind around it, no matter how hard he tried.

"Come with me." She grasped his hand. It was very warm.

"You actually did it, didn't you?" he asked.

"You sound surprised."

"I didn't think it was possible."

"All things are possible."

"Please tell me where we are."

"It is called the Forbidden Place, and, in time, you'll forget it as well."

"Where is it?"

"It doesn't matter. You'll never come back. Besides, we're about to leave. Close your eyes."

Just as he did, he thought he heard someone yelling, but the voice sounded far away. "*Dude!*"

His eyes shot open. "I just...heard someone."

"Ignore it. It will soon be gone, and you'll never be bothered again."

The voice shouted again a moment later, sounding much farther away.

"I can't believe this...*any* of this..."

"Is it time to conclude our transaction?" Jessica asked.

"Yes."

"You're sure?"

"Yes."

"Then close your eyes. From now on, everything will happen the way you wish it to."

Once again he did as she'd instructed. However, this time he felt as if something had been lifted from his shoulders, something that had been weighing him down for a long time.

"Open them one last time…"

When he opened his eyes again, the colors returned much brighter than ever before. When they finally dissipated, he saw her face. He was lying on top of her. Her eyes glistened. Sweat pitted her face and neck, and her hair matted her forehead and part of her cheek. She was smiling, and her strange fragrance enveloped him. She pulled his face closer. Their lips mashed together, and everything turned intensely hot. Tongues of angry flame danced around them.

"Now give it to me one last time," she whispered, her fiery breath engulfing him. "The rest of it. Your spirit. Your soul. Surrender it *all* to me!"

The heat rising from his center began to grow, bubbling over, searing his flesh. His muscles stood out in knots the moment he exploded inside her.

The flames vanished, and everything ebbed into nothingness. Violent waves of cold shimmered up and down his body. She screamed beneath him, her limbs squeezing him in a death grip that literally tore his breath from his lungs.

He shivered as if someone had dumped a bucket of ice water on his back, and for one long, terrible moment he felt an overwhelming sense of loss as something warm and comforting slipped away and was immediately replaced by a sliver of cold piercing his heart.

Then he collapsed and surrendered to the blackness.

CHAPTER SEVEN

A little groggy, Aaron sat up in bed.

Except for the usual traffic sounds humming outside the building, he heard nothing else. Nothing from the next room, or bathroom. As far as he could tell, no one else was in the apartment.

He had the strangest feeling that someone had been here with him. He stared at the bed sheets—the mattress, the pillows. Was it his imagination? Or did the room have a strange smell?

"Anyone here?"

Silence.

He lowered his legs over the edge of the bed and sat there for several minutes, trying to grasp the situation—to decide what had happened, why he felt so strange. He could tell by the tiny glints of silver light peeking between the blinds that it was morning. The digital clock on the dusty end table said: 7:29.

His clothes lay in a scattered heap about five feet from the bed. He looked down at himself; he was naked. He always slept in his undershorts. Why were they lying on the floor with the rest of his clothes?

He struggled to recall the previous night, cringing when the shadows came back.

He'd seen a mugging, or some sort of scuffle, in the alley on his way to the liquor store. Instead of walking away, he'd stayed right there, staring into the darkness of the alley. Logic and reason eventually took over, convincing him that he needed to get away, but before he was able to, the scuffle had ended, and someone rushed from the alley. The man was extremely enraged that someone might have seen what he'd done.

The bastard slammed me against the wall, and when I tried resisting, he tossed me to the concrete and walked away. And when I got back up, I came back here and went right to bed...

No. That wasn't what happened.

As if on cue, the throbbing just above his right eye supplied the missing details to the mystery.

He reached up and felt the bandage. The memories trickled back. A girl with dark hair, dark eyes and a pretty face applied antiseptic and gauze to his wound. She was slender and efficient, and easy on the eyes.

The scene, clear as day, flashed in his head.

He found it very strange that he could remember so much of the previous night but hadn't been able to tell the cop anything right after it happened. Stress, no doubt. And shock. The blow to the head had rattled his brain.

Everything had become a blur--a big, black emptiness. I must have shed my clothes as soon as I came back home, fallen into bed and gone to sleep.

Had he been so exhausted and stressed that he'd blacked out completely? For an instant he thought he remembered going to the liquor store after talking to the cop, but the emptiness in his head told him nothing.

The blow to his skull had obviously done some damage. Hopefully, his thoughts would eventually clear in a day or so.

51

He got up from the bed. His hips and lower back protested, and a spike of pain sliced through him, rushing down his legs. He sat down and rode it out. When the pain subsided a few minutes later, he got up carefully and padded naked to the bathroom.

He decided to have a shower and then make breakfast. He suddenly remembered that he hadn't fixed breakfast in a while. He couldn't even recall the last time he'd eaten. Was it two days ago? Three? His gut made a rumbling protest. He couldn't remember the last time he'd used the oven or when he'd last used the burners on top of the stove.

But that was of no consequence. Fixing breakfast wouldn't be much of a problem.

However, he had something else to tend to first.

He found the card the cop had given him the night before and called the Orlando Police Department. After being placed on hold and waiting for nearly five minutes, the cop who'd questioned him at the scene came on the line. "Remember anything this morning?"

"A few things," Aaron said. "Got a pen?"

"Go 'head, I'm listenin'…"

"My attacker's six-five, two-forty, muscular and strong." As he spoke, the picture in his head grew crystal-clear. It was almost as if he was watching it all over again. "He's around thirty-five, with thick black hair combed straight back, dark eyes, and a broad nose that was obviously broken. He's got what looks like a two-inch white scar running vertically through his right eyebrow, and two tiny teardrop tattoos just below his right eye, about a quarter of an inch above the cheekbone. He has large hands and big knuckles, and two or three of the knuckles on each hand showed evidence of being broken. We could be looking for an ex-boxer or strong-arm for the Mob. He was dressed well— Versace, I think—and I believe he was wearing *Obsession for Men*."

Silence.

Hopefully, the cop hadn't gotten bored and left the room.

"Hello?"

"Is that all?" the cop finally said.

"Well, I didn't catch his shoe size because it was dark… "

"I was kidding. Tell me something… Like you said, it was dark. How could you have noticed the nose thing…or the prison tatts?"

"My subconscious might have caught some details. The man was pretty close. By the way, I smelled vodka on his breath."

"Damn…when your memory came back, it sure did open up the floodgates!"

"Think it'll help?"

"Mr. Grill, this is probably the best damn description I've ever heard in my twenty-two years on the Force. Of course it'll help. Based on what you've just told me, I can already nail down the suspects to three or four. We'll definitely catch him now."

He stood in the shower for ten minutes, letting the heavy warm spray massage him from head to toe. Afterward, he toweled himself dry and stood in front of the mirror. He was about to apply the shaving cream to his cheeks and chin when he realized that he felt better than he had in quite a while. He also noticed that the swelling on his forehead had gone down, and when he touched the bandage above the wound, it no longer hurt. In fact, it wasn't the least bit tender. Curious, he peeled back the adhesive. Aside from a slight two-inch jagged scratch that looked nearly healed, there was nothing. No bruising, no discoloring. His forehead showed no signs of the recent brutal attack that had nearly killed him.

How could I heal so quickly? How could anyone heal so quickly?

If Lou Connor could see me now, he'd probably want me to come back to work...

He spread the foam over his cheeks, chin and neck and picked up the razor. Ten minutes later, he splashed on cologne, brushed his teeth, dressed and went out to the kitchen to make breakfast. He was in the process of taking the eggs out of the carton when his cell phone rang.

It was Lou Connor, his former boss from C&H Software Systems. "Aaron, how're you doing?"

"Just fine." It was strange, the man calling him out of the blue just moments after he'd entered Aaron's thoughts...

This was almost as strange as looking in the mirror and seeing no signs of the blow to his head.

"What's up, Lou?"

"I'll make this short and to the point. I want you to come in this morning."

"Come *in?*" For some reason, he couldn't quite understand what the man was telling him.

"To C&H."

"To the *office*?"

"Yes."

"Why?"

"I'd like you to have your old job back."

CHAPTER EIGHT

Short, broad, and about fifty-five, with thick gray hair and a ruddy round face, Lou Connor looked him up and down before extending his hand. "Good to see you, old friend."

"Good to see you, too." Aaron shook his former boss's hand.

"You're looking well." Connor nodded. "You've obviously gone back to therapy, after all."

As Aaron faced Connor, he noticed that he'd forgotten how short his former boss was. Connor seemed much shorter than the last time they'd seen one another. Or maybe Aaron just felt taller. Right now, the situation was so confusing, he couldn't tell if his observation was genuine or if his mind was playing tricks. He had to remind himself that it hadn't been very long since he'd worked here. In fact, it had been a little more than a year since he'd walked outside into the hot Florida sunshine, got behind the wheel of the Crown Vic and stopped at the first bar he came to before driving home a few hours later to find the house empty.

But why would his former boss think Aaron had been back to therapy? Both Connor and Jimmy Holmes, the co-founder of C&H, knew how Aaron felt about therapy. Even now, he couldn't think of one good reason to share his troubles with an overpaid, unconcerned professional.

"What makes you say that?" he asked.

"You *haven't* been back?"

"Not since those first two sessions." He wondered if he'd just killed his chances of coming back to work.

"You've been working out, then." Connor nodded approvingly. "You definitely look stronger, more confident. Intense physical exercise forces those stubborn endorphins to work overtime, kicking stress and ridding the body of toxins and other harmful elements that will eventually tear down the works." He gave Aaron one last quick once-over. "Good work."

"Actually, I really haven't been doing much." He felt the need to explain even though he had no idea why anything was different. Telling Lou Connor that he looked and felt better because he'd been physically assaulted by a crazy man the night before would not be bright.

"Well, whatever you've been doing is obviously working, so keep it up." He turned toward the open doorway. "Let's chat."

Aaron followed the man into his office. From the opposite side of the large room, the brightness of the new day shone in a subdued cast of gold as it pushed gently against the large, tinted window.

Connor closed the door and pointed to the padded chair facing his metal desk. Aaron sat while the other man took his seat in his leather chair behind the desk. Connor thumped his elbows onto the green blotter and placed his hands together, as in prayer. A serious expression took over his features and he regarded Aaron in silence before speaking again. "As I told you on the phone, I think it's time you came back."

Aaron sat in puzzled silence. This was really strange. He'd left the company under extremely unpleasant circumstances. Now that everything had retreated into the past, he discovered that he couldn't remember exactly what happened, although he knew that his breakdown was triggered by his marriage problems. He and Lana had been fighting constantly for several months. He'd been working many hours during those months and frequently came home late at night. Lana constantly complained that in a good marriage, the people involved did whatever was necessary to spend as much time together as possible. He also blamed the disintegration of their relationship on his hit-and-run injury. But now, for some reason, he couldn't remember the details.

Strangely, all those past events now seemed so distant. The memories of what their relationship had once been remained with him, but now it seemed like everything had happened to some other guy—someone he no longer knew. And now, as he faced his former employer for the first time in many months, he discovered that much of the unpleasantness that had consumed his life had mysteriously retreated into the darkness of his subconscious.

Those dismal days were obviously not worth remembering. This was a new day and a new period in his life. He had no idea what had changed—just that it had, and he felt much better. And, judging by Connor's reaction, he apparently looked better as well.

But none of this explained Lou Connor's phone call earlier that morning.

"Look at you," Connor said, smiling. "You're alert and look one hundred percent better. You're clean-shaven, your hair's perfect, and that sparkle in your eyes has returned. Whatever you've been doing is working."

"What made you call me this morning?" He couldn't stop thinking about it.

Connor sat forward and frowned. "That's a really good question. The answer is, I honestly don't know. I just found myself thinking about you. That's the only intelligent way I can explain it. Nothing was different or even slightly off until this morning, when I was getting ready for work. Then your image popped into my head. I was sitting down at breakfast with the wife and just blurted out your name—just like that." He clicked his fingers. Then he laughed. "Of course, the wife thought I might be losing my mind, and I really can't blame her, the way your name popped right out. But that's how it happened. I explained to her that things hadn't been the same since you left—that your department has been dropping in sales for months. So, when I got to the office this morning, I decided to call Johnson in Personnel to find out how you were doing." He shrugged.

"What did he tell you?"

"He said he hadn't heard anything for months. He'd sent you to one of our associate therapy groups, but that turned out to be just a couple of sessions, and you hadn't been back. You know C&H's policy on that, right?"

"I was required to attend a specific number of visits before he signed off on me and approved my return. He wanted to see me twice a week for eight weeks."

"But you obviously didn't go to him for the duration."

"During the two times I saw him, all he did was ask me about my dreams and why I thought I was having them. I told him I didn't want to talk about them, and he told me that was a definite sign that something more serious was wrong."

"Then what did he say?"

"Didn't you read his report?"

"Holmes did. I didn't."

"He told me my reluctance to work with him was good enough reason for me to visit a psychiatrist for a more thorough treatment. I told him I didn't intend to see a psychiatrist."

"So that's when you left?"

"I called him an asshole first. *Then* I left."

Connor grinned and immediately turned serious. "What about the nightmares? Still having them?"

"Nope." It wasn't necessary to tell the man something that no longer seemed important. "I haven't had them in a while."

"How long?"

"I don't remember. In fact, I don't even remember what they were about. I assume they were brought on by my divorce, but since I can't even remember the details, I guess it no longer matters."

Connor sat silently for nearly a minute, watching him closely. "That's very strange."

"I know it is."

"The mind has been known to do some miraculous things to heal itself. Perhaps yours did just that."

"I can't think of anything else that would explain any of this."

"So unless you've been lying to me, I'd say you've actually achieved some sort of miraculous recovery."

"I'd say so, too."

Connor watched him silence. "Whatever happened is very strange, to say the least, and even stranger that I had that sudden flash that you were okay, and were ready to come back."

"You're not psychic, are you?"

Connor laughed. "Hardly."

"But that really *is* strange..."

"The important thing—that is, to me—is that you look as fit as a fiddle."

"I feel great."

"Any objection to a physical exam before starting?"

"None at all…"

"Good. Then I want you to come back."

"But when I left, I said some things I shouldn't have said…"

The man's bushy gray brows dropped abruptly. "That's in the past, Aaron. Let it die. You're a good man. You always were. We all knew you were going through a rough patch. Holmes knew it as well. He and I got together right after you left and

61

realized you'd need a few months—perhaps even a year—to sort it all out. Well, it looks like you've mended completely, because you've obviously turned back into the same bright talent we originally hired on ten years ago."

"Then...I can have my job back?"

"If you want it, you've got it. I've even prepared a signing bonus for the occasion. Holmes and I discussed that as well. We both figured you could use it. We decided on ten K, if that's all right with you. The point is, we want you back. C&H needs you." He stood and extended his hand. "So...what'll it be?"

Aaron straightened and reached across the desk. "I guess you could say I'm back, then."

CHAPTER NINE

After his meeting with Lou Connor, Aaron drove back to the depressing two-room dump that had been his home for the last twelve months.

The moment he entered the dark, musty living room, a cloud of gloominess nipped at him, and he decided that it would be in his best interests to move to a more prosperous section of town. A new chapter of his life had begun. The signing bonus C&H had deposited into his meager bank account enabled him to afford a better lifestyle. For the first time since Lana had walked out on him, he could see his life getting back on track.

He left the apartment shortly before dinnertime and drove to the nearest supermarket. He went straight to the deli and picked up a carton of freshly prepared pot roast, a couple of broiled drumsticks and a large slice of vanilla cheesecake. He also grabbed a six-pack of dark beer and drove back home.

After dinner, he rinsed off the dishes and plates and stacked them in the drainer. He found two large empty boxes near the dumpsters behind the complex, brought them into the apartment and began packing them with the few odds and ends he'd dumped into the drawers and cabinets when he'd first moved in.

It took him less than half an hour to discover that he'd packed just about everything he wanted to keep, so he went into the living room and had a shot of bourbon. It took only one shot to discover he was exhausted. But it was no wonder. It had been a busy day—much busier than what he'd been used to. The excitement of returning to the C&H offices—and, of course, the signing bonus—had taken its toll. Without hesitation, he got up and shuffled off to bed.

He awakened in the middle of the night in a cold sweat, sitting up and gawking stupidly at the darkness surrounding him. He vaguely recalled dreaming of a beautiful dark-haired woman visiting him in the night. It was so vivid that, for one frightening moment, he sensed someone lying in the bed beside him. He fumbled for the lamp on the end table and flicked it on. He was alone, of course, and cursed himself for letting his imagination run wild.

For the next twenty minutes he lay there with the light on, thinking about the dream. At first, it had been very clear. But after a few minutes, it dissolved into nothingness.

Flustered, he flicked off the light and spent the next hour or so staring at the dark ceiling, wondering about the dream.

He finally drifted off and fell into a dreamless sleep.

***

He awoke at nine the next morning, had a shower, dressed, fixed breakfast, and finished packing.

While gathering up what few kitchen utensils he wanted to take with him, he caught himself thinking about that dream again. This time, he drew a complete blank. He thought he remembered a female being in it, but when nothing else came, he decided it wasn't worth his time. He had better things to do. He was a man, dammit—he'd dreamed about women hundreds of times before. In fact, he dreamed about them all the time. As a boy, he'd dreamed about movie stars, swimsuit models and cheerleaders. He dreamed about women he'd seen on the street...and working the register at the local 7-Eleven...and in TV commercials. When he was married, he dreamed about women he'd known earlier in his life, and even dreamed about Lana much of the time.

Wrenching himself back to reality, he took the last of his things from the cabinets and put them on the counter so he could sort through them. He was in the process of gathering up the two skillets he wanted to keep when the phone rang.

It was the police. "Mr. Grill?"

"Yes?"

"Mr. Aaron Grill?"

"Speaking..."

"Sorry to bother you, but this concerns the assault you reported two days ago."

He sat down on the sofa and waited for his pulse to slow down. The assault. The police were calling him about the assault. This was obviously something he needed to hear, so he knew he should calm down and pay attention. "Yes?"

"We'd like you to come to the Morgue at your earliest convenience."

"The *Morgue*?" The back of his neck tingled.

"The building's on East Michigan. We'd like you to identify a body that was just brought in this morning."

"Did you say…body?"

"We think it could be your attacker."

"What happened?"

"Could you come in sometime today and identify the body?"

"You're saying he's really dead?" He realized how stupid that sounded, but he wasn't thinking very clearly at the moment. Of course the man was dead. Why else would this cop refer to the attacker as a "body?"

"We think the man matching your description is the same man who was brought in a couple of hours ago. This man was killed in a shootout with the police, and we'd like you to come in and see if he's the same person you described in your formal complaint."

"Wow…" This was unbelievable. Could this really be happening? Could the psycho who'd nearly killed him actually be dead?

"Mr. Grill?"

"Yes?"

"Will you come in later today and identify the body?"

"This is really far out…" He couldn't help feeling strange about this. It was even weirder than Lou Connor calling him that same morning.

"Does that mean you'll come in?"

"I'll be there."

***

The front lot of the Medical Examiner's Office was more than half-filled by the time Aaron pulled into a space at a little after one o'clock.

Inside, men and women in uniforms and long white jackets shuffled up and down the corridors carrying folders and briefcases. The building was very cool and dark, and smelled strongly of antiseptic.

Aaron signed in at the door, and a man in a police uniform met him and led him silently down the corridor. Another man met them halfway down. He wore a long white jacket over his light-blue shirt and black trousers. He was around forty, slender and at least six-three, with a receding hairline, black hair and black thick-rimmed glasses. He opened a door and they entered a large, dark room smelling even more strongly of that same antiseptic. Thirty feet away, several rows of polished metal storage cabinets covered the opposite wall. A big-boned middle-aged man sat at a small metal table, poring over a stack of papers. He wore a police uniform and didn't look up or acknowledge their presence.

The man with Aaron went on ahead and approached one of the drawers on the bottom row. He bent at the waist and unlatched it, sliding it out about three feet, which revealed the head and face of the corpse lying inside. Then he straightened and motioned Aaron closer.

Suddenly nervous, Aaron moved rather stiffly to the open drawer.

"Please...have a closer look."

Swallowing a lump in his throat, Aaron peered over the top of the drawer and gazed at the corpse. Despite the blood, the unhinged jaw and the rather large bullet hole in the forehead, it was definitely the same man who'd nearly killed him.

Aaron wanted to smile at the irony. This was a strange sort of justice—an almost remarkable sense of karma that gave clear indication of a natural order to the Universe.

Something else occurred to him, and he nearly shuddered when he thought of it. This made the situation much more than ironic, and he wanted to dismiss it as soon as it popped into his thoughts.

The morning after the street attack, he woke up feeling better than he'd felt in a long time. He had no headache and the wound on his forehead had nearly disappeared. He even wanted breakfast—something he hadn't had in a long time. Then, of course, the call came from Lou Connor, asking him to come back to work.

Finally, this psycho showed up dead just a couple of days after attacking Aaron and nearly claiming his life...

Was this some sort of karma at work? Or was it merely a series of unrelated coincidences?

He knew better than consider this as some miracle. The corpse in the drawer had led a violent life and undoubtedly had made more than just a few enemies. This instance strongly indicated the "eye for an eye" mentality—not something out of a silly book of magic spells that gullible, desperate people consulted when they wanted to believe in something that defied simple logic.

"Sir?" The attendant was waiting. "Can you identify this man?"

He shook himself out of it. He needed to focus. More than that, he wanted to get out of here. The place was making him nauseous. "That's definitely the guy who attacked me."

The man slammed the drawer shut and gestured toward the table. "If you'll follow me, we'd like you to sign some papers before you leave."

***

Aaron spent the rest of the afternoon packing, cleaning the place as best he could and waiting for Goodwill to stop by and pick up the furniture he no longer wanted.

At around ten o'clock that night, he realized he was tired and needed to relax. He picked up the bourbon bottle and a glass from the kitchen, went out into the living room and collapsed on the couch. He poured two inches of the stuff, sipped, and sighed in relief as the whiskey burned its way down his throat.

He sat back and let the whiskey work its magic. His thoughts went back to the night of the attack. This time, he picked out minor details he hadn't thought of before and tried sorting them out in an effort to put more meaning into them. He found that he was suddenly desperate to understand why a simple street attack would prove instrumental in changing so many things.

Nothing made sense, so he went back a few hours before he'd left the apartment. As he recalled, he'd spent the day zoned out on the couch while soaps and other mindless stuff silently filled the TV screen. He couldn't remember if he'd had anything to eat that day. He could only recall that he'd finished his last bottle and needed more. This was when he'd decided to take the trip to the liquor

69

store. Sleep was on its way and he didn't want to be caught off-guard. Without enough bourbon to knock him out cold, sleep would bring on the nightmares.

That night seemed no different from any of the others, yet something had obviously happened to shift future events. Once again he went back into the thick of it, combing his memory for clues.

After the paramedic babe had fixed him up, he'd gone to the liquor store, bought two bottles and came straight back to the apartment.

Or *did* he?

This was the precise moment when he discovered that his brain refused to cooperate. His thoughts became muddled, with total confusion setting in.

What was going on? He'd never been so confused before—what was different now?

He had more bourbon and thought about it for another half hour. When he realized he couldn't come up with anything new, he decided to call it a night.

He switched off his overworked brain and went to bed.

CHAPTER TEN

He spent the next morning poring over the real estate section of the Yellow Pages and making inquiries.

By 11:30, he'd found three suitable prospects for condos, one of them located in one of his preferred locations.

The complex sat in an exclusive area of Winter Park, less than two miles from Semoran Boulevard and just a few miles north of Colonial Drive. It was a nice area, and less than thirty minutes from the C&H offices in downtown Orlando. The furnished two-bedroom condo included a comfortable living room, dining and bar area, and a spacious kitchen in the rear. A Florida room extending from the kitchen led to a small private back yard. It also provided direct access to an Olympic-sized complex pool and recreation area. The Party & Activities building included a pool room, game room, and a large area toward the back, where four rows of long tables had been set up for weekly bingo. Shuffleboard and a tennis court sat in a separate area in the rear of the property, behind the recreation building. The bulletin board, displayed prominently in the entrance of the building, announced weekly activities, such as poker and canasta. Private parties were encouraged but were required to be booked at least one month in advance, subject to approval by the Homeowner's Association.

The complex manager, a tall, slender woman in her late sixties, smiled at him beneath her large puffy cloud of frosted white hair. She had bright blue eyes and a friendly face. Her nameplate said *ELIZABETH BRENNAN*. The glittering silver rings on her fingers and the many silver bracelets on her bony wrists suggested wealth. She studied his application and stopped when she'd reached the bottom. Then she looked up at him. "Mr. Grill, you provided only one reference."

Since Lou Connor had offered him his old job back, he'd included the man's name as his only reference. He'd left C&H under tense circumstances and realized he couldn't provide the names of those people he'd antagonized or disappointed the last few months he'd worked there. He hadn't bothered with anyone or developed any relationships since his breakdown. He knew better than include the name of his former therapist. Lana was out of the question, as well. "The only name I could provide is my former boss. I've been keeping to myself lately and don't really know anyone else I could use as a reference."

She studied his face before re-examining his application, adjusting her thick-rimmed glasses as if to make sure she hadn't missed anything the first time around. Then she frowned, and a small bubble of tanned flesh appeared between her cultured white brows. "The Association requires three references, Mr. Grill. We've got many elderly people living here. As you can well understand, we've got to make sure that whoever we accept meets our—"

"It's all right."

She smiled in relief. "I'm so glad you understand."

He shrugged and got up. "I shouldn't have taken up your time. I can't expect you to sign your own name for me, can I?" He'd known there could be a problem the moment he'd seen the proviso but decided to try anyway. He knew he'd probably have to settle for a cheaper, less prestigious place. But anything would be better than the dump he'd come from.

"One moment, please..." She sat in silence, staring at the application. When she raised her head and met his gaze, her face paled, and fear filled her eyes.

"Are you...all right?" he asked.

She didn't reply. Snatching up her pen, she lowered her head and began scribbling something on his application.

"Mrs. Brennan?"

Once she'd finished scribbling, she dropped the pen on the blotter and looked up at him. The fear had disappeared from her face. She was smiling. "Congratulations, Mr. Grill. You may move right in whenever you like."

***

That afternoon, he loaded his few belongings into the trunk of the Crown Vic.

He wanted to keep busy because he didn't want to drive himself crazy thinking about what had happened in Elizabeth Brennan's office at the Winter Park Isle Estates.

All he knew was that she was about to reject his application when her face suddenly paled, and her eyes filled with fear. Then, once that moment had

73

passed, she wrote something down and told him he could move right in.

What happened? And what had put that fear in her eyes?

What did she write down on the application?

More important, what had she seen in his eyes that frightened her so much?

I can't expect you to sign your own name for me, can I?

He possessed no super abilities—nothing that would suggest a hint of subliminal mental suggestion. How could he possibly think he had the ability to change another human being's mind merely by suggesting such a thing?

Was it coincidence? Or was the woman so sympathetic that she hadn't wanted to reject him?

That was it; she'd felt sorry for him.

What else could it be? How could he possess any strange mental capabilities when he'd never seen evidence of them before?

However, some inner sense suggested that this had nothing to do with sympathy. Sympathy wouldn't have made her pale so quickly, and it certainly wouldn't have put that fear in her eyes.

Yet nothing else could explain any of this.

Before leaving, he went down the hall to settle his account with the building manager, a short, stocky man in his early forties everyone called Mel. Smelling of cigars and B.O., the little guy always wore a sloppy blue grease-stained mechanic's shirt and tattered jeans hiked down, exposing four inches of his hairy butt crack whenever he bent over. He lived alone in his tiny one-room efficiency, had no friends, and left his place only for booze and groceries, to collect rent, dump his trash or repair something. He seldom spoke, usually mumbling one- or two-word sentences with the stub of a smoldering cigar wedged permanently between his tiny yellowish teeth.

Aaron stepped up to the door and pressed the buzzer. About ten seconds later, the door creaked open and a thick bubble of cigar smoke rushed out, engulfing him. The little man stood there, looking up at him, the cigar smoke forming wiggly ringlets as it slithered up toward the top of the threshold, becoming a grayish cloud.

Aaron coughed twice before he could speak. "I'm moving out."

Without a word, Mel turned and plodded back into his apartment. Aaron turned away and began desperately searching for fresh air. Mel shuffled back out, sorting through a stack of receipts.

Aaron quickly found that he didn't want to stand here, inhaling smoke from Mel's putrid stogy. The rank smell of the hall and the building itself disgusted him, and he suddenly realized how disappointed he was with himself for living here. He didn't want to pay any more money for living in this horrible place. He wanted to get out of here and forget about it. But it was the first week of October, and he owed them a full month's rent.

Mel squinted at his stack of receipts. "You're paid up."

"You sure?"

Mel studied the receipt, squinting again and scattering more smoke. "All paid up." He scribbled something on the receipt and handed it to Aaron.

Aaron glanced at it and saw that it was what he'd already paid for September. He held it out. "You say this is for October?"

Mel scowled and scattered more smoke. "That's what it says." Then he turned around, scurried back inside, and slammed the door behind him.

***

That evening, after carrying the last of his belongings into the new condo, Aaron collapsed onto one of the two barstools in the kitchen.

He hadn't eaten since lunch and needed to give his aching knees and back a break. After a drink and some rest, he decided to go out for a pizza or grab a hot dinner at one of the supermarkets on Semoran.

He poured two inches of bourbon into a glass, but as soon as he raised the glass to his lips, he began thinking about his meeting with Mel. What happened seemed just as bizarre as the episode with Elizabeth Brennan.

There had to be a logical reason for this.

I can't expect you to sign your own name for me, can I?

I don't want to pay any more money for living in this horrible place.

Mental suggestion? Hypnosis?

Had the street attack caused all this? Had the pounding he'd suffered from being slammed to the pavement done something to his brain? Had it jarred loose some hidden power that had been there all along?

Why is this troubling you?

That was a very good question. In fact, most people would think him weird for giving any of this a second thought.

He'd always considered himself an honest person—one who paid his own way and didn't depend on others. Things like this made him feel guilty. He felt as if he'd stiffed someone.

But he hadn't stiffed anyone.

His thoughts were innocent. Most everyone reacted in the same sort of way and would jump at the chance to turn their hidden desires into reality.

He forced himself to admit that whatever this was, it wasn't his fault. Thinking something didn't necessarily make it so. If that were the case, the world would be in an even much bigger mess.

His thoughts went back to the last few days. He started thinking about the meeting with Lou Connor and immediately began wondering about the call from the police. Right after that, his thoughts shifted to Elizabeth Brennan, who'd obviously done something risky and unethical to help him move in. He ended his deliberations with his former landlord, who'd obviously misread his last rent receipt.

Were these nothing more than unrelated coincidences? Was it a series of random good luck? Was it Karma? Fate? Some sort of glitch in the universe?

What other explanation could there be?

CHAPTER ELEVEN

Suddenly needing a change of scenery, Aaron got behind the wheel of the Crown Vic at around ten-thirty and drove south on Semoran.

He went west on Colonial for several blocks, until he passed North Mills. He drove another a block and parked along the curb about half a block from Visconti's, a bar he'd been to a few times before, and walked down the street, taking in the coolness of the night.

Although it was getting late, Colonial Drive resonated with the sounds of steady traffic. Knots of rowdy people staggered to and from the other bars in the area, giggling and hanging onto one another. A slight chill lingered in the air. It was much like the chill he'd experienced the night he was attacked on his way to Frank's Liquor Store.

He shivered—not from the chill, but from the memory of that night. He kept on walking. He didn't want to spend the evening sitting alone in his new apartment, wondering why his life had suddenly turned weird. He was tired of feeling sorry for himself and wanted to take his mind off his troubles.

He almost laughed at the thought. For the first time in his life, things were happening in his favor. How could he possibly find fault with this current state of affairs?

The answer was simple: His life had suddenly become perfect. Even so, it was causing him stress and anguish. Something strange and wonderful had apparently taken control but he saw no valid reason for any of it.

That was it, in a nutshell. He'd somehow lost control of his destiny and wasn't quite sure what he could do about it. What made it so frustrating was that everything had become so dreamlike. Obstacles were pushed aside or eliminated. People were not only listening to him, they were treating him better than they'd ever treated him before.

No matter how he looked at the situation, it made no sense whatsoever.

He was halfway down the block when he heard approaching voices. There were two of them. They both sounded male and were giggling stupidly as they drew closer.

In no time they were right behind him. The heavy reek of weed and whiskey permeated the air the moment one of them slipped past him and quickly spun around, blocking his path.

The haze from the streetlamp straight ahead enabled him to see a leather vest and frayed jeans, several tatts and piercings, a large silver dog collar and two black wristbands with a row of inch-long silver spikes protruding from them. The kid was about Aaron's height and skinny—probably no more than one-thirty on a good day. But the gleaming switchblade in his left hand made him much more intimidating.

The boy's right hand lashed out, stopping about two feet away. It was held open, palm up, facing the dark sky.

"The money and the plastic, motherfucker." The kid's voice was high-pitched and nasal.

Pimples and a sprinkling of chin hair covered his gaunt face.

The punk behind him jabbed Aaron in the small of the back. "Now, asshole." He moved closer and Aaron took in another foul cloud of weed and whiskey. "Don't got all fuckin' night."

Aaron realized he should be terrified. The first punk held the switchblade dead-steady, just two feet away. He had the sinking feeling these boys had done this same thing before. But something about all this had failed to instill any fear in him. Perhaps it was because of what had been happening the last few days. He was confident that the punk behind him was also armed, but that didn't matter, either. He just didn't think he'd be hurt.

"Get a job." The words came out before he realized he'd opened his mouth. "Then you won't have to risk your neck robbing people." He moved onto the grass and walked around the boy.

"Hey! Don't fuckin' walk away from us!" The boy reached out and grabbed Aaron by the upper arm. The blade of the knife glinted in the haze of the streetlamp as it dove down into the darkness. Aaron guessed that it would come back up in an arc before hitting its target. *Be careful with that knife*, he thought wildly. *You're liable to cut yourself.* Then he tensed his body and closed his eyes.

Nothing.

When he opened his eyes, he realized he was approaching the walk that led to Visconti's. Gasps and moans resonated loudly directly behind him.

80

Two figures dressed in dark clothing lay on the sidewalk, wrestling with one another. Two stilettos lay on the pavement just a few feet away.

"What's goin' on, dude?" one of them said as his friend pushed him away.

"I fuckin' *cut* myself! Shit...I almost sliced open my fuckin' *gut!*"

"How'd ya do *that*, dude?"

"I knew *that*, I wouldn't be sittin' here, bleedin' like this, moron!"

"Where'd that guy go?"

"He's walkin' away, you idiot!"

"What the fuck happened?"

"Leggo of my fuckin' arm!"

One of them sat up and looked around. "This...this ain't right, dude... somethin's really fucked up..."

"Ya think?"

***

Nearly all the barstools and most of the tables in Visconti's were filled.

From the far corner, the juke thumped out a heavy, persistent beat over someone's low-pitched, barely audible mumblings.

Aaron found a small table about fifteen feet from the door, next to a smudged window looking out at the dumpsters behind the deserted supermarket across the street.

The husky middle-aged waitress showed definite signs of boredom behind her thick glasses and small, squinty eyes. She took his order and without a word plodded lazily back to the bar.

About five minutes later, she brought over his drink. He sat staring at the glass, his mind on the scuffle. Something just wasn't right.

Two punks with switchblades were following me. One of them went on ahead, said something, and then--

What happened?

That was just it—he didn't know. Everything went black, and now he couldn't remember a damned thing.

He picked up the glass and drank half of it.

How'd I manage to get out of that? Did those two take anything from me?

Suddenly worried, he got out his wallet. It was still there. He opened it. His cash was there as well. So were his credit cards. He obviously hadn't been mugged.

Things were getting way beyond strange. After what he'd seen the last few days, he no longer knew *what* to think. All he knew was that ever since that psycho had attacked him the other night, nothing bad happened to him anymore.

He downed the rest of the drink, put it back down and let the rest of his thoughts intermingle with an avalanche of bright images. Then he stared at his empty glass and thought, *I really need another drink, and I need it now...*

The waitress came right over.

He sat back and watched curiously as the woman lumbered back to the bar. As the realization settled over him, something occurred to him that perplexed him even more.

He didn't think he'd have a problem getting whatever he wanted from now on.

***

When he returned to the condo shortly after midnight, he was completely exhausted.

He shuffled down the carpeted hall to the master bedroom, collapsed on the big double bed and fell asleep in minutes.

In no time at all he was watching beautiful light-haired angels flying amongst the clouds, their translucent wings fluttering wildly. As they frolicked in the sky, he experienced a sudden calm, and a lightness of spirit he hadn't felt since he was a child.

Seeing him, one of the angels fell from the sky, her wings fluttering wildly as she lowered herself gently to the ground. Once she landed, her wings vanished, her golden hair darkened and her large, deep-set blue eyes glowed while gazing at him.

He felt totally mesmerized in her presence. He'd never before seen such a beautiful creature. He tried to speak, but the lump forming in his throat prevented him from getting the words out. He cleared his throat and the words trickled out thickly, like warm molasses. "Are you…an angel?" he asked.

"What do you think?" she asked in a soft, breathless voice.

"I don't know…but you sure are beautiful…"

Her long, curly lashes fluttered. "Then I guess I'm an angel."

"I've never seen a genuine angel before. I don't think I ever truly believed in them."

"You do now, don't you?"

"I must. You're here. I'm talking to you."

"You're talking to me because you must believe in me."

"This could be a dream, couldn't it?"

"Do you want it to be?"

"I want it to be real. I want you to be real."

She laughed. "I am real, then. And if I'm real, you belong to me."

"I belong…to an angel?"

"No, but you belong to me."

"I don't understand."

"Maybe not now, but you will…in time…"

"When?"

"Soon." She moved closer, and an aura of cold nipped at him. Her arms encircled him. It felt as if long ropes of ice had tightened around him. His flesh stood out in knots. Laughing, she pulled him to her, and her icy touch made him go completely numb.

"Who…a-are you?" he whispered, his teeth chattering.

Just before her lips met his, she said, "If you really want to know who I am, there is a price."

"A *price*?" Somehow, the word sounded ominous.

"I think it would be better if I reminded you." Her lips pressed against his, and the intense cold enveloping him turned into an overwhelming blackness.

CHAPTER TWELVE

He awoke just before eight the next morning and had the strange feeling that he'd been visited again during the night.

Instantly alert, he sat up and scanned the room. His clothes lay in a crumpled heap on the floor beside the bed. As was his custom, he laid them neatly on the chair before retiring. The last time he'd found them tossed on the floor was a couple of days ago, in his old apartment. But now they lay there once again, as if they'd been tossed in a hurry.

Yet he had no recollection of leaving them lying there.

Had he woken sometime during the night and removed them?

That seemed doubtful. He assumed that since he'd been so exhausted, he'd slept straight through the night.

Or *had* he? As this shred of doubt lingered, he recounted the events the day before. Judging by his activities, he was satisfied that he'd been much too exhausted to do anything but come straight home and shuffle off to bed.

So why did he shed his clothes and leave them on the floor?

He simply could not remember. From the moment he'd come into this room last night, everything had become a total blank.

Except for the dream...

It came back in a flurry—the meadow, the beautiful golden-haired angels frolicking amongst the clouds.

As these visions swirled around in his consciousness, he wondered if what he'd imagined was really a dream. The images were all so breathtakingly real—especially the golden-haired creature that had come down from the clouds.

Her hair was brilliant—like spun gold. But the moment she touched down and approached him, the gold disappeared and turned dark.

Now, as he struggled to remember, the vividness of the dream quickly faded.

"No!" He vigorously rubbed his temples. He *had* to remember. This was important. For some reason he couldn't quite understand, he sensed that it was vital that he remembered every single detail of that dream. But the harder he tried, the quicker it dissolved, like sand through an hourglass. Just before the last bits vanished, he caught a flash of the dark-haired vision wrapping her arms around him, her soft, caressing voice whispering, "*There is a price…*"

Then the blackness came, swallowing up what was left of his memories.

***

After a warm shower, he fixed breakfast and sat at the small drop-leaf kitchen table near the window overlooking the back yard, where the morning sun cast bright images on the complex, the freshly mowed grass, and glittering specks of the pool on the other side of the picket fence.

As he ate his eggs and toast, he mulled over the dream he'd had the previous night.

Once again he struggled to remember, but the darkness filling his mind prevented anything from coming through, and all he gathered was a sense of intense cold, and that sensuous voice whispering, "There is a price," very close to his face.

What the hell was that all about?

And why couldn't he remember more of it?

Why did he fear some invisible presence lurking close by had forbidden him from bringing back these memories?

***

At around ten, his cell buzzed.

The loud, gruff voice of a man he didn't recognize said, "Mister Grill?"

"Yes?"

"I'm Arthur Ridgemont, Vice President of the Homeowner's Association, and I'd like to talk to you at your earliest convenience."

"What's this about?"

"It concerns your application for residency, of course."

"What about it?"

"If you don't mind, I think we'd better talk about it in person."

"All right."

"When can you come to the office?"

"I'm free right now."

"Splendid. I'll be waiting."

Click.

He pocketed the phone. The man definitely sounded upset. If his guess was correct, Ridgemont

87

had seen his application and wanted to question him about it. Apparently Elizabeth Brennan had done something the man didn't like.

He slipped through the sliding glass door of the kitchen and went down the winding path that led to the complex grounds.

***

The strong smell of fresh-brewed coffee filled the small office.

The man sitting behind the desk was around seventy, with thinning white hair combed straight back, a gaunt face and small, blinking blue eyes looking suspicious behind his square-framed glasses. A white mug half-filled with coffee sat on the green desk blotter next to the phone. The man stood sharply when Aaron came in. He was about six-four and very slender. His white dress shirt and gray pinstripe slacks were clean and pressed. The dark-blue bow tie hung impeccably beneath the man's prominent Adam's apple.

"Mister Grill?"

"Yes?"

"Arthur Ridgemont." He offered his hand. It was large, warm, and surprisingly firm. "Please sit."

Aaron sat as the other man lowered himself behind the desk and picked up some papers.

"On the phone, you mentioned my application." Aaron thought it best to get right to the point.

"Yes." He picked up another paper and studied it while squeezing his right earlobe with the thumb and index finger of his free hand.

"What about it?"

Arthur Ridgemont glanced at Aaron and turned right back to the paper. His forehead wrinkled. "This is, er, awkward, Mr. Grill."

"What's awkward?"

"Elizabeth's name—Mrs. Brennan's name, that is, as well as her husband's name—are listed as references on your application..."

"Really?" Aaron was surprised. But at least now he knew what she'd done to push his application through...

Arthur Ridgemont dropped the paper onto the blotter and gazed at Aaron. He clasped his hands together. "This is highly irregular."

"What's highly irregular?"

Arthur Ridgemont unclasped his hands and sat back. Aaron could tell by the other man's frown that he was about to say something unpleasant. "Mr. Grill, since you're new to our family, you obviously aren't aware of the protocol the Association must stick to in order to maintain its high standards."

"Obviously not."

"But I'm sure you can understand our position here."

"Just tell me what's on your mind."

"Mr. Grill, Elizabeth Brennan has been President of the Homeowner's Association for the last three years and has been doing a wonderful job. She has a spotless record, an untarnished reputation, and we all think highly of her."

"She seems like a nice lady."

"She is highly regarded and extremely well-liked. She and her husband have been playing weekly bridge with my wife and myself for the last fifteen years. I consider her a dear friend, and I don't want anything to jeopardize our relationship."

"That's all very nice, but I don't see what you're trying to tell me."

He frowned at the interruption. "We also attend Mass together and have been directly responsible for organizing the nightly bingo festivities here."

"What are you trying to say?" Aaron wanted this windbag to get to the point.

Arthur Ridgemont sat forward. "Just this. I'd like to know why she signed her name and her husband's name as references on your application."

"I honestly have no idea why she did that."

"Are you trying to tell me you weren't aware of this?"

"I remember her having an issue because I put down only one reference. But no, I didn't realize what she'd done."

"It's right here." He picked up the application and held it up.

Aaron leaned closer. Sure enough, the woman had signed her own name, as well as the name William Brennan. "I guess you're right."

Arthur Ridgemont dropped the application once again. "You're trying to tell me you had no knowledge that she did this?"

"That's exactly what I'm saying."

"I find that difficult to believe."

"Have you discussed this with her?"

"Yes…"

"What did she say?"

"That's what puzzles me about this. She was extremely distant when I brought it up. Very hesitant. In fact, she seemed afraid, and clammed up the moment I started asking questions."

"You said she was afraid?"

"I'd like you to tell me what you did or said that would cause her to react in such a way."

"You think I *forced* her to write down those references?"

Arthur Ridgemont tapped the application three times with his index finger. "This is her signature. I recognize it."

"As I already told you, I was right there with her. But I honestly had no idea what she wrote down."

"Let's not be glib here, Mr. Grill. You know exactly what I'm talking about. I'm not stupid, so I suggest you tell me why my friend would sign her name as a reference for someone she doesn't even know."

"I did absolutely nothing to get her to do it."

"Of course. You don't remember. It happened only a day or so ago, but you don't remember. As I've told you, Elizabeth and William are my dear friends. I know their friends, their relatives. I've never seen you before. And I'd hazard a guess to say that, before you came into this office, neither did Elizabeth. You've come to us completely out of the blue, with only one valid reference. That is totally unacceptable."

"Did you call Lou Connor, by any chance?"

"Of course. Mr. Connor had good things to say about you, although he did mention that you'd left his company about a year ago for medical reasons."

"Did he say anything else?"

"I asked about the circumstances, but he refused to tell me. He did say that you were returning to the company."

"Then what's the problem?"

"Unfortunately, that has nothing to do with Elizabeth or why she put her reputation on the line to attest to someone we've never heard of."

"She's President, right?"

"I'm sure you already know that..."

"What she says goes, right?"

"Under normal conditions..."

"What's abnormal about this?"

"It's very clear to us at the Board that Elizabeth should not have breached protocol. She should have told us about this before making any decision."

"She has to tell you everything she does?"

"We don't know you, Mr. Grill. We've never heard of you before. And judging by her behavior, I'd wager Elizabeth had never heard of you before you filled out this application."

"It doesn't matter, does it?"

"Of course it matters."

"Why should it?"

"I have the strong feeling that you somehow forced her into this."

"How could I possibly do something like that?"

"Mr. Grill, let's not insult one another's intelligence any longer. I strongly suggest that you move out of the condo before—"

"I just moved in. I'm quiet. I never bother anyone. I've been living alone for more than a year. I don't go to parties and never have them myself. I'm starting a high-paying job with tremendous benefits. Lastly, I have no friends or pets. I'd say that makes me a pretty damned good risk."

"It doesn't matter. Protocol was breeched. A meeting will have to be called. We do things a certain way, and since you obviously forced Elizabeth into opening doors that should not have been opened—"

"Why are you making such a big deal about this? I'm not a bad person. In fact—"

"It's not that at all. Protocol is at stake here. We're a tight little community. We like it that way. I'm sorry, but if we let just anyone come in by conning us into doctoring their application, this community will never stay as relaxed and as organized as it has been since it was first built. The system must stand."

"You sound like a politician."

"Mr. Grill, I insist that you take this matter seriously."

"It's much too ridiculous to be taken seriously."

"I'm sorry, but we just can't let something like this get out of hand." He reached for the phone. "I'm going to call Security and let them know that because of protocol violations, you've been ordered off the property. They'll escort you safely off the grounds as soon as you've finished packing. This will be discussed with Elizabeth at an emergency board meeting, and unless she tells us exactly what happened, I'm afraid our decision must stand—"

"I wish you wouldn't do that."

"Pardon me?" Arthur Ridgemont froze; his hand remained inches from the phone.

"I said I wish you wouldn't do that."

Arthur Ridgemont stared at him for long moments. Then he sighed and pulled his hand away from the phone. He sat bolt upright in his chair. "Are you...*threatening* me, Mister Grill?"

"I'm trying to make this situation more tolerable for both of us."

"And just how could you make this more tolerable for *me*?"

He stared directly at the man and thought: *You'd better not make that call.*

Arthur Ridgemont's face paled. He trembled and slumped in his seat. After a long, tense silence, he sighed. In a tired, raspy voice, he said, "Maybe I did act...a little...foolishly."

"You almost made a terrible mistake."

Arthur Ridgemont went back to staring at Aaron's application. "I think I've been a little harsh with Elizabeth as well."

"I believe you owe her an apology."

Arthur Ridgemont raised his head and appeared dazed—as if he'd just awoken from a sound sleep. "I believe I owe you one as well, although I have no idea why..."

"Don't question it. Just do it. You'll feel much better."

"All right... I'm sorry, Mister Grill."

"Aaron stood. "Then my application is approved?"

"Of course."

"It's been nice doing business with you."

Arthur Ridgemont didn't reply. He pulled a handkerchief out of his pocket and began mopping at his forehead as Aaron opened the door.

CHAPTER THIRTEEN

The next morning, Aaron drove to downtown Orlando.

After leaving the Crown Vic in the parking garage down the block from the C&H Offices, he stopped at the First National Bank on Orange Avenue and asked to see the bank president.

One of the cashiers—a skinny blonde in her early twenties—told him the man was busy. Aaron told her to check again. A little shaken by Aaron's insistence, the girl whisked away. Less than two minutes later, she came back and gestured for him to follow her down the carpeted hall.

The bank president was about fifty, tall and broad, with a reddish-brown comb-over that barely did its job. He had tiny blue eyes and a complexion that suggested heavy drinking, high blood pressure, or both. The brass nameplate on his desk said *MELVIN OSBORNE, BANK PRESIDENT*. He'd just put down the phone when the blonde led Aaron into the office. His expression was a mixture of anger and disgust. He looked like someone who'd been rudely interrupted in the middle of something important.

The blonde quickly pulled the door closed behind her. She obviously wanted to make herself scarce.

"What can I do for you, sir?" Melvin Osborne asked. "We don't know one another, do we?"

"I don't believe we do." Aaron sat without being asked to.

Melvin Osborne scowled. He followed suit and kept his scowl, strongly indicating that he was having trouble tolerating this interruption. "I hope we can end this quickly. I've got an important meeting." He raised his left arm and consulted his Rolex. "In fifteen minutes."

"This won't take long."

"That suits me just fine. As for Miss Hollenbeck interrupting my last call... Bank policy clearly states that I'm not to be disturbed unless—"

"You're not going to do anything to Miss Hollenbeck," Aaron said flatly.

"Excuse me?"

"She had no choice but to do as I told her."

Melvin Osborne stood abruptly. "Listen...whoever you are—"

"My name is Aaron Grill."

"Er...Mister Grill, whatever your reason is for coming here—"

"I'd like to transfer money into my account."

Melvin Osborne groaned. "Sir, you do not need my assistance to make such a transaction. Miss Hollenbeck has been specifically trained to handle such tasks. Even if she was busy with another customer, there are four other tellers out in the main area at all times. Any one of them could have—"

"I actually need you to do this for me."

A pause. "Now why would you need *me* to transfer money?"

"Two reasons, actually. One, I don't have an account at this bank."

The man shrugged and sat back down. "Again, you don't need me for that."

"No, but I do need you for something else."

"And what might that be?"

"I want you to arrange to take your twelve-dollar monthly banking fee, deduct two dollars of it from everyone's account, as you do each month, and transfer it automatically into a new account. This new account will be in my name."

Melvin Osborne sat in silence, his eyes fixed on Aaron. After several uncomfortable moments, he squinted and tilted his head as if he'd heard something he couldn't quite understand. "What in hell are you suggesting, sir?"

"Did you not understand any of that?"

Melvin Osborne's face splashed crimson. "Sir, what you are asking me to do—"

"I'm not asking." Aaron stood up and approached the desk. "This is something you have to do."

Melvin Osborne stood again and watched Aaron in stunned silence. His eyes lowered briefly to the phone on his desk before returning to Aaron. "Sir, I don't know who you are, but if you don't get the hell out of my office in the next five seconds, I'm going to call Security and have you escorted outside, where the Orlando Police Department will be waiting for—"

"Listen to me, you idiot…" Aaron glared. "If you don't do exactly as I say, several things will happen. First of all, you'll have difficulty breathing. Then you'll suffer a heart attack and probably die in just a couple of minutes."

Melvin Osborne's broad face turned a blotchy red. He then began gasping for air and reached up to loosen the knot of his tie.

"Get the idea now?" Aaron asked.

Struggling for breath, Melvin Osborne nodded.

"Now...will you do as I say?"

Melvin Osborne nodded once again. A moment later, he began breathing easier. Then, without another word, he collapsed in his chair.

***

At eleven o'clock, Lou Connor sat at his desk, talking on his phone.

Aaron approached the doorway and waited anxiously for his former boss to finish his call. He was looking forward to this meeting but felt somewhat guilty. C&H had always been a good company to work for. It wasn't fair to Lou or the company what was about to happen, but Aaron just couldn't see struggling through the same grind he'd endured in his former life, before Providence had intervened.

After about a minute, the man hung up and wrote something on his notepad. Aaron tapped the door. Connor put down his pen and looked up. When he saw Aaron standing there, he motioned for him to come in.

"I was just about to call you." He stood and reached over the desk to shake Aaron's hand then sat back down and gestured for Aaron to follow suit. "It's been several days since our last talk, and you mentioned that you might be moving."

"I already moved." Aaron sat.

"Oh? Where?"

"I found a nice two-bedroom condo in Winter Park. It's just a few miles north of Colonial."

"So you've already settled in?"

"Yes."

"I was going to call and ask when you'd decided to come in, but since you're here—"

"That's why I'm here. I decided to tell you in person that I've decided not to return to C&H."

Connor froze in his chair. "You're *not* coming back?"

"That's right."

Connor went silent. Aaron could tell the man was trying to analyze the situation. Connor considered all problems challenges and went out of his way to solve them. He'd always boasted that he could solve any problem presented him. "What exactly are you getting at?"

"It's very simple. I don't need to come in. I don't have to work anymore."

His face flushed, Connor sat up in his chair. "What about that substantial signing bonus we just gave you?"

"I sure did appreciate the gesture, Lou. Thanks again."

Connor took a breath. "You were given ten thousand dollars on the condition that—"

"I'm aware of the condition."

"Then you must know that, by law, you're required to—"

"I know what I'm required to do. I signed the papers."

"Then what's all this about?"

"I just told you. I don't have to work anymore. Why should I work when I no longer have to?"

"You just signed a contract with us!"

"I realize that."

"This company can sue you for the signing bonus, as well as for breach of contract. We can also arrange it so you won't be able to find another job in this town."

Aaron sighed. "Haven't you been listening to me? I already told you I don't have to work anymore. Why should I worry about getting another job when I no longer need to work?"

"Aaron..." Connor suddenly sounded tired. "This isn't making any sense. Surely you realize what that contract means—what it can do. How it can hurt you..."

"There *is* no contract."

"*What* did you say?"

"I said, there *is* no contract."

"I witnessed it. I co-signed and even notarized—"

"That doesn't mean anything."

"How can you possibly say that?"

"I can say it because you're going to rip it up as soon as I leave."

Connor's right eyelid twitched. "I beg your pardon?"

"You heard me. As soon as I leave this office, you're going to rip up that contract and toss the pieces in the trash."

"What makes you think I'll do something like that?"

"You have to. You've got no choice."

"I don't think I quite understand what you're—

"

"It's very simple. If you don't rip up the contract, you're going to be sorry."

"Seriously? A threat?"

"Just a warning."

Connor continued sitting perfectly still, watching Aaron. Then he lowered his voice. It was a tactic Aaron had witnessed many times before. The gentle approach. And it usually worked.

"Aaron, I'd like you to tell me what's going on."

"I told you what's going on."

"You just gave me some cockamamie story about not having to work anymore. What happened? Did you hit the Lottery? Inherit a fortune?"

"Better than that." He got up.

"Aaron, talk to me!"

"You wouldn't believe me if I told you."

"Try me."

"All you need to know is that you have to rip up that contract. Rip it up—as well as any and all other copies. And don't tell anyone you did it. If anyone asks, just tell them we made other arrangements."

Connor jumped up. "You can't *do* this!"

"I wouldn't have a fit if I were you. You might have a coronary."

"Aaron Grill, if you leave this office right now, I swear I'll—"

"You'll what?"

Connor opened his mouth, but nothing came out. He began gasping for breath. Then he grabbed

101

his left arm with his right hand and fell back into his chair.

"See what I mean?"

Connor continued gasping in his chair.

"All you have to do is nod that you agree to my terms, and everything will be okay again."

Choking and coughing, Connor struggled to loosen the knot of his tie. His gasping grew more frequent; slobber gathered at the corners of his mouth.

"Just nod and it'll all go away," Aaron said.

The other man fought for breath. His bulging eyes focused on Aaron and he nodded. A moment later, he took a deep breath and lowered his head in a coughing fit. About thirty seconds later, he began breathing easier. He sat back and gawked at Aaron with an expression that was a mixture of shock and fear.

"You okay now?" Aaron asked.

Connor closed his eyes and nodded.

"Good deal." Aaron turned and approached the door. "Don't forget to rip up that contract and all the copies. And thanks for the signing bonus. It really came in handy."

***

On the way back to his condo, Aaron stopped at a liquor store and picked up two bottles of their best bourbon.

He walked up to the register, placed the bottles on the counter and waited as the man rang it up. Seconds later, the man waited for Aaron to hand over the cash.

Aaron smiled pleasantly. "I didn't bring any money with me."

The cashier, big and burly, had the look of a former Marine. Judging by his grim expression, he obviously didn't appreciate nonsense. He stepped away from the register, rested his huge fists on the counter and gave Aaron a look that clearly suggested that he was not in the mood for bullshit. "*What* was that?"

Aaron shrugged. "I said, I don't have any money."

"Then why'd you pick up these bottles?"

"Because I want them and I'm taking them with me."

"Without payin'?"

Aaron winked. "You got it."

The man straightened, closed his hands around the necks of the bottles and dragged them closer to him. His small black eyes glistened. "Get your sorry ass the hell outa here and don't ever come back."

"You're not being very friendly."

"Mister, if you don't get your ass the hell outa here right now, I'm gonna pick you up and toss you out the door. Then I'm gonna call the cops and have them haul away what's left of your worthless carcass."

"You really don't mean that, do you?"

"If ya don't think I mean it, just keep standin' there. I'll give ya a live demonstration."

Aaron sighed. "You don't want to do anything like that. It'll turn out seriously bad for you."

The man glanced at the two corner convex mirrors bolted to the ceiling, then at the front door.

He leaned toward Aaron and lowered his voice. "You sonuvabitch…if you don't get outa my store right now, I'm gonna take your pathetic ass out back and beat the livin' shit—"

"You know you don't really mean that," Aaron said.

"You stupid sonuvabitch—"

"You don't mean it because you won't be able to do it. If you try, you'll be sorry."

"Listen to me, you fuckin' idiot—"

The man didn't finish. He doubled over and began choking and hacking away.

Aaron waited until he was convinced the man got the message. Then he picked up the bottles and left the store.

***

Later that evening, after a large dinner he'd selected from the deli at the supermarket down the street, he watched the local news on the new sixty-inch widescreen that the tall, skinny young guy working at the electronics department at the local Walmart had given him at his request.

He knew he should be at least moderately tired from such an eventful day, but after he stepped into the shower for a few minutes and approached the mirror to dry his hair, he realized that he was bored and needed some excitement. He hadn't had a night out since his stop at Visconti's and found that he craved fresh air and scenery. He decided to drive to one of the clubs in the area, have a few drinks and hook up with a stripper, or waitress.

It had been a long time since he was with a woman. When Lana walked out, sex quickly became something he associated with his past. He'd wanted only to be left alone—to crawl deep inside his bottle and hide until the hurt, the anger, and the nightmares disappeared.

But now that things had settled in comfortably and began moving in an exciting new direction, he wanted to start having fun again. Since he no longer had difficulty achieving anything he desired, he saw no reason why finding and bringing home a sexy, willing babe would be difficult.

CHAPTER FOURTEEN

At nine-thirty that evening, Colonial Drive roared with heavy traffic.

Six solid lanes sat at the intersections, waiting tensely for the light to change. Aaron pulled into Shannon's, a new nightclub that displayed a giant shamrock blinking in bright neon over the front entrance of the red brick building. The front lot was packed. He drove around the building to find a place to park in back. The club was definitely doing a booming business; only two empty spaces were available.

Inside, a brightly-lit foyer, its green walls covered with large prints of Irish landscapes, highlighted the open area leading to the carpeted hall. A tall, slender redhead dressed in a long black dress and open-toed black spikes met him with a dimpled smile. Her nametag said *Hi! I'm AUDREY!* She wore a sparkling silver necklace, glittering bracelets and several earrings glinting at him from each ear. The tiny tatt of a red heart showed visibly on the inside of her left wrist.

"Where would you like to sit?" She moved closer so he could hear her above the thumping of the p.a. system.

He took in her large cornflower blue eyes and her sweet lavender perfume while trying to decide if he wanted to take her back to the condo. The wedding ring on her finger probably went for two or three grand. It also suggested that she might not be his most sensible choice for an evening companion. "A booth would be nice."

She smiled and led him down the hall.

His waitress took his order and came back with his bourbon on the rocks a couple of minutes later, setting it carefully on a coaster on the table in front of him next to the flickering white candle. Her black hair was pulled back and tied in a thick ponytail. Her nametag said *WENDY*. Her breasts were as large as Audrey's, but the squiggly name *FIONA* tattooed over her left breast, near the cleavage, gave off red flags. She smiled and said she'd be back to check on him in a few minutes. Then she was gone.

Three booths down, on the other side of the aisle, a couple sat, having drinks. The man's back was to him. The woman faced him. She looked about twenty-five and was slender and fine-featured, with long, thick blond hair. Her ears were pierced; silver studs glinted from each lobe. She wore a sleeveless black blouse, red skirt and black open-toed spikes. Her legs were long and shapely. He could see them clearly beneath their table.

The man facing her was broad-shouldered, with thick black hair professionally styled and cut. Aaron couldn't see his face but could tell by the fit of his jacket that he was expensively dressed.

His first impulse was to walk right over and tell the man to leave. That would be a huge mistake. It wouldn't go over too well with the woman and would start the evening on a sour note. This had to be handled just right. Otherwise, he'd have to look for someone else.

107

She was a little young, but perfect in every other conceivable way. He decided it would be foolish to go after someone else when he'd already spotted a woman meeting his criteria.

He decided to wait until her date made a trip to the restroom. They'd obviously been here a little while; it wouldn't be long before one of them needed a potty break.

His waitress came back and peered over his shoulder. Her ponytail dangled between them. "Not ready for a refill?"

"Not yet."

"I'll come back in a few." She whisked away.

Ten minutes passed.

Twenty.

His waitress came back with his refill. As soon as she left, the man and woman slid out of their booth, got up and went down the hall leading to the restrooms.

Aaron got up from his seat and followed.

**

The man was about thirty, tall and broad-shouldered, with the build of a former linebacker.

He stood in front of one of the six urinals on the other side of the brightly lit room, whistling something by Elton John while relieving himself. Aaron walked over to the sink and washed his hands.

The man flushed, approached the sink at the far end and turned on the tap.

"Is that your wife you're with?" Aaron asked.

The man turned his head but kept scrubbing. "Pardon?"

"The woman you're with. Who is she to you?"

The man stopped scrubbing. "What business is it of yours?"

"Is she your wife? Girlfriend?"

"Listen, bud—"

Aaron gazed into the other man's eyes. "You really need to answer my question."

The man immediately went pale. His eyes filled the sockets.

"Wife? Girlfriend?"

He swallowed with difficulty. "She's...a colleague..."

"That wasn't so hard, was it?"

Sighing, the man leaned against the sink. He looked like he'd just lost a long, grueling race.

"You'd better wash the soap off your hands. You're spilling some suds on your slacks. Those threads look pricey."

The man turned awkwardly back to the sink. Shaking a little, he put his hands beneath the thick stream of water.

Aaron grabbed some paper towels and dried his hands. "How'd you two get here? Did you drive? Or did she?"

The man turned off the tap and snatched a few paper towels from the dispenser. He didn't look at Aaron as he wiped his hands. "I drove."

"Okay...here's what I want you to do. Go out to your car. Call her from your cell and tell her you had to leave unexpectedly. Then drive straight home. Understand?"

Startled, he turned to face Aaron. "I can't just leave her here...by herself..."

"She'll be fine."

The man didn't reply.

"Understand?"

The man paled again. After a few moments, he nodded.

"One other thing. The moment you leave this room, you won't remember me at all—get it?"

***

The blonde was gawking at her cell as Aaron approached her table. "Want some company?"

She glanced up at him and turned right back to her cell.

"Were you stood up?"

She kept staring at her cell.

He jabbed a thumb toward his booth. "I was sitting over there and couldn't help noticing that you were here with someone. Judging by your present mood, he's not coming back, is he?"

She closed the cell and dropped it in her black leather bag. "I'm all right, thanks."

"Are you sure you don't want company? You look like you could use some stimulating conversation right now."

"I appreciate your concern, but—"

"You'd rather sit by yourself?"

She didn't reply.

"You're obviously pretty upset. I really think you need some company."

She looked up at him. A mixture of hurt and anger filled her big blue eyes. "Listen...I'm not in the mood right now..."

"You're not in the mood for stimulating conversation?"

She didn't reply.

"I know what it's like to be stood up. It happens. However, in our case, I just can't understand it. A woman as beautiful as you?"

"I haven't been stood up!" Her tone was sharp.

"He's not here, is he?"

She didn't reply.

"Is he coming back?"

She just sighed.

"*I'm* here. That's *some*thing, isn't it?"

"Listen…I know you mean well…"

"I do, I really do."

She turned to her drink and frowned at it.

He gazed at her and let his thoughts drift her way. *I suggest you ask me to join you…*

Confusion showed clearly in her eyes. After a few moments, she looked around the room as if she'd come out of a trance.

"May I?" He gestured to the seat facing her.

She stared at the empty place for a moment. Then she nodded. "Please…"

***

She said her name was Brittany Michaels and that she'd been working as a paralegal aide the last two years, since graduating from Rollins.

She was twenty-four, and the man with her was a defense lawyer she'd been working with the last six months. His name was Alan Jenkins, and she loved working with him because he treated her well and didn't have the condescending attitude of most other attorneys she knew.

"I just don't understand why he left so suddenly," she said. "He's *never* done that before."

111

"A family emergency, maybe?" Aaron asked.

"He still wouldn't have left me here alone like this. He's just not that way. He's always been a real gentleman—the kind of guy who opens doors for a girl and stands up when she enters a room. I hope nothing bad happened..."

He caught himself staring at her neck again—and her breasts, which were small, but round and full. She had a tiny waist, and her toned arms and legs suggested tennis or aerobics. Judging by her gorgeous diamond-shaped calves, he guessed aerobics, or maybe even weights. He visualized pulling off that top, unbuckling the belt and sliding the skirt down those long, firm thighs—

You'd better not...

The sudden thought came from out of nowhere. It sounded like a woman's voice, but he couldn't be sure, and he wondered if he'd just imagined it. Was it just nerves? His insecurity rearing its ugly head? It was possible, wasn't it? It had been quite a while since he'd picked up a woman.

I'm just a little rusty. My subconscious is trying to warn me not to make a fool of myself.

He picked up his glass. The whiskey went down smoothly, and he began feeling a little better.

"Are you all right?" she asked. "You look a little nauseous."

"I'm okay." He sat quietly, waiting for his pulse to settle down. After a few deep breaths, he felt much better. It had been a long day, but he suspected it was about to get much better. "Please go on. You were saying?"

"All I was saying was that Alan's much more considerate than most others—especially in this profession. Attorneys can be a handful." She glanced at her watch. "I really need to give him time to get home. Then I'll call to see what happened."

"I'm sure nothing's wrong."

"Then why'd he leave me here without a word of explanation?"

"Like I said, it could've been a family emergency. Can I get you another drink?"

"I really shouldn't. Tomorrow's a workday, and I should be getting back home."

"I can take you home."

"I couldn't ask you to do that..."

"You need a ride. I'd feel guilty if I knew you had to take a cab when I've got my car out back."

"I hate cabs. Besides, I don't think I could afford one to take me all the way to my apartment. I live just a few miles south of Altamonte."

"Like I just said, my car's outside, in back..."

"We only just met."

"Does that matter?"

"Listen...Aaron...I'm really not that kind of girl."

"The kind who doesn't accept rides from strangers?"

She smiled. "You know what I'm talking about."

"I'm talking about driving you home—nothing else."

She stared at him. She was obviously trying to decide if he was telling her the truth. "Look, I've been around. I really like guys, but if I had a nickel for every time one of them tried that stupid just-ran-out-of-gas trick…or anything else just as equally lame…"

"Just one more drink, and I promise I'll take you wherever you want to go. I'll even stay in the car if it'll make you feel better."

He imagined her in his bed, naked and eager, and envisioned how her breasts would look in the dim hall light…how her hair would glow in the darkness—

You've already been warned…

The strange voice had returned. It was definitely a woman's voice and sounded vaguely familiar. Although he couldn't place it right off, he decided this had nothing to do with his nervousness or insecurity about picking up a strange woman.

But he had no idea what it *was* about…

"Aaron?"

He closed his eyes and lowered his head, struggling to clear his mind and calm himself. When the confusion disappeared, he remembered where he was and what he was doing. "I'm okay. Probably just something I had for supper earlier."

"I've got some Tums in my bag…"

"Thanks. I'm all right. Really." He wiped his forehead with a napkin and sat back in the booth. "What were we talking about?"

She paused a moment. "It…sounds silly now…"

"Go on. I'm a good listener."

"I was just saying that I really can't trust guys because they lie so much."

"I don't lie…"

114

"Not ever?"

"I used to…when I was young and stupid."

"But not now?"

"Brittany, look at me…"

Her eyes met his. His thoughts were loud and clear as they drifted toward her. *It's okay, Brittany…you can trust me…*

She sat very still. She looked like she'd just slipped into a trance. Then, blinking, she snapped out of it. A smile touched her lips. "Okay. I'll trust you. But only on the condition that we leave now. I really shouldn't have another drink. I have to be at the office early in the morning."

"That's fine." He smiled back, knowing that once he got this beauty in his car, she wouldn't be going straight home. When they were on their way, he'd slip another thought into her head—something that would excite her, appeal to her sense of adventure, and—

This is your final warning…

A fit of nausea swept violently through him. Something hot and sharp sliced him in the gut, and he doubled up.

"Aaron? Should I call nine-one-one?"

He shook his head and tensed his body, struggling as the spasms raged through him.

"You don't have an ulcer, do you?"

He shook his head again.

"Are you sure? I can get the paramedics here—
"

"I'll be all right." His thoughts looped, going back to the last few days.

Did this have anything to do with the strange new karma that had changed his life?

All I want is to take this beautiful babe home…

Once I get those clothes off and—

Stop it. That voice filled his head again…

He was upset and nervous. This could be indigestion, for all he knew. He had a big dinner. Maybe the baked fish wasn't quite fresh enough.

After a while, the storm within him vanished and he was able to sit up.

"You okay?" Brittany asked.

"I'm just fine."

"You're sure?"

"I'm sure."

Watching him closely, she picked up her bag and got up. He got up and followed her outside. As they went down the walk, he took in a healthy whiff of her perfume and felt his blood boiling. *Easy. You don't want another episode.*

Don't be silly. You've had a long day and need release. Once you've got her home with you, things will be just fine.

As they approached his car, the dizziness came from out of nowhere, sweeping through him.

Then he blacked out.

***

When he opened his eyes moments later, he was kneeling on the cold pavement between his car and the one parked beside it.

Brittany lay beneath him. His hands were locked around her neck. He was choking the life out of her.

What the fuck?

116

His mind screamed at him, and to his horror he quickly realized that he could not pull his hands away. Some invisible force held them fast. As hard as he struggled, he just could not release his viselike grip from her throat. She gasped and choked, her body squirming and twisting wildly beneath him. Her knees pounded his back and her hands clawed at his forearms as the life steadily drained out of her.

No...this isn't happening...this is a dream...I'm not doing this!

Close your eyes.

He'd done this before, hadn't he? Inside the club, just minutes ago, when he kept hearing the strange voice. And it had worked, hadn't it? Yes. It made things as they'd been before.

No reason why it shouldn't work again, was there?

When you open them again, everything will be as it was before...

He closed his eyes and visualized himself pulling away...and straightening...and making sure Brittany was breathing again before he got in his car, drove a safe distance away and then dialed 911 to get someone here to help her.

But when he opened them again, he realized instantly that he'd been deceiving himself. He was standing over her, gazing down at her motionless body.

She was dead.

Then he heard the voice once again. It was the same voice he'd heard before, in the club. It sounded like it was coming from somewhere deep inside him.

"This is the price you must pay…"

CHAPTER FIFTEEN

Waking early, Aaron pushed the sheets aside and realized he was naked.

Again? How many other times had this happened? Two? Three? And why was it happening in the first place?

He swung his legs over the side and sat there, staring at the heap on the floor while trying to figure out what was going on.

Something happened last night. It was something he couldn't quite remember...something bad...

His thoughts went back to Shannon's...to the booth where he'd seen the beautiful young blonde sitting with a big guy in an expensive suit.

Yes. The blonde. He wanted to bring her back to the condo with him for the night.

He struggled to remember. To his delight, the details came back quickly. Once she and her companion got up and went to the restrooms, Aaron followed the man into the men's room and convinced him to leave the building without the woman. The man, of course, was reluctant but, with the added incentive of Aaron's suggestion, did as he was instructed. Once he'd left, Aaron went back out into the bar and began chatting with the woman. Her name was Brittany, and she worked at a law firm in Orlando. She was distrustful of men, but once he'd convinced her he meant no harm, she accepted his offer of driving her home.

His memory of the event remained clear right up to the time he'd escorted her outside and down the walk, where his car was parked behind the building.

Why couldn't he remember what happened after that? Each time he tried, his mind turned the rest of the evening into a muddled darkness.

Did he drive her back to her apartment? Surely he'd remember stopping outside her building or escorting her up the walk, to her front door...

He possessed a unique gift. Strange things he couldn't possibly explain had been happening to him. It wouldn't have taken much to convince Brittany or any other girl to invite him into her home and eventually into her bed.

He'd obviously come home alone. Otherwise, there would be signs of someone else in the condo with him. But as far as he could tell, there were no signs whatsoever. He saw no evidence of a woman's clothing lying on the floor or on the chair in the corner. No scent of a woman's perfume lingered in the room. No aromas of coffee or food drifted down the hall from the kitchen.

He was naked, but he'd obviously come home alone.

Why couldn't he remember anything?

***

He decided to consult with a doctor.

The matter of his life turning in a different direction had suddenly become minor; the prospect of losing his memory was what terrified him. He had to find out what was happening to him and how he could deal with it.

But first, he decided on a long, hot shower and breakfast. Then he'd consult the Yellow Pages and spend some time trying to find a specialist who might be able to help him.

He got up and took a couple of steps toward the bathroom when a heavy wave of dizziness swept through him. Frightened, he sat back down on the edge of the bed. *Relax, close your eyes, and ride it out. It's just nerves—it'll pass.*

In moments he felt himself relaxing and fell backward onto the mattress. He lay there on his back, letting the soft waves of darkness wash over him.

What seemed like just moments later, he opened his eyes and felt completely revitalized. The exhaustion had vanished, and his energy levels had reached a new high. Briefly he thought he'd forgotten something, but the complete blankness in his mind suggested that it could simply be residual fatigue.

After a shower and a big breakfast of three scrambled eggs, buttered rye toast and six strips of crispy bacon, he discovered that he not only felt a hundred percent better, but he was also even more eager to start the day. For some reason, the short rest was just what he'd needed. Whatever had happened the night before no longer mattered. The important thing was that he and the blonde— whatever her name was—hadn't been able to connect. It didn't matter why; the only thing that concerned him was that he'd come home alone.

He got behind the wheel of the Crown Vic just before twelve and drove to the Mall on Colonial and

Maguire. It was a great day to get some new clothes and pick up some DVDs he'd always wanted. Since he no longer had to pay for anything, he couldn't think of a more pleasant way of spending a sunny afternoon.

He stepped into the first electronics store he came to and went right over to the Bargain DVD bin. He picked up a dozen movies and approached the counter, where the skinny young redheaded cashier popped gum while studying a graphic novel through the thick, red-rimmed glasses perched on the tip of her short upturned nose.

He placed the pile on the counter. Scowling at the interruption, she reluctantly turned away from her mindless reading material. With one heavily tattooed hand, she logged onto her register, scanned the DVDs one by one and rang them up. She gave his button-down shirt a quick look of disapproval and turned back to the display on the register. "That's two-twenty-five-seventy-six, with tax." Her voice was flat, disinterested.

"That's all right. I'll let you pay for it." Aaron gave her a friendly wink. "I'll give you and your register a moment alone while you do it. Then you can go right back to your comic book."

She directed her next scowl at his face. "*Huh*?"

"Did I stutter?"

Her thin black brows mashed together. "Listen. Dude...you friggin' *kiddin'* me?"

He gazed into her large cornflower blue eyes and pushed his next thought into her lame brain. *Do I look like I'm kidding, you stupid twit?*

122

Her eyes grew; her facial muscles tightened. A sick pallor had taken over her features.

He moved closer. Luckily, no one was close, but he lowered his voice anyway. "Ring it up with your personal code. You'll feel much better."

She swallowed audibly. Then, nodding, she rang up his purchases.

***

Thirty minutes later, after leaving Elegant Wearhouse for Men with a pair of two-thousand-dollar imported Italian suits wrapped very carefully in the store's stylishly monogrammed garment bag, Aaron went back outside and headed briskly down the long aisle of the front parking lot, where his car was parked.

As he opened his trunk and carefully laid the garment bag flat, he heard the approaching clicks of high heels on the pavement behind him. Just as he straightened, his elbow bumped into someone, and he spun around. Just a couple of feet away, a woman tripped, dropping her handbag as well as a large bag of purchases.

"Damn! I'm so *sorry*!" His pulse racing, he bent, took her arm and carefully helped her back up. While she wiped off her sleeve, he grabbed her bag from the pavement and handed it to her. She took it and checked it for damages. He picked up the other bag where it had landed in front of the rear bumper of a white Lexus and checked the pavement to make sure nothing had fallen out. Then he turned around. "I really am very sorry. I didn't mean to…I guess I wasn't paying attention…"

He stopped talking and stood perfectly still, holding her bag in front of him like an idiot. But he didn't care. He quickly discovered that he didn't care about anything but the woman standing just a couple of feet away, fixing the sleeves of her jacket and pushing her hair away from her face.

She had the clearest emerald-green eyes he'd ever seen. They were large and long lashed, and very calm, possessing an almost dreamlike quality. Her hair was a rich chestnut brown and barely brushed her shoulders. She had full, pouty lips, and her cheekbones were large and round. She was tall—nearly his own height—and slender, with long legs and a tiny waist. Her breasts were small, and her simple outfit—short-waisted tan jacket, turquoise blouse and black skirt two or three inches below the knee—made her a knockout.

"To what?" she said suddenly, in a soft, low voice.

Her voice wrenched him right out of his fantasy, and he realized what had happened and what he'd done. *Think, Grill... Start using that brain again.*

"I obviously wasn't paying attention to what I was doing," he said, hoping it came out all right.

She smiled. It made him glad that he'd been so clumsy. Otherwise, this beauty would have walked right on by. He wouldn't have had the opportunity to get close to her...or talk to her...or watch her gorgeous face break into such a breathtaking smile.

"I've done that once or twice, too," she said.

"What? Not pay attention? Or suddenly turn into a total klutz?"

124

"Both, now that you mention it."

"Could I possibly ask if I could make this up to you?"

"Make what up to me?"

He shrugged. "Bumping into you. Knocking you down. Tossing all your stuff onto the pavement. Making you late for whatever you were doing..."

"All you did was bump into me. You didn't exactly turn my future into a cosmic disaster... *I* was the one who wasn't paying attention. If I *had* been, I wouldn't have bumped into you in the first place. I guess I was walking a little too close..."

He wanted to tell her that he was grateful she'd been walking so close but decided that would be tacky. Best try and maintain a *little* dignity. "Anyway, I'd like to make up for it."

She regarded him for a few moments, her beautiful eyes taking him in. She was obviously thinking it over. Then he eyes lowered. "Well, for starters, you can give me back my bag." She sighed. "I kind of put my credit card into a serious coma with the stuff I just bought."

He realized only then that he was still holding it. He felt himself reddening. "*Damn.* I'm *such* an idiot." He handed it to her and was grateful that she found this amusing. "I'm not usually this...I don't normally...that is, I usually—"

"Function as a normal human being when you're not busy being an idiot?" she finished for him, and they both laughed.

Moments later, he realized he was gawking again. "Do you...have time right now?"

"For what?"

125

"For anything."

"You'll have to be just a teensy more specific."

"Coffee? Tea? A latté, maybe? Lunch? Maybe a drink at one of the bars?"

She checked her watch. "Well, actually, I've really got to be going back to work..."

"It would mean a lot to me." The prospects of watching her leave so soon saddened him. Her smile—as well as her bright air—had made him feel much better than he'd felt in a long time. He hoped he wouldn't have to use his strange new gift to force her to share a few minutes with him. He didn't want to do anything that would remove the smile from her face.

"All right, then. But I've really got to be back to work in an hour."

"How far away do you work from here?"

"Fifteen minutes, if traffic isn't too bad."

"Then maybe you can spare half an hour or so with me?"

Her smile remained. "I guess I can handle that."

***

Inside the Mall, they stopped at a small latte shop down the hall from the busy Food Court.

The waitress took their order and brought over their lattes a couple of minutes later, where they sat in the corner just inside the open entrance, overlooking the hectic activity on the other side of the glass wall.

Her name was Roxie Nash, and she owned and ran a bookstore called Classic Reads on Curry Ford and Crystal Lake Road. Using what money she'd saved from a small trust fund her parents had left her, she'd bought the office space next to a strip mall five years earlier and opened the store. She was thirty-four and didn't wear a wedding band. He didn't see much other jewelry, either. When she opened her jacket, a small copper necklace peeked at him through the two-inch slit in her blouse. Aside from her watch and a small gold stud in each earlobe, she wore no other accessories.

"What sort of books do you carry?" He hadn't read in years and was intrigued that she was doing something so old-fashioned in today's high-tech, digital society.

"All kinds, but mostly fiction. I love fiction—especially the classics. That's why I named the store Classic Reads."

"Do they sell?"

She had a sip of her latte and frowned. "People don't read like they used to. The Internet has just about killed the desire for a good, quiet read."

He felt sorry for her and wanted to visit her store to buy a few books just to see her smile again. "There will probably always be book lovers."

"It'll never be how it was before the Internet, but yes, there will always be devoted readers. What about you? What do you do?"

He stared at his latte and thought about what he should tell her. He couldn't very well tell her the truth. No one in his right mind would believe him, for one thing. He found his current streak of good luck too fantastic to understand, let alone share it with someone else.

"I've been taking it easy lately," he said.

"Lucky you…"

"I'm very fortunate. It seems that I don't have to work anymore."

"Did you hit the Lotto or something?"

"Actually, an investment paid off and pretty much changed my life."

She nodded.

"But I don't intend to go crazy."

"Crazy?"

"I won't go on a wild spending spree...or buy things I don't really need. I can't see getting a brand-new Porsche or Lamborghini or buying a mansion in Aspen."

"That sounds very wise."

"I've always been sensible and conservative. Even in high school, I never went out much. I never even liked going to parties. I was always the guy standing in the corner, watching everyone else have a good time."

"That's sad..."

"I didn't mind, but it killed my chances when I tried dating."

"But look at you now. You're a nice-looking guy. You're quiet and reserved. And you obviously take care of yourself."

He found himself growing uncomfortable. But it made him realize how different things were right now—how different *he* was. "Thank you."

"I really mean it. Those girls who considered you boring back then might think differently about you now."

"The funny thing is, I don't care about that stuff anymore."

"You shouldn't. You should only care about the here and now."

"You're not married, are you, Roxie?"

"Divorced. How about you?"

"My wife divorced me last year."

"It was rough, wasn't it?"

"Most divorces are."

"Yours was obviously pretty bad…"

"Why do you say that?"

"I saw the pain in your eyes when you said it."

"It *was* bad."

"Did you go off the deep end? Chase any woman within earshot? Drink? That sort of thing?"

He wondered if she'd just had a peek of what was going on inside him. He knew it was probably just his imagination working, but she'd still managed to nail it on the head. "I started drinking."

"Men tend to do that. Women usually go out and get picked up."

"Is that what you did?"

"At first. But then I sobered up and realized what I was doing. There are a lot of dangerous guys out there. I just wasn't ready to hook up with someone bad and end up lying dead in a ditch. I'm much too young for that."

"There are a lot of crazy women out there, too."

"You can say that again…"

He wondered if she'd go out with him. They seemed to be hitting it off; he didn't see any reason why she wouldn't agree to a date. "What are you doing tonight?"

"Probably having dinner and curling up on the sofa with a good book. Why?"

"I was wondering if you'd like to go out. We could have dinner..."

"I wish I could, but not tonight. We're open until nine, and by the time I've finished tallying up the receipts and straightening up the store, I'm usually home around eleven. That's why I'm taking a long lunch today. I usually get a sandwich to go, drive back to the bookstore and take a twenty-minute break in my office..."

"Tomorrow night, maybe?"

"Why don't you call me tomorrow and I'll see if I'll have time to drive home, change clothes and go back out before it gets too late?"

"Why change? You'll look fabulous."

"Twelve hours in the same outfit?" She wrinkled her nose. "Besides, I can't go very long in these heels. I need to take them off and switch to something comfortable..."

He could tell she wasn't just making excuses. "Can you give me your number?"

She snatched up her bag, pulled out her wallet, opened it, took out a card and handed it to him. On it was her name, the name of the bookstore and her phone number.

"You don't have a private number?"

She blinked. "We've only just met..."

He nodded.

She got some bills from her wallet.

"Please. Let me get this."

"No, that's—"

"This date was my idea, wasn't it?"

She sighed. "As you wish."

He signaled for the waitress. "I'll be with you in a moment."

"I'll go on out, then." She got up and went out.

The waitress came over. Keeping his back to the glass wall, he handed her the check. "This is on you."

She blinked. "P-Pardon me?"

"You heard me." *You're paying for this…*

She gawked at him. Her eyes widened, her mouth gaped open, and she reached up and covered her throat.

"Understand?"

She began gasping for air.

"Did you hear me?"

Gasping, she nodded with difficulty.

He turned and left.

Roxie was walking down the crowded hall when he rejoined her. "Was there a problem?" she asked.

"Everything's fine."

She smiled and they went down the hall and back out into the sunny afternoon.

She waved as she got in her car, a fairly new copper Honda Accord. Then she backed up and drove down the aisle, away from him, toward Colonial.

For one frightening instant he wondered if she'd seen what had transpired in the latte place. He decided he was worrying over nothing. If she *had* seen something, she wouldn't have smiled or waved as she left.

Excited at the prospect of seeing her again, he fired up the Crown Vic, pulled out and headed back to Winter Park.

CHAPTER SIXTEEN

Sandy sat at her desk in front of the laptop, finishing up her latest transaction.

She looked up when Roxie came in. "I take it you didn't bring back lunch."

Roxie smiled sheepishly and came right over. "Sorry, I guess I forgot." She bent, opened the bottom desk drawer and dropped her bag inside. Then she straightened. "What was your first clue?"

Sandy shrugged a bony shoulder. "The only thing you're carrying is your bag." She glanced at the clock on the opposite wall. "What happened? Was there some ginormous sale at the Mall you didn't tell me about? I also can't help noticing that you're nearly an hour late."

"I did some shopping and left everything in the Honda."

"You're still an hour late."

Roxie smiled sheepishly. "I met someone."

Sandy blinked. "You mean...someone of the other gender? As in, maybe, an actual *man*?"

"I just bumped into him—literally. We got to talking, and he bought me a latte. That was it."

Sandy didn't look convinced. "Sounds a little more involved than that."

"Because he bought me a latte? Don't be silly."

"Me? Silly?"

"What was I thinking?"

"Tell me this couldn't possibly lead anywhere, and I'll apologize profusely."

Roxie gazed at her friend and wondered how Sandy could read into such things so well. "How could you tell?"

"I was just going by your smile." Sandy shrugged. "You seem to be putting a little more into it than usual."

"Aaron's a really nice guy. I enjoyed his company."

"So I can safely say Henry's out of the pic?"

Roxie frowned. She and Henry Bowen had gone together three years earlier but broke it off when Henry's business demands required him to spend so much time in Miami. Henry ran a software business and frequently spoke at conventions. His lecture circuit had been pretty heavy for the last couple of years and kept him out of Orlando eight months of the year. Since he hadn't been speaking or lecturing much lately, he and Roxie had had dinner a few times, but both of them considered their relationship far from serious. Roxie had once thought she and Henry could be the perfect match, but the man's devotion to his business commitments prevented him from sustaining a permanent relationship. "Henry and I are just friends, Sandy. You know that."

"Does Henry?"

"Of course. We've known one another for years. Sure, we dated, but that was a while ago, and his job keeps him out of town most of the time. We both knew that one of us would have to sacrifice his career if we wanted something permanent to develop."

"I always liked Henry."

"I like him, too, and we'll always be great friends, so…"

"Whatever you say. So tell me…when are you gonna see this new guy—this Aaron—again? I take it you gave him one of our cards, right?"

Roxie nodded.

"Good. Maybe he'll even turn out to be an actual *reader*…"

"One can always hope. So…did anything happen while I was gone?"

"Hardly. We might've had a dozen customers come in."

"Anyone buy anything?"

Sandy shrugged. "I sold a couple of Tolstoy's and a John Fowles."

"That's better than nothing."

"Now that you're back, I'd better go mind the store and make sure no one tries to slip outside without buying anything." Sandy got up and left the room.

Roxie sat in the chair and thought about her visit with Aaron. Once again, that tiny morsel that had popped up after leaving Aaron reared its ugly head yet. This time, she tried a little harder to analyze what happened in the latte store when she'd left Aaron with the waitress. Although she'd been several yards away, she knew what she'd seen—rather *hadn't* seen. And what she hadn't seen was Aaron giving the woman any money for their lattes.

This was very strange indeed…

***

Aaron got home shortly before 3:00 and spent the next twenty minutes removing the imported

135

suits from the garment bag, hanging them neatly in his bedroom closet, then unwrapping and storing his DVDs.

After making a pot of coffee and fixing a turkey and cheese sandwich, he sat down on a barstool and thought about Roxie Nash.

He considered it an incredible stroke of luck to have bumped into such a great lady. She was fun to be with and terrific to talk to. It reminded him of his early days with Lana. Like Lana, Roxie was easy on the eyes, but much more independent. The way Roxie looked at him made him believe he was the center of her universe. He couldn't remember the last time a woman had made him feel so special.

His thoughts went right back to the previous night, when he'd met the woman at Shannon's. He tried remembering her name but once again found that it had vanished from his memory. He couldn't even remember what she looked like or if they'd left the place together. Part of his memory suggested that they might have, while the other part—that dark, fathomless abyss that had been swallowing up important images and making them disappear—told him that they'd parted their ways once they'd left Shannon's.

That latter possibility seemed most likely. He had no recollection of anything once he'd slipped behind the wheel of the Crown Vic. He figured that since he'd had two strong drinks at the club, he hadn't been in the right frame of mind to drive the girl home. It seemed most likely that she'd called a cab.

Maybe that was the answer all along—his reason for the gaping hole in his recall. Booze had affected his memory before—why wouldn't it be the culprit this time?

He took her card out of his shirt pocket.

CLASSIC READS
1775 CURRY FORD ROAD
ORLANDO, FLORIDA
"Show some class--come visit our store and check us out!"

And, of course, the phone number at the bottom.

He could visualize her approaching customers, smiling, answering questions. Walking past the rows of books, straightening things, bending over to pick up a paperback some careless customer had accidentally dropped…

Smiling, he slipped the card back into his pocket and finished his coffee.

The wall clock said 3:55. With the beginnings of the late afternoon rush hour turning traffic into its daily nightmare, it would take him at least thirty minutes to reach Curry Ford Road. That would get him there a little after 4:30—or maybe five o'clock, if he washed up and changed clothes. Either way, she wouldn't be expecting him.

He decided to clean up and change clothes. If any girl deserved extra effort and attention, it was Roxie. He couldn't wait to see the surprise on her gorgeous face when he walked through the door.

He was whistling as he climbed down from the barstool and hurried down the hall to get ready for his first visit to a bookstore in years.

***

At five-thirty, the bell above the front door of the bookstore jingled.

About a minute later, Sandy poked her face in the office doorway. "Rox? Got a minute?"

Roxie looked up from the invoices she'd been poring over the last half-hour. She dropped her reading glasses on the blotter. "What's up?"

"There's a guy out there who wants to see you."

"A *guy*?"

Sandy winked devilishly. "I'm pretty sure it's that new someone you bumped into at the Mall. He says his name's Aaron Grill."

***

Roxie was obviously very proud of her store.

It showed in its neatness and its brightness, and in the tasteful way the books were displayed. Posters of classic movies made from such books as *Doctor Zhivago, Gone with the Wind, Wuthering Heights, Anna Karenina, To Kill A Mockingbird, Captain Blood,* and *The Collector* graced the walls. A collection of Hitchcock movies adapted from such classics as *Rebecca, The Thirty-Nine Steps, Marnie, The Birds,* and several others sat in a neat arrangement on a table in front of a collage of movie posters and collectible theater cards. Plaster busts of Tolstoy, Dostoevsky, Poe, Shakespeare, Kafka, and other masters rested peacefully on shelves, watching over their masterpieces.

The storefront windows faced Curry Ford Road and the strip malls directly across the highway, and the late afternoon sun adorned the displays in a golden tint, highlighting boxed sets of Dickens, Algernon Blackwood, Rafael Sabatini and Victor Hugo.

"This sure is a surprise." Roxie had come out of her office and was staring at him, her arms crossed in front of her. Her forced smile suggested that she was slightly less than delighted by his unexpected presence. He realized right then that he should have called before driving over.

He chose the awkward approach. "Sorry, but I couldn't help myself. I just had to see your store for myself."

She made no comment.

It was time to toss in some flattery. He looked around and nodded. "It's really a great-looking bookstore."

"Thank you. Is that the *only* reason you came over?"

He didn't want to lie to her. Although they'd just met, he thought too much of her to play silly games. "I guess I just wanted to see you in your element."

She uncrossed her arms. "So now that you have, what's next?"

"Next?"

"It probably took you at least half an hour to drive here and maybe thirty seconds to see me in my element. There must be something else on your agenda…"

He discovered that he had no idea what to tell her that wouldn't make him sound like an idiot.

She took a few steps toward him. "Let me help you out. Maybe you actually came here to *buy* something?"

He felt genuine relief that she'd bailed him out. "You know, I really did intend to buy a book or two while I was here…"

"Good. All you have to do is pick your favorite author or someone who looks interesting. Just find his display, take your time to see what we've got available, and grab something."

He found himself gripped in embarrassment. He hadn't read a book in years and couldn't even remember the last one he'd read. He'd done a lot of reading in college but got out of the habit when he graduated and started his career. Then he met and married Lana, who liked only TV reality shows, soaps, and football games. But now that he'd met Roxie, he found that he had the strong desire to start reading again.

"You're not moving." She was watching him.

"There's a reason for that."

"And that is…?"

"Uncertainty, for a start."

"This is a small store. You can probably look at every single title in this room in half an hour. Besides, everything's marked."

He wanted her to show him around but didn't want her to think he was helpless or stupid. He could tell she was busy. Part of him was glad he'd made the trip, but he was silently cursing himself for not waiting until tomorrow to arrange his date with her.

The tall, skinny blonde who'd asked what he wanted—Roxie's partner, no doubt—slipped out of the office at that moment and approached a middle-aged woman browsing the shelves marked *YOUNG ADULT*.

"Who's your favorite author?" Roxie asked.

He shrugged. "It's been a long time."

"Who did you read last?"

"I'm not sure…"

"What category did you like?"

"Category?"

She smiled but he could tell she was growing impatient. "Fiction?"

He nodded.

"All right, at least we've got that out of the way. Now…let me guess… I'll bet Romance wasn't your thing, was it?"

"How can you tell?"

"Not many guys like Romance."

"You're right."

"Military?"

He shook his head.

"How about fantasy?"

"I remember getting into science fiction in high school and college."

She pointed toward the table display next to the front door. "Over there."

"I'm not really big on novels, though."

"Why not?"

"They take too long to wade through. I really liked short stories. I preferred something I could

141

finish in fifteen minutes. Now that I'm thinking of it, I used to read several a day in college."

"Anthologies, then…"

"That sounds about right."

"Over there." She pointed to her left, next to the front window.

He knew he'd better do as she'd suggested. She was obviously much too busy and too distracted to be interested in anything but business. But the moment she turned to go back to her office, he cringed when he felt the compulsion taking over. "Roxie?"

She turned around.

"I'd like you to have dinner with me."

Sighing, she lowered her voice. "As I told you at the Mall—"

"I know, but I'd still like to take you to dinner."

"Listen—"

"There are steakhouses and restaurants up and down this stretch. Most of them are less than five minutes away."

"That's not the point…"

"Can't your assistant handle things for an hour?"

"She's my partner, and yes, she can handle things."

"Then why can't you spare one hour with me? I'll take you wherever you want to go…"

"I already told you. Tomorrow would be better for me."

"Please?"

"Aaron, it's really nice that you want to take me out to dinner, but…"

I want you to go out with me. His gut tightened, and his thoughts rang loud and strong the instant they left his brain. *The blonde can spare you. I won't take no for an answer*...

His throat became constricted as the words came out: "Tell her you're going out with me."

"Aaron..."

"I insist..."

"But—"

You're going out with me...

Roxie stopped talking and stood stiffly, her eyes on him. A mix of fear and pain took over her features.

He hadn't wanted to do it this way but felt his defenses going up. As long as he was capable of getting what he wanted, he was going to use his strange new gift.

When he felt she'd had enough and was ready to give in, he heard himself say, "Just one hour, and I promise you'll be right back here."

She snapped out of it and stood there, dazed. When she noticed him watching her, she was no longer smiling. She seemed totally confused and disoriented. After a few moments she shook herself and rubbed her temples. "All right. Give me a minute to tell Sandy, and we'll be on our way."

"Take your time." His pulse fluttered as he watched her move unsteadily to the rear of the store, where her friend was talking to a middle-aged female.

CHAPTER SEVENTEEN

"Sandy?"

Sandy turned away from the lady she was talking to. The moment she met Roxie's eyes, she stiffened. "You okay, Rox? You look kind of weird. What's wrong?"

"I'm...all right." She didn't feel all right at all. In fact, it took all her strength to stand there without collapsing. The dizziness had subsided somewhat, but she still felt unsteady and a little nauseous.

Sandy obviously wasn't convinced. "You sure?"

"Listen...I've got to go. I'll be back in an hour."

"Did something...is there anything I can do?"

"Everything's okay." She made sure her voice was loud enough just in case Aaron was listening. "I've just been invited out to dinner, but I promise I won't be long. Will you be okay?"

Sandy's gaze shifted slightly to where Aaron was apparently standing. Sandy didn't say anything, but Roxie could see the suspicion in her friend's large blue eyes. "I'll be fine."

"Thanks." Fighting off the last remnants of dizziness, Roxie shuffled back into the office and leaned against the desk for support. Still shaking, she waited anxiously for her nerves to steady. Once the room stopped swaying and her vertigo subsided, she began thinking more clearly.

What on earth just happened out there?

This was just like that time she'd gotten off the rollercoaster as a kid and hurried away too soon. The dizziness, the nausea, the confusion—everything had hit her at once, and she nearly threw up. She'd immediately staggered over to a bench and sat down for a couple of minutes. When everything eventually returned to normal, she got back up and ran back to where her friends were standing in line to buy cotton candy.

But this was totally different. For one thing, she was no longer a child. And this happened in her bookstore. There was no rollercoaster to blame this on—nothing that would tax her nerves or equilibrium or spike her adrenaline system.

Once her mind cleared, she struggled to evaluate what happened. Aaron offered to take her to lunch, but she'd told him she didn't have the time. That was simple enough, wasn't it? The message was short and sweet, and easy enough to understand. A grade school kid would have grasped its meaning. She was certain Aaron understood. Anyone else would have just nodded and said, all right, we'll do it tomorrow.

But it hadn't happened that way. During the exchange, a strange feeling had taken over, and a growing nausea settled deep in her gut. Then she heard a strange voice.

Your partner can spare you. I won't take no for an answer...

Now she wasn't sure if it was an actual voice or just a strong feeling. Whatever it was, she knew she had to do it. A strange compulsion had accompanied

145

it, and she sensed that if she didn't satisfy this urge, something bad would happen.

During all this, she'd scanned her surroundings and felt her blood turning cold. The bookstore had darkened, the shelves and displays had become blurred grayish images, and the man facing her had transformed into an indistinguishable shape covered in a filmy black shroud.

Was this an omen? Some terrifying message?

All she knew was that some unseen force had transported her to a strange dark place where she was all alone and unable to move.

Then, before the panic could take over, she heard the familiar voice: "Just one hour, and I promise you'll be right back here…"

The darkness immediately disappeared, and she found herself in the bookstore once again. The sun was back; so were the shelves, the books and the displays. The black shroud had disappeared, and Aaron was standing there as before. He was smiling, but there was something in his eyes that disappeared the moment she saw it. They'd somehow changed from chestnut to a very deep, piercing dark blue, remaining like that an instant before returning to their natural color.

What was going on?

"Roxie?" It was Aaron calling. "You okay in there?"

His voice snapped her right back to the present. Everything else came back with it—the store, the strange feeling of uneasiness, of helplessness. She had to clear her throat to get her voice working again. "Be there in just one minute…"

146

For long, uncomfortable moments she remained frozen, afraid to move.

I don't want to go with him. I have to get out of this, somehow. But how?

It doesn't matter, does it? I can't go anywhere with a man who just did something terrifying to my mind.

Aaron appeared in the doorway. "You sure everything's okay?" He looked worried.

Her heart sank. For one moment she opened her mouth to protest, to tell him she didn't feel well...but the moment she did, the nausea came right back, and she knew right then that there was only one way to deal with this. "I'm just about ready..." She bent, opened the desk drawer, and groped for her handbag.

"Let's go, then."

Her heart was halfway up her throat when she slipped past him and led the way out through the store.

***

The Crab Hut sat at the far end of Curry Ford Plaza, a large, busy strip mall just a couple of miles down the road from Roxie's bookstore.

Aaron parked about six spaces down from the front of the large storefront window, which advertised their large fried shrimp basket for $7.95, which included twelve medium shrimp, scallops, fries, and coleslaw.

"Ever eaten here?" he asked, switching off the engine.

"A couple of times."

"How was it?"

"Very good."

He waited for her to elaborate, but she pushed open her door and got out. He followed her up to the entrance and held the glass door open for her.

It was almost six, and the dark, air-conditioned place swarmed with hungry customers. Two harried waitresses hauled around large metal trays covered with steaming plates of seafood. Three sweaty busboys pushed carts and frantically cleared off the tables. Luscious smells of sautéed shrimp, baked fish, steamed crab and garlic-flavored toast hung heavily in the air.

"This place smells terrific," Aaron said as the hostess led them to their table.

Roxie remained silent as she followed the tall brunette to the other side of the room, where a corner booth awaited them. Once the hostess left them alone, he waited for Roxie to slide into the seat before joining her. As he drew closer, she placed her large leather handbag on the seat between them.

He couldn't help viewing this as some sort of message. It was as if she was trying to distance herself. He told himself he was being silly. His imagination had obviously kicked in again. He felt guilty for coaxing her here and told himself he was making something out of nothing.

While Roxie studied the menu printed on their glossy place mats, he told himself that he needed to stop this stupid paranoia. She came here with him, didn't she? That was all that mattered. He'd promised her he'd have her back at the bookstore in an hour. He intended to fulfill that promise because he knew what it meant to her and because he wanted her to know he was honorable.

He rubbed his temples and forced himself to concentrate on dinner. And, of course, Roxie. "What are you in the mood for?" he asked.

She was still studying the menu. "I'm not sure. Like I said before, I wasn't really planning to have dinner out."

"What *were* you planning to do?"

"Sandy and I usually run over to the Chinese place at the shopping plaza next door for takeout. That way, we can eat in the office and keep an eye out on the store." She hadn't looked at him at all; she'd kept her gaze on the menu.

"When was the last time you went out for a regular sit-down dinner?"

She shrugged.

The waitress came to take their orders.

Roxie said, "I'm still not sure what I want, but I would like some coffee…"

"Make it two."

The waitress rushed off.

"Do you like shrimp?"

She nodded.

"Oysters?"

"Sure…"

"Scallops?"

"Yes…"

"Raw musk ox in giblet gravy?"

She looked up from the menu.

He smiled sheepishly. "I was hoping to get your attention at least once before taking you back."

She smiled but said nothing. Then went right back to the menu.

"What's wrong? You've been awfully quiet since we got here."

"I guess I'm still trying to decide why I agreed to come here with you."

His heart raced. *Focus*, he told himself. *Downplay this.* "I guess I sort of...pressured you, didn't I?"

"Yeah, you did."

"I'm sorry. But as I promised, we won't be very long."

The waitress brought their coffees. Roxie ordered shrimp salad and a slice of charbroiled salmon. Aaron ordered half a dozen chilled oysters on the half shell and a dozen fried shrimp.

After the waitress left, Roxie said, "Why *did* you pressure me?"

"Why do you think?"

"I'm serious. I told you my schedule, but you wouldn't take no for an answer. It was as if you didn't care."

"I cared." Now he felt even worse.

"You sure didn't come across that way. You actually made me feel nauseous...and dizzy. It was very strange."

"I'm really sorry, Roxie. I didn't mean to make you feel that way." He felt his pulse pounding and hoped she wouldn't be able to see the guilt in his eyes.

She sat back and rubbed the back of her neck. "I guess I'd put in a few too many hours and got sort of light-headed. That's the only thing I can think of that would explain something like that."

"That sounds reasonable." He felt relieved that she'd unwittingly managed to let him off the hook.

"But it wouldn't have happened if you hadn't pressured me. Do you always act like that?"

He decided to let her win the argument. If it made her feel better, the dinner would go more pleasantly. "I'm sorry. I guess I was just a tad too eager to get you alone."

"How long have you been this way?"

"My divorce practically destroyed me, and I guess I just gave up on life. I even quit my job and moved to a tiny two-room apartment in West Orlando. I needed to be by myself. I think it was a form of self-punishment. I really believed I had to be away from people."

"Well, something obviously happened to change all this."

"I just woke up one morning and realized that I didn't want to spend the rest of my life alone." He shrugged. "You reach a point where you're tired of waiting for things to happen. Everyone knows most good things in life don't come without a helping hand. The only way of getting them is to step up and take the reins."

She had more coffee. "Well, I sort of got that idea myself a few years ago. But I also realized that you can't have everything and that it should be enough if you can latch onto whatever you *can* get and forget about all the things that are just unreachable."

"I prefer thinking that I *can* get what I want, and if I'm unable to, then what I *thought* I wanted just wasn't worth the trouble."

"How's that working for you?"

"You're here with me, aren't you?"

"It's *dinner*, Aaron—*not* a life-changing miracle."

"I'm just saying that life is a series of triumphs and failures. For most people, it's minor triumphs and major failures. But if you can accumulate an impressive number of triumphs, I think you can consider yourself a success in your own right."

"That all depends on what you consider a triumph."

"Anything that you can get for yourself is, in my view, a triumph."

Their dinner came. The food was fabulous. Roxie finished in fifteen minutes then sat quietly, sipping her third cup of coffee while he finished the last of his shrimp. She'd glanced at her watch twice.

The waitress came with their check. Roxie grabbed her handbag.

He waved her down. "I can take care of this. If you need to go to the powder room—"

"It's all right, I don't mind..."

"No, I'll take care of it. I brought you here, invited you to dinner..."

"Aaron, I *want* to pay for this..."

He shook his head. "You go on ahead. I'll get this."

The waitress chuckled. "Why don't the two of you split it?"

152

Both women stared at him. He noticed something in Roxie's eyes—something dark and disturbing. It looked like suspicion.

"Yes, Aaron…why don't we split it?"

He glanced at the waitress. The woman immediately paled and coughed.

Catching himself, he snapped out of it. *Easy…you don't want to blow this…* He pulled his gaze abruptly from her and turned his attention to his empty plate.

The waitress sighed and cleared her throat.

He felt a wave of panic. He never carried money around anymore because he no longer needed it. But he had to do *some*thing, and quickly. He was going to have to compromise but had no idea how he could manage it without attracting Roxie's suspicion. He couldn't very well handle this with her sitting beside him, watching.

Maybe he could have her spill the contents of her bag. When some of it disappeared under the table, he could—

No. If he scared Roxie in any way, she'd be too frightened to agree to see him again. He'd already narrowly escaped suspicion from what he did to her in the bookstore…

But he had to do *some*thing.

He just couldn't figure out why Roxie was so insistent about paying for this meal.

The bookstore. She wanted to get back and didn't want any more delays.

"All right," he said. "If you really want to pay…"

"Thank you." She opened her bag. Then she stopped and gazed at him. That same darkness showed in her eyes. "I'll let you take care of the tip. Will that help?"

His pulse fluttered; he felt his skin flushing. "I don't…that is, all I've got are hundreds…"

"I'll be happy to get your change." The waitress was smiling again.

He wanted to melt into the seat as his trembling hand slowly dug into his empty pocket.

"Don't worry about it, okay?" Roxie was taking money out of her wallet. "I really have to get back." She handed the woman three twenties and told her to keep the change.

Relieved but highly embarrassed, he slid awkwardly out of the booth. His legs trembled as he followed Roxie outside.

CHAPTER EIGHTEEN

Although the trip back to the bookstore took only five minutes, it seemed considerably longer for Roxie.

She couldn't stop wondering what happened at the restaurant. Whatever had transpired had taken quite a toll on Aaron. She could tell by the way his white knuckles gripped the wheel that he'd just been through something horrific.

She couldn't imagine why he was acting this way. He'd been all right up to the time the waitress brought over their check. The moment Roxie chose to pay, he'd come unglued.

She'd volunteered to take care of the check because she wanted to get back to the bookstore. She had no idea something so trivial would set him off.

Was it a simple macho thing? Had she somehow challenged his attempt to be chivalrous? Had this bruised his ego in some way?

Somehow, this seemed totally different.

Since he'd been just fine until the waitress came with the check, she could only assume that that was what pushed him over the edge. He'd been on edge ever since they'd left and hadn't spoken at all since he got in the car.

What sort of traumatic event could make an otherwise considerate, respectable man freak out in the blinking of an eye?

As she replayed the scene one last time in her head, he pulled off Curry Ford, turned into the parking lot and eased up to the front of the bookstore. He put the car into park and just sat there, gazing at the tinted storefront window. His white-knuckled hands remained gripping the wheel. Something was still obviously traumatizing him.

However, logic told her she shouldn't let on.

"Thank you for taking me to dinner," she said softly.

He remained gazing at the store and seemed oblivious of her presence.

"I enjoyed it." She hated lying, but she couldn't tell him she'd been uneasy and somewhat frightened since they'd left the bookstore.

"Would you...like to go out with me...again?" he asked suddenly, still staring straight ahead.

Once again, she knew better than tell him the truth. In his present mood, her rejection might turn into something terrifying. She certainly didn't want to say anything that would worsen this. "Sure. Why not?"

He looked shocked. "Really?"

"Just because I was a little upset with you before doesn't mean I don't want to see you again..."

"You *were* upset, then..."

"You didn't listen to me. No girl likes that."

"Once again, I'm truly sorry. I guess I was just too excited. Meeting someone as classy and as beautiful as you has always been hard for me. Since my divorce, there hasn't been anyone. My loneliness apparently hit me harder than I thought."

156

Moved by what he'd just said, she placed her hand gently on his wrist. The severe iciness of his flesh made her pull away.

"Something wrong?"

She swallowed. "You're *cold*..."

He shrugged. "It's probably the a/c."

No. This was more than that.

His skin felt like ice...

Suddenly even more frightened, she fought down more nausea. *I've got to get out of this car...* "Well, thanks again. I need to...get back to work...and see how Sandy's doing."

"Roxie...when can I see you again?"

"Call me."

"How about tomorrow?"

"I'll be here till six." She slipped out, slammed the door, and hurried inside the building.

***

Aaron sat in his car in front of the bookstore for the next fifteen minutes, debating if he should go back inside and talk to Roxie again.

He wanted to make amends, but he also realized he couldn't possibly tell her why he'd acted that way.

He finally decided that he was making entirely too much out of this. Things had been tense for a little while but the crisis had been abated, ending satisfactorily. Roxie had paid for the meal and they'd left without anyone getting hurt.

So why was he so uneasy? Was it because he'd come so close to being discovered?

He remembered the look of suspicion he'd seen in Roxie's eyes.

157

Suspicion was the enemy—the one thing that could destroy the status quo. He considered himself fortunate that there hadn't been any repercussions so far. With Roxie, he had to tread very carefully. She was a very bright, perceptive lady. Because of his impatience and lack of self-control, he'd already manipulated her; it would be disastrous to do it again.

He had to start doing things more sensibly. He didn't want to do or say anything else that might arouse her suspicions. To start off, he needed to stop at a bank first thing in the morning. To prevent a repeat of what happened at the Crab Hut, it was necessary to have plenty of ready cash to carry around. Five hundred would probably be enough for dinner and drinks at most of the better places in town. Once he ran low, he could simply stop at another bank.

Feeling confident and somewhat relieved, he flicked on the ignition and backed out of the space.

***

"Tell me what happened, Roxie…"

Sandy had apparently followed her into the office and stood very close, staring. "You look…well, like you've just been through some sort of severe traumatic experience."

"I'm all right."

"You're sure?"

"I'm fine."

Sandy looked skeptical. "Okay… Then tell me why you were acting so spacey when you left with that guy."

158

Roxie collapsed in her chair and leaned her head back. Her pulse still fluttered, and she found that she couldn't stop shaking. She hadn't even noticed what Sandy was doing when she'd come back inside. But she certainly didn't want to tell her best friend what happened. For one thing, she didn't know what happened, so she had no idea how she could explain her sudden trip to the Crab Hut. For another, she didn't want to burden Sandy with her problems. Sandy was a worrier and wouldn't rest until she knew everything that was going on. "Aaron took me to the Crab Hut."

"Then why do you look like you've just had a pregnancy scare?" Sandy scowled. "He didn't...try something, did he?"

In spite of the situation, Roxie wanted to laugh. "Sandy, I'm thirty-four. You're thirty-five."

Sandy frowned. "What's *that* have to do with anything? And by the way, I won't be thirty-five for two more months."

"It only means that at our age, it's time to worry when a guy *doesn't* try something."

"So he *did* try something?"

"Sandy..."

"This is me, Rox. Your best friend. At least I *thought* we were best friends. You can tell me anything—you know that."

"Aaron's one of those control freaks." It was best to give Sandy a generic detail or two so she'd ease off. "Get it?"

Sandy nodded. "I think I do. He's an asshole. Is that what you're saying?"

159

"Aaron's a nice guy, actually. He just…well, he—"

"He likes to call all the shots."

"That's basically it."

"Let me guess…he tried ordering for you—irritating things like that?"

Roxie nodded.

"Then I don't have to worry about that sick pale color on your face?"

"No, Sandy… As I just told you, I'm fine."

Sandy watched her a few more moments. "Then I guess we can get back to work?"

"Yes, Sandy. We can get back to work."

***

On his way back to Winter Park, Aaron pulled into the hectic shopping plaza on Curry Ford and Semoran, went down the two-lane road that led to the liquor store and parked two spaces down from the door, about ten feet from a beat-up brown van. He got out of the car and went up to the front entrance.

At seven-fifteen, the place was packed. Several customers crowded the register with their purchases while a dozen others browsed the aisles. Not wanting trouble, Aaron decided to wait until tomorrow, when he had enough walking-around money to pay for his purchases in case someone else was within earshot. He turned around and went back to the car. He was about to open the door when he heard footsteps approaching him.

A man in ragged, loose-fitting clothing stopped a few feet away, his left hand out, palm up. His right arm remained at his side, his hand gripping a rusty steak knife. He looked about forty; his bloodshot eyes and the way he twitched and shifted his weight suggested he was high.

"Money," he muttered, his left hand shaking.

Aaron shrugged.

"The money. Hand it over."

Aaron sighed. He wasn't in the mood for this. "You really don't want to do this, you know…"

"I'll cut ya if ya don't shuddup and give me the fuckin' money!" The man's left arm shook. "Cut ya up real good…"

"What are you on?" Aaron asked.

"No crap, man. Just gimme the fuckin' money!" He jerked his head toward the right, where traffic was coming from Curry Ford. "Ain't got all fuckin' day…"

"Like I just said, you really don't want to do this."

"I *mean* it, fucker!"

You're going to be really sorry…

Just then, the man began coughing and gasping.

Turning back to the Crown Vic, Aaron reached for the door handle and got back in. An instant later, he felt very strange. He sat behind the wheel for a few moments, his eyes closed while waiting for the moment to subside.

What seemed like just a few moments later, he opened his eyes and found that he was heading north on Semoran Boulevard in heavy traffic.

***

Fifteen minutes later, Aaron parked in front of his condo and got out.

161

The instant he turned to walk up to the entrance, something caught his eye. A slender arc of blood spatter about three feet long embellished the driver's door, starting from the running board and ending a few inches short of the side mirror.

He stiffened. What the hell?

He moved closer and squatted, inspecting the door by touching it very gently with his fingertip. It was blood, all right, and fairly fresh. Some of it had been smeared into microscopic red strings pushed by the air current during his drive home while others remained tiny droplets. But nothing explained how they'd gotten there.

After about a minute, he straightened and let his thoughts go back to the last half-hour or so but couldn't recall anything unusual that had happened on his way home. As far as he was concerned, the short trip had been completely uneventful. Traffic was heavy, as usual, but there had been no pedestrians to be concerned about. No rowdy kids, no stray dogs—nothing out of the ordinary. If he'd hit someone, he'd certainly remember. Yet nothing registered to make him think otherwise.

So where did this blood come from?

He took a breath and tried to clear his mind while struggling to remember what happened after he'd left Roxie.

I stopped at the liquor store but decided not to go in. Then I got back in the car and drove right home.

He suddenly remembered a brief exchange with a stranger. The man wore filthy clothes and obviously hadn't showered or bathed in a while.

162

The man wanted money. Aaron vaguely recalled a dirty, shaking hand extending in his direction. That was most likely the extent of it. And since Aaron couldn't remember much else, he figured he'd probably told the bum to get lost.

But this didn't tell him about the blood spatter on the side of his car.

He'd possibly picked it up in the parking lot of the liquor store. He'd seen how people acted in public—how they tossed trash in the beds of parked trucks, left food wrappers on the pavement, and showed total disrespect for other people's property. Any number of things could have happened.

Satisfied with his reasoning, he approached the front stoop of the condo. Just as he reached out to insert the key into the lock, he noticed something on his shirt sleeve.

Another sweeping arc of blood, this one extending from his shoulder, ran all the way down to his wrist. There were even droplets on his skin, near the knuckles.

What was going on? How had he picked up blood on his shirt?

He checked his hands, his wrists. Finding nothing, he felt his neck, his chin, his cheeks. No cuts, no nicks. Then he examined his shirt again.

It certainly looked like blood…

But how did he get it? What the hell had happened?

CHAPTER NINETEEN

Stripped to the waist, Aaron started up the washing machine in the laundry room of his condo.

In just twenty minutes, the shirt would be fresh, and the blood stains would be gone. Then he could relax and forget all about it.

Or could he?

Whatever happened was obviously very serious—something he needed to consider. For that, it was necessary to remember what happened. He didn't know how much blood there was, or who it belonged to. He only knew that it didn't belong to him.

If there had been enough to spray the side of his car—as well as his shirt sleeve and the back of the shirt—it meant someone had been seriously hurt.

But how?

A traffic accident? A bodily assault?

That made no sense at all. If someone had actually been close enough to spray him with their blood, he would have heard the commotion.

However, he had the windows closed and the air on. The radio wasn't on, but the a/c did muffle most traffic sounds.

The wash began its cycle. He went back out into the kitchen and poured more bourbon then took his drink out into the living room, flicked on the widescreen and began watching the local news.

The moment the commentator began to talk, he was cut off when the channel went to a commercial break. A car commercial came on. Thirty seconds later, something that removed unwanted hair by laser filled the thirty-second spot. Another car commercial came on. Afterward, a thirty-second spot for McDonald's showed on the screen. Arby's followed, then some special shindig at Disney came on. Two more car commercials followed.

The news finally came back on. The feature opened with an apparent suicide in the Conway area. The camera settled on the ABC Liquor Store on Curry Ford and Semoran, showing a beat-up brown van, two police cruisers, a medical unit, a flurry of activity in front of the building and small groups of gawkers coming out of the strip mall down the aisle. Two uniformed men were placing a body encased in a body bag onto a gurney. A tall, slender, smartly dressed brunette holding a microphone stepped up to the camera. "The man hasn't been identified yet, but…"

He didn't hear the rest. The brown van looked frighteningly familiar. He'd parked in front of that very store. He could even remember parking next to the van.

This was very strange. While he was just a few feet away, someone had committed suicide.

He tried remembering the details, but as usual, his mind quickly turned into a dark mass of emptiness. Aside from opening the door and getting back in the car, he couldn't recall—

No. Something began squeezing out of the dark mass.

Someone had walked up behind him. Yes. That smelly, sloppy-dressed guy he'd remembered. The guy wanted something…

What had he asked for? Directions? Money?

He couldn't remember. His mind clouded over again.

It must not have been important. But it made him wonder if it had been the same guy who'd killed himself—the corpse the paramedics were shoving into the medical unit.

He thought about that for a minute or so but soon found that he no longer cared. He finished his drink and stretched out on the sofa. Then he wondered if he should grab a shirt from the bedroom. He decided he was too lazy and too comfortable to get back up. He picked up the remote and flicked on an old movie with Ronald Coleman and Jean Arthur. Moments later, he closed his eyes and nodded off.

When he opened his eyes, a different movie was playing, this one starring Clark Gable and Myrna Loy.

I must've been more exhausted than I thought...

He sat up and discovered that he was naked. His trousers, undershorts, shoes and socks lay on the carpet a few feet from the sofa.

He rubbed his eyes and yawned.

When did I take off my clothes?

Once again, his mind went dark. A vague image drifted past, and he tried remembering if this had ever happened before. A fleeting memory suggested that he'd woken up naked several times before, but as soon as he tried retrieving the details, whatever had been up there immediately vanished.

Frustrated, he decided that he was agonizing over things that didn't matter. He got up and put his undershorts and pants back on. He noticed his shirt was missing, but told himself that didn't matter, either. Suddenly hungry, he plodded barefoot into the kitchen to make a sandwich. As he crossed the hall, he saw that the laundry room light was on. He was about to flick it off when the closed washing machine lid grabbed his attention. He usually left it open. He opened it and peered inside.

What was his shirt doing in the wash? And why was it the only item in the washer?

Why didn't he remember putting it in the machine?

He'd apparently tossed it in there when he came home then forgot about it.

He tossed the shirt in the dryer, set the cycle for fifteen minutes and went back into the kitchen to fix his sandwich. And, of course, think about the strategy he'd use on his next date with Roxie.

***

Shortly after nine that night, as Sandy locked the front door, flipped the OPEN sign to CLOSED and pulled the blinds shut, Roxie straightened up the bargain discount bin then stacked and lined up the hardcover books so the titles on the spines all faced upward.

Roxie heard the clicking of her friend's high heels on the tile floor but wasn't paying much attention. She was concerned only about straightening up and getting things ready for the next day. She was also thinking about what she could do about straightening up her own personal agenda with Aaron and wanted to curse herself for getting involved with him in the first place.

She told herself she had to look at this objectively. Aaron was quite possibly involved in something that defied the laws of logic and caused people pain and discomfort. The concept of such a scenario was both scary and totally ridiculous, but that didn't mean it wasn't happening, did it? It also didn't mean she should just turn her back and walk away.

How could she? It would be like knowing someone was in serious trouble and not telling anyone. She'd have to live with herself knowing that the person involved was headed for trouble, and she'd done nothing to stop it.

Aaron obviously possessed some sort of frightening ability that could hurt people. And it had. It had affected her right there in the bookstore. She'd been thinking about it ever since and reasoned that whatever had happened had nothing to do with her blood sugar or stress level. She'd been affected by something Aaron had done to her mind. It was as simple as that.

"You okay?"

Startled, she spun around. Sandy was watching her.

"I'm fine. Why?"

"You seem on edge."

"I was…thinking."

"You've been distracted for hours, girl."

"I guess I've got a lot of things on my mind."

"Do you even remember when I told you I was going out to grab some Chinese for dinner?"

She suddenly felt stupid and clueless. "When did we talk about *that*?"

"A while ago."

"I'm *really* sorry, Sandy…"

"Don't worry about it. Are you sure you're okay?"

"I'm fine. Really."

"You haven't been the same since you got back from dinner."

"I'm really okay, Sandy…"

Sandy smiled in relief. "Good. I mean, it *is* good, isn't it?"

Roxie wondered why Sandy seemed so concerned. "It was just dinner…"

"I'm *so* glad."

"What's wrong? Aaron's a nice guy."

"I just think he's weird. You must think that way, too. You seemed confused and distracted when you came back."

"Confused and distracted how?"

"I can't explain it. You're not your normal carefree self."

"He really is a nice guy." She hoped she'd sounded convincing enough.

"You're not going out with him again, are ya?"

"Why do you ask?"

"He seemed, well, obsessed, for want of a better term. I've been around the block a few times. I can tell. So what are you gonna do if he calls and asks you out again?"

Roxie shrugged.

"And that means…?"

"It means I'll figure something out when the time comes."

169

Sandy just nodded and went back to dusting off the counter.

"I'll lock up, Sandy. You go home. We've both had a long day." She went back in her office and stood there, staring off into space. Her pulse raced and the back of her neck felt damp.

Yes. It was painfully obvious. She couldn't let this go. She couldn't for one reason. The very thing Sandy had mentioned.

You're not going out with him again, are ya?

That was the reason. He was going to call her tomorrow and ask her out again.

How could she let this go if he planned on seeing her again? And how could she forget about all this if Aaron wanted to be a part of her life?

Most important, how could she let Aaron know she didn't *want* to be a part of his life? She couldn't even turn him down for a dinner date without becoming a helpless victim of his strange, frightening power.

She didn't want to pursue this—at least, not tonight. Maybe tomorrow, after she'd had a good night's sleep. It had been a long, tiring day, and she was exhausted. That was by far the best reason in the world to go home and hit the sack.

As Scarlet O'Hara once said, "After all, tomorrow is another day."

She locked up, got in her Honda, and drove straight home.

***

Half an hour later, Roxie got into bed and immediately drifted off into a deep sleep.

Just moments later, she found that she was standing in a cold, dark room. Dampness enveloped her and she wondered if she'd entered a cave or tunnel. A strong, unpleasant scent drifted in from somewhere behind her, and her eyes watered. She turned. An oval opening appeared about twenty feet away, leading out to a star-filled sky.

Just as she approached the opening, the stars disappeared behind a long, slender shape approaching the opening. The shape came closer, growing more vivid with each step, its limbs becoming long and slender, its shoulders narrow. When it was less than ten feet away, it became a woman with long black hair. The darkness penetrating the area prevented Roxie from distinguishing the woman's features, but as the woman drew closer, the repulsive scent grew stronger. Cold emanated from the woman, drifting toward Roxie, and she shivered.

When the woman was just a few feet away, she stopped moving. Roxie tried backing up but immediately discovered that she couldn't move her legs. Her limbs had grown numb.

The woman spoke. Her voice was low and harsh, bouncing off the jagged rock walls of the cave. "Stay away from him. He belongs to me. He is mine."

"Wh-Who…wh-what…are you talking about?" Roxie could barely get the words out.

"He is mine," the woman repeated.

"*Who* is yours?"

"You know what I'm talking about."

"This is a dream. It makes no sense…"

"It is no dream."

"Wh-Who *are* you?" Roxie asked, the words thick and heavy in her throat.

"He belongs to me. He has paid the price."

"What price? *Please* tell me what you're talking about."

The woman chuckled—a sharp, unpleasant sound ricocheting off the rock walls like bullets. "If you do not comply, you will be sorry."

"I don't know what you're talking about..."

"I will show you what I'm talking about." She reached out and placed her hand on the top of Roxie's head. Roxie gasped at the icy touch. It felt as if someone had just dumped ice water on her head. She tried pulling away, but her legs still wouldn't function.

A moment later, her mind exploded in brightness. She saw herself at seventeen, driving her parents' car in the country in the middle of summer. The road, the car, the brightness of the day—everything was frighteningly familiar—and she began tensing up because she knew what was going to happen. She took the next sharp bend at fifty miles an hour and saw the familiar sight.

The large, square head of the Golden Retriever poked out from the bush next to the road...and in the next second, stepped out in front of her.

Her mind went berserk with the memories. When it had first happened, she'd slammed on her brakes and swerved, nearly sliding into the ditch on the other side of the road as the car tilted, rising up and staying that way until she was able to regain control of the wheel and correct the skid.

Later, when she'd gone another hundred yards and her heart slid back down where it belonged, she glanced in the mirror and saw that the dog had safely turned back around and retreated into the bush—

But no...this time it was different—horribly so...

The sickening loud thud exploded in her ears, shaking the car. She clutched her stomach with one hand, nearly losing control of the car as she swerved into the next lane and then raised her wet eyes to the rearview mirror a quarter of a mile later to see the dying animal lying in the middle of the road, twitching in its final moments as it grew smaller in the distance...

No! This is all very wrong! It didn't happen like that! I missed the dog! I practically killed myself and totaled the car, but I missed the dog!

Who *was* this wicked woman? How did she have the power to alter a bad memory to create such a disgusting horror? How would she even *know* about this?

"Who *are* you? And what did you do to my head?"

The woman had vanished. Roxie found herself in the cave alone.

No. This wasn't happening. This had *to be a dream...*

She opened her eyes and, shivering, woke up in a cold sweat. Her eyes had filled with tears. She sat up and, holding her breath, switched on the light and nervously scanned the room. Nothing looked different or even slightly disturbed. As expected, she was all alone.

Still shivering, she brought up her right hand to her throat and gasped.

Her hand was numb with cold.

PART TWO
"NULL & VOID"

CHAPTER TWENTY

Aaron woke early, shuffled into the bathroom, and stepped into the shower.

After toweling himself dry, he shaved and dressed, then plodded into the kitchen to make breakfast. The wall clock said it was 8:25. As he sat down to eat, he immediately began thinking about Roxie.

She was probably still sleeping. The previous day had been a long one; she probably hadn't gotten home until late. He couldn't blame her for sleeping in.

He'd memorized the store hours from the neatly printed sign on the glass door of Classic Reads. The place opened at nine on Monday, Wednesday, and Saturday, and ten on Tuesday, Thursday, and Friday. He didn't know where she lived—not yet, anyway. He assumed she didn't live far from the store. She no doubt had a place within half an hour of her business, possibly in the Conway area.

He imagined her lying in bed, sleeping peacefully, her hair spread out like reddish-brown feathers on her pillow...

He wondered if her pillow was blue or white...or maybe pink. She didn't seem to be a "pink" type of lady; it would be too girly. And judging by her taste in clothes, he figured she liked

175

darker, bolder colors. For her bedroom, she'd stick to neutral stuff. Eggshell-white, or maybe a light gray.

Then he wondered how she looked lying in bed...

Did she sleep naked?

She'd no doubt prefer modest, or less showy. She might sleep in an oversized tee shirt. As he'd learned through the years, women were complex and oftentimes impulsive. Lana had slept naked when they'd first met. Once they were married, she insisted on sleeping in bra and panties, and went through a six-month period where she wore a sheer light-blue nightgown. But during the last few months of their marriage, when they were having problems, she'd worn a baggy sweatshirt over her bra and panties to bed.

He couldn't visualize Roxie in a baggy sweatshirt. She'd sleep in bra and panties, those long, shapely legs forming a figure 4 as she lay on her right side, her right arm flung straight out, her left arm resting over her bosom. Her hair would cover her face, forming a shiny reddish-brown veil...

He closed his eyes and surrendered to the blackness. Roxie disappeared and he saw nothing, thought of nothing, felt nothing, heard nothing.

His eyes snapped open; it took him several shaky moments to realize where he was, what he was doing.

He was sitting on a barstool in the kitchen, a plate of toast and two eggs on the counter in front of him.

I'm eating breakfast, but I can't remember fixing it...

What was he thinking about? What had been so important that he'd totally lost all comprehension of the last few minutes?

More importantly, why couldn't he remember? Had he actually fallen asleep at the breakfast table?

What was wrong with him?

While struggling to remember, he stared at the half-eaten eggs and the jagged chunk of toast on his plate as if they'd suddenly appeared with the wave of a magician's wand. Then he noticed the fork in his left hand. A sliver of egg white dangled from it.

Weird...

He put it in his mouth. It was cold.

How long had he been daydreaming? He glanced at the wall clock. 9:17. He must have done a great job of zoning out. Something was wrong; he couldn't even remember what he'd been daydreaming about.

Was it Roxie? What else could it be?

He finished his breakfast and drank another cup of coffee. Then he thought about the day ahead.

He decided to call her later—maybe after lunch—and work out the details.

But first, he needed to do a little shopping. It was important to select a special outfit to wear for the special new lady in his life.

***

"Classic Reads, this is Sandy. How can I help you?"

"Sandy? This is Henry. How're you doing?"

Sandy dropped her reading glasses onto the desk blotter and sat back. "Henry, it's really great to hear from you! How have you been? I take it you're in town?"

"I took a well-deserved break."

"You mean a vacation?"

"Call it what you like, but it all comes across as a guy looking burnout in the face and not liking what he sees."

"How long has this been going on?"

"Actually, I've been going full-tilt the last eight months and decided that it was time to say hell with it and try and get my life back. As I just said, I needed a break. I also needed to come home and see if I remembered where I left my condo."

Sandy laughed. "The same old Henry. Did you find it?"

"Eventually, but I also discovered that I had to toss most of the food in the fridge."

"I can imagine. So how's the software business going? Other than ruining your life…"

"As well as can be expected. I'll breathe much easier once I can find a way to con a couple of my idiot partners into buying me out so I can retire in style."

"Retire? At your age? I didn't think you were much older than Roxie or me."

"I'm just tired of working."

"That's how I feel sometimes—especially when the store is empty—or full, and I'm the only one on the floor."

"I guess we're all just a little tired of the grind. How's she doing, by the way? She there?"

"She hasn't come in yet."

"What happened? She have a hot date last night?"

Sandy didn't reply. She didn't know if she should tell him Roxie's personal business. She wasn't quite sure if she should even mention this Aaron guy. For one thing, he seemed to be freaking Roxie out. For another, she didn't like the negative vibes she'd gotten from Roxie when Aaron came to pick her up for dinner, and she certainly didn't like how Roxie was acting when she'd come back. There was definitely something going on, and the fact that Roxie refused to confide in her only made her more suspicious. But even so, she didn't think it was her place to tell Henry.

"Sandy? Still there?"

"I'm still here."

"Is something wrong?"

"Well, no, but…well—"

"Well what?"

Sandy wanted to slap herself. She should have figured Henry would pick up on her silence.

"Roxie's doing just fine…"

"I sense a *but* hanging in there, somewhere."

"There's really nothing to worry about. It's just that, well, Roxie started seeing someone, and I just didn't know if I should tell you."

A short pause. "That's great that she's seeing someone—provided he's an okay guy. He *is* an okay guy, isn't he?"

Once again, she didn't know what she should say.

"Sandy…why are you taking so long to answer my questions?"

"I'm just not sure if I should say anything, but if you want the honest truth, I'm kind of leery about this man."

"Leery how?"

"It's kind of hard to explain…"

"Are you trying to tell me she might be hooking up with someone who might hurt her? Someone who might not be good for her? Or both?"

"I don't know. She just doesn't seem herself when he's around. She seems…well, frightened."

A pause. "Frightened? Or just uncomfortable?"

Once again, she didn't know how to reply.

"Sandy, this is me. Roxie and I…well, we haven't actually been close the last year or so, but that's only because I haven't been in Orlando much. But I still consider her my very close friend, and I'm sure she thinks the same of me."

"She does."

"Then tell me…is this something I need to follow up on?"

Sandy sighed. This was a tough call. "Well, maybe…"

"Just maybe?"

"Listen, Henry…I know all about how close you and Roxie are. You two practically grew up together and probably would have married one another if your careers hadn't gotten in the way. But I also know how private a person Roxie is, and that she doesn't like people butting in—"

"You're not telling me anything I don't already know."

180

"I just think we should let her handle this herself."

"If Roxie's in any danger, butting in is exactly what I intend to do."

"But she'll strangle me if she finds out I told you anything about—"

"She won't find out, Sandy."

"How can you be sure?"

"Don't worry about it, okay? I promise that whatever I do will be my idea alone."

Sandy didn't like what Henry was suggesting but knew she couldn't stop him if his mind was made up. Besides, she found herself secretly hoping Henry would step in and do something. She didn't usually get such bad vibes about people, but she couldn't help feeling this way about Aaron. "You don't want Roxie to know anything about this conversation, do you?" she asked.

"I'd prefer you didn't even tell her I called."

Sandy didn't like where this was going but decided Henry probably knew best. Even with her reservations, she knew Henry had only Roxie's best interests at heart. "Whatever you do, you *will* be discreet, won't you?"

"Sandy, my dear, discreet happens to be my middle name."

***

After a brief stop at the bank for some cash, Aaron drove to the Winter Park Village at around eleven to pick up a new outfit for his date with Roxie.

He stepped into the priciest men's store he could find, selected a beautiful form-fitting

181

cashmere dress shirt, black silk slacks and a pair of hand-stitched Italian imported casuals. The price of the outfit totaled $2,000.

The skinny well-dressed guy standing behind the register smelled strongly of *Obsession for Men*. He flashed a beaming smile. "You have very good taste, sir."

"Thanks. I think so, too."

The young man began clipping off the tags and placing them neatly on the counter beside the register. "Will this be cash or charge?"

"Actually, neither."

"P-Pardon me?"

"This is all on you."

"Sir...I don't understand—"

All you need to know is that you're going to pay for this yourself. You have to. Otherwise, you're going to feel really bad...

Aaron took his new purchases outside and headed down the sidewalk, where the Crown Vic was parked halfway down the block.

"Aaron?" called a familiar voice behind him.

He turned. It was Lana.

His pleasant thoughts of Roxie immediately vanished. He began trembling as she came closer, her tense smile lighting up her pretty face. He couldn't understand why he should be so nervous. His life had taken an upward swing. He had nothing to fear, nothing to be bitter about. He reminded himself that he owed at least part of this new life to Lana. If she hadn't left him and forced him into the gutter, whatever had changed him would never have happened. He really should thank her.

This new realization made him feel better. The trembling stopped; so did the anger he'd experienced when he'd first seen her.

She looked different. Her hair, about an inch shorter, was frosted in some places. Her makeup wasn't quite as heavy as he remembered, and her clothes fit her more snugly. She wore a simple black skirt just below the knee and a red blouse with long sleeves and an open neck. She'd always had great legs, and her white open-toed sandals made her thighs and calves much sexier. She'd dropped a couple of pounds and was wearing more jewelry than usual.

He also noticed that her smile was different. Her face seemed brighter than he remembered. He could tell she was genuinely happy.

"How have you been?" Her eyes sparkled. "I didn't think I'd see you *here*, of all places."

"I do shop once in a while." For some reason, her statement had raked on him.

"I didn't mean *that*… I meant, well, this is quite a coincidence."

He could tell she was taking inventory. Lana had always been able to size up a man at a glance. She checked out the clothes first—how they fit, how they looked. Then she eyed the waist to compute a weight gain. Then, of course, the hair, before settling on the man's face. "You're looking good," she said, nodding her approval.

"So are you."

"Thank you." She smiled. "I'm glad we're both doing well."

He just nodded.

"So…what's going on with you? Still with C&H?"

He wondered if she was trying to irritate him. She knew what happened after their split—why would she bring that up? He reminded himself that he'd be seeing Roxie in a few hours. No one could spoil that for him. Not even the woman who'd done so much to wreck his life.

"I left them not long after our divorce. I thought you knew that."

"I figured that maybe you went back."

"Why would I do that?"

She shrugged. "Well, you look like you're back on your feet, obviously." She glanced at his bag. "That store isn't known for bargain prices, so I figured that since you could afford their stuff, maybe you went back to your old job. Besides, you and Louis were always good friends, so…"

"I'm doing all right on my own."

"I'm really happy for you."

He wanted her to stop talking. She was keeping him from getting back to the condo. He had to call Roxie and make arrangements for their date and couldn't do it while he was standing here, talking to his ex-wife.

"Would you like to have coffee or something?" Lana asked. "There's a quiet little shop down the street, not far from where I work. I'm working at a cute little dress shop just two blocks from here. That's why I'm here. I'm only working part-time, and I was going to do a little shopping when I spotted you. Anyway, we could, you know, catch up on how we're both doing—"

184

"I really have to go. I have a bunch of things to tend to."

She nodded. "Sure. I understand. I just thought maybe you and I could have a little chat. It's been a long time since we've seen one another…"

"That tends to happen after a divorce." Despite his warm thoughts of Roxie, he couldn't keep the cold darkness—as well as the anger and the hurt—from taking over and clouding his mind.

Lana didn't reply right off. She was still studying his face. "I just thought we might, you know, chat…"

"About what?"

"Well, we *were* married, Aaron. For nine years. We did share a life together. I thought maybe we could spend a few—"

"We did share a life. You decided you didn't want to share it with me anymore." The darkness continued, growing colder and heavier. He soon found that he could no longer fight it off.

"Listen, Aaron, I know now that was a stupid idea. I just thought—"

"Why suggest it, then?"

She bit her lower lip—as she usually did when nervous or caught off-guard. It made him feel a hundred percent better. "I just thought it was kind of nice to see you again. Just forget about it, okay? Have a nice life." She turned to walk away.

The sight of her turning away from him ignited a spark that transformed the darkness in his mind into a raging inferno.

She was turning away from him…again!

Calm yourself. You can't let this destroy you…

185

Lana turned at the corner and disappeared.

He closed his eyes and felt the storm inside him subsiding. *That's it... Let the calm run through you... Go back to the car...and think of Roxie and your evening together...and forget about Lana—*

He opened his eyes and realized that he was standing beside Lana's car. She was parked down the block, in front of a delivery van. A middle-aged woman hurried by without glancing in their direction. The only traffic he heard came from the intersection half a block straight ahead.

How the hell did he get here? Just moments ago, he was nearly a block away, calming himself...

Lana started up the car.

She needs to know, a strange voice inside him said. *She needs to know about you...and that everything in your life is now great...and that it's all great because of her...because of how things changed when she walked out on you...*

All his former thoughts of getting back to the car and driving home vanished. The darkness had returned and, with it, an overwhelming anger he'd never experienced before.

I need to turn around and leave before I do something I'll regret...

No, the voice said. *Lana has to know about your triumphs and your new happiness. You can have anything you want, and no one will be able to hurt you anymore.*

He watched his hand reaching out as if it had a mind of its own...and motioned for her to roll down her window.

She hesitated, staring up at him with that same hurt expression he'd seen so many times before. Then, after a few moments, she sighed and did as he suggested. "I'm sorry, Aaron. I didn't mean to bring anything back—really. I was just happy to see you and thought we should talk and at least try and clear the air—"

"I know what you meant, but you know something? It no longer matters. Life's been great for me since our divorce."

"I'm really happy for you, Aaron—"

"I've got everything I want, everything I'll ever need, and I don't need you anymore. I don't even think about you anymore."

"I understand. And I'm very happy everything's going good for you. Now *please* let me—"

"No. You *don't* understand. You can't *possibly* understand." He held up the bag. "I just got this new outfit because I'm meeting someone tonight. Her name is Roxie, and she's a great lady."

"That's nice, Aaron. Like I just said, I'm happy for you."

"I got this outfit and I didn't even have to pay for it. I no longer have to pay for anything, Lana. People let me take things because they have no choice. Something happens to them if they piss me off."

"Aaron, *please* let me drive away…"

"I'll tell you what we're going to do, too. Roxie and me? As soon as I pick her up—"

"Aaron, I don't want to sit here and listen to this!"

187

The obsession had taken over. "I'm going to take her to the priciest eatery I can find, and when we've finished having dinner, we're going to have sex. Lots and lots of sex—"

"Aaron, *please*…"

"And when we're finished, we're going to go at it again—"

"Aaron, *stop it!*"

The window started sliding back up.

A thicker, heavier blackness took over. The raging inferno came right back, filling his mind and making everything else go away. The anger returned…and the hurt…and something he'd never experienced before…and a strange feeling of warmth and joy drifted up amongst the turmoil, making everything soft and quiet again…

Sighing deeply, he opened his eyes.

Lana lay across the front seat, her lips parted, her bluish tongue protruding from her mouth. Her face was deathly pale. Shards of glass glittered on the seat near her face, in her hair and on her red blouse.

There is a price, the voice inside him said. Then it vanished, and all he heard was the traffic behind him and the fast-moving footsteps of someone passing on the sidewalk, on the other side of Lana's car.

CHAPTER TWENTY-ONE

At one o'clock, Sandy came into the office. "How about taking a break for lunch?"

Roxie finished entering the latest transaction into her laptop. She sat back and rubbed her temples. The morning had been terrible. She couldn't get back to sleep after her horrible nightmare and had spent the rest of the night trying to figure it out—to make sense of it as well as trying to understand what it had to do with Aaron. She convinced herself it was just mental trash and meant nothing, and she should just forget about it. It might have been the result of her weird experience with Aaron earlier in the bookstore, for all she knew. The important thing was that she hadn't killed that dog, and nothing could ever change that.

Anyway, she'd survived the night, and this was a brand-new day. Lunch sounded like a terrific idea. "Sounds great. Chinese again?"

"I was thinking more along the lines of pizza. How about it?"

Even better. "You're asking *me* if I want *pizza*?"

Sandy laughed. "I figured I'd be polite."

"When have you *ever* known me to turn down pizza?"

"I never have, actually…"

"It's nature's perfect food. Of course I want pizza. I always want pizza!"

"Well, all right…since I had to force you into it…"

"Sausage and pepperoni?"

"Of course."

Just then, she thought of Aaron. When he called, he'd certainly ask her to dinner. She didn't want to insult him by going to an expensive restaurant with him on a full stomach.

"Something wrong?" Sandy asked.

"I just remembered. I'm probably going out to dinner later on."

"When?"

"I'm not sure. Aaron knows our hours. When he calls, he'll probably set it up so we're having dinner by seven, or seven-thirty."

Sandy glanced at the wall clock. "That's more than six hours from now."

"It could take half an hour to get it and bring it back…"

Sandy sighed tiredly. "That still leaves you five and a half hours to scarf it down and get it digested, right?"

"I guess you've got a point."

"I'll call first. That way, it'll be ready by the time I get there." Sandy got out her phone. "Unless, of course, you don't actually *want* pizza…"

"Perish the thought, silly. It means I'll probably only want a couple of pieces, rather than my usual habit of sucking up half."

Sandy laughed. "Then I'll just get a medium, rather than our usual extra-large." Sandy made the call, grabbed her bag, and left.

Fifteen minutes later, the phone rang. It was Aaron.

Her heart racing, Roxie took a deep breath and told her nerves to settle down. She could handle this. It was just a phone call—nothing that would kill her or change her life. "Hi, Aaron. How are things?"

"Actually, everything's just great." He sounded unusually chipper. "Have you thought about where you'd like to have dinner tonight?"

"I thought I'd leave it up to you." She figured he'd be more relaxed if she left him in charge of the arrangements. She knew from experience that most men appreciated things like that.

"Terrific. Do you want me to pick you up at the bookstore? Or should I come over to your place?"

She still didn't want him knowing where she lived, but she knew to be tactful. "That depends on where we're going."

"You just left it up to me, right?"

"I guess I did…"

"Then it'll have to be a surprise."

Roxie sagged in her seat. She hadn't expected this to work out that way. But since she'd just set the ground rules, she couldn't very well squirm out of it. Now she had to keep her fingers crossed and hope everything would turn out okay. "I guess so, then."

"Good. So where should I pick you up?"

"The store will be fine."

"You close at six, right?"

"Yes…"

"I know you have to straighten up and do the cash and receipts and everything. How long should I give you?"

"It's been pretty busy today, but I'm sure Sandy and I can finish up in twenty or thirty minutes."

"Great. I'll be there at six-thirty, then."

***

After lunch, Roxie found it difficult to pay attention to what she was doing and even suffered a memory blip when a customer asked her to find an out-of-print novel by Ross MacDonald. She just couldn't stop worrying about her date with Aaron.

Although she tried to remain positive, she couldn't help thinking something would go wrong. The simple facts made failure inevitable. There was something frightening going on with Aaron. She had no idea what it was; she only knew that it involved other people's minds.

Could he actually *read* minds? Could he sense suspicion in other people? What would happen if he picked up something that told him she knew about his ability?

If he really possessed the ability to get into her mind, did that mean that he had something to do with her nightmare the previous night? If so, what would be the purpose? Would he think that by scaring her, she'd be more malleable? More submissive to his demands? Would it give him more control over her?

That reasoning seemed totally ridiculous. How could he or anyone else enter someone's mind in the first place? Even if he *was* capable, how could he possibly worm his way into her mind and find what he needed to instigate a nightmare? How would he even know what happened to her that sunny afternoon so many years ago? And lastly, why would he do such a nasty thing to someone he obviously wanted to be involved with?

She realized right then that she had to rid her mind of all these suspicions. She couldn't possibly bring them with her when she saw him again. If Aaron did indeed possess such a powerful ability, he'd undoubtedly sense her fears and suspicions.

She had to convince herself that this was nothing more than a regular date with a nice, personable guy she'd just met. And once the date was over, she'd tell him that although she liked him, she just didn't want to get serious with anyone.

As six o'clock approached, she grew more and more uneasy. She wanted to cancel but knew that would be unwise. It would not only drag things out, it would also irritate him.

She kept busy until closing time finally arrived, and once the last customer had left, she reluctantly flipped the sign on the door to *CLOSED* while Sandy straightened out some of the displays.

Aaron showed up precisely at six-thirty in a form-fitting cashmere shirt, black slacks, and a pair of expensive-looking tan casuals. He looked very neat. He'd washed his hair, and the scent of his mint shaving lotion was quite strong. If things had been different, Roxie would have been excited about the prospects of the evening.

"Ready to go?" he asked.

"I'll just be a moment. I've got to get my bag."

"Take your time."

Sandy was sitting at the desk in front of the laptop when Roxie came in. "Where are you two going?"

193

"I don't know. It's a surprise."

Sandy frowned. "Why aren't you more excited? You look like you're on your way to visit someone at the hospital."

She'd hoped her fears wouldn't show but realized she was probably much too nervous and upset to hide her true feelings. "I guess I'm just a little tense."

"It's only dinner, right?"

"Right…"

Sandy lowered her voice. "If it doesn't go well, you can always tell him to get lost. We've both been handling men since high school. We both know they're really not that difficult. Some are more fragile than others, but they always seem to be able to cope. And no matter what happens, they *always* manage to find someone else."

She wanted to tell Sandy that she couldn't possibly tell Aaron to get lost. You just couldn't avoid or get rid of someone like him very easily.

Smiling weakly, Roxie nodded and waved on her way out.

I can do this, she thought as she slipped through the doorway. *I started it. Now I have to find some way of finishing it…*

***

Aaron kept with the heavy northbound flow, until they'd crossed Aloma Avenue.

He wanted to take Roxie to the new steakhouse that had just opened a couple of weeks earlier. Beef Handlers specialized in more than two dozen different cuts and styles of steaks and would prepare your meal any way you wished. The large stucco

194

building consisted of four separate dining rooms with paneled walls, giving the appearance of a Spanish villa from the outside.

Aaron could tell something was on Roxie's mind. She hadn't said a word since they'd gotten in the car. She was acting just as she had when he'd taken her to the Crab Hut the day before. She sat very still in the seat beside him, her hands in her lap.

When he'd caught her glancing at the side mirror, he decided to try a little levity in hopes of helping her relax. "Are we being followed?"

She turned her head sharply. "What makes you say *that*?"

"I was just kidding. It's just that...well, you seem distracted. Did everything go all right at work?"

"Nothing's wrong. Everything's fine—just fine." She smiled. "That's a very nice shirt you're wearing. Is it new?"

"Just picked it up this afternoon." He sat up proudly and pretended to flick something off the sleeve. "Winter Park Village. They have some nice shops there."

"I've been there once or twice, but I really don't like shopping in that area. Their stuff's way too pricey."

He winked. "You gotta know how to talk them down."

"I didn't think that was possible."

"When you know what you're doing, anything's possible."

She nodded but didn't reply.

He turned back to the road ahead and thought about Lana. It brought a smile to his face. If only she could see him now... He glanced at the auburn-haired beauty beside him and felt triumphant all over again. *I really wish you could meet Roxie and see how great I've been doing since you walked out of my life... Maybe I'll bring her back with me the next time I'm shopping, and we can bump into one another again...*

His thoughts went back to their accidental meeting on the street. Once again, he was very proud of the way he'd handled her. He'd been cool and casual about the whole thing when he'd told her how well he was doing and how terrific things were. He knew he should've held off mentioning Roxie, but Lana's attitude had raked on him, and he'd felt the need to brag. Telling Lana about his recent success had been the best thing for him. It had compensated for much of the torment he'd endured because of her.

He wondered for a moment if he'd gone overboard. He didn't think so—not really. Telling her about Roxie and their dinner date hadn't been *too* obvious, had it?

Lana needed to know I've moved on. Now she knows for sure.

I probably knocked her right off her pedestal.

He smiled, remembering her reaction. Lana hadn't appreciated that sort of talk. She hadn't wanted to hear how great he was doing. He could tell by how she'd stiffened in her seat...how her eyes had filled their sockets...how she'd chewed her lower lip...how her cheeks had turned red. Lana never liked hearing about people doing better than she was. And she especially hadn't wanted to know that Aaron, of all people, was able to survive without her.

Well, Lana, you were wrong this time. Dead wrong.

And when he'd left her sitting there in her car, the look of shock covering her face, he realized how great life could really be...and how sweet revenge really was—especially if you let it take its natural course.

As the saying went: Living well is the best revenge...

He realized once again that life could not possibly get any better than this...

"Now *you're* the one who's quiet." Roxie was watching him. "Everything okay?"

"Everything's just great. In fact, things couldn't be better." He couldn't help grinning like a stupid kid. The whole world felt truly wonderful at the moment. Although he didn't want the day to end, he found that he couldn't wait for the evening to embrace them.

CHAPTER TWENTY-TWO

Dinner—an eight-ounce charbroiled steak, twice-baked potato, asparagus, sautéed mushrooms, and a vintage red wine—was excellent. The service was quick, the servers attentive, friendly, and committed to their work.

Roxie and Aaron sat in the main dining room, enjoying their meal as the embers crackled and winked at them from the fireplace just a few feet away. As they ate, chamber music whispered soothingly through the speakers built into the ceiling.

Despite her initial anxiety, Roxie found that she was having a good time. This meal was the best she'd had in quite a while.

She was also pleased to find that Aaron was a really nice guy after all—very considerate and attentive to her every need. They chatted away as they ate, discussing all sorts of things. She quickly discovered how comfortable she was with him and that he was not someone she should have feared at all. She began having doubts about what she'd really seen outside the latte shop and wondered if her wild imagination had made her see something that actually didn't happen.

This, of course, led to what had happened the day before, in the bookstore. For all she knew, she could have been stressed from the long, busy workday and was experiencing queasiness from not eating. And she shouldn't forget that his sudden appearance had surprised her, knocking her slightly off-balance. What had happened might not have been anything to worry about at all.

And her nightmare might have been merely another weeding out of mental trash, this time fueled by suspicions of Aaron and what she'd feared about him.

Even so, she felt her pulse hastening when the waitress brought over the check. If anything would put an end to her suspicions, this would. It would clear up the mystery of what happened at the latte shop and also at the Crab Hut.

Without hesitation, Aaron pulled a roll of bills from his pocket, removed a hundred-dollar-bill, slipped it on the tray and told the woman to keep the change.

A warm wave of honest relief billowed through her, and she wanted to scold herself for suspecting him in the first place.

Soon they were getting back in his car. He pulled out of the crowded lot and headed south on Semoran, turning right at the intersection of Colonial then making a left on Primrose just fifteen minutes later. Aaron remained silent, his eyes on the road in front of them. Roxie could tell he was deep in thought.

Ten minutes later, he made the left onto Curry Ford, pulled off the main drag a minute later and eased down the narrow one-lane road that went past the strip mall, where her car was parked behind the bookstore.

While he put the car in park and switched off the ignition, she began to suspect once again that she'd been imagining things. Aaron had not done anything frightening or out of the ordinary, making her wonder yet again why she'd suspected him of anything underhanded in the first place. She kept telling herself that she'd been wrong about him. Nothing was scary or weird about him at all.

She could tell by the luminous numbers on the dash that it was nearly nine o'clock. Then she noticed that Aaron had switched off the lights and turned in his seat. He was smiling at her. It took her only a moment to realize that he probably wanted a kiss.

No problem. He was a nice, personable guy. Kissing him would not be that difficult.

"I'll follow you back to your place, if you like." His smile remained.

"Pardon me?"

He shrugged. "Our date's going well—wouldn't you say?"

"Well, yes..."

"Didn't you have a good time?"

"I had a great time, Aaron."

"Then let me follow you back to your place."

She had no idea what to say. She hadn't thought he'd want things to move so quickly.

"What's wrong?"

"Nothing's wrong..."

"You like me, don't you?"

"Of *course* I do..."

"Then tell me what's wrong."

"Aaron, I think this might be going a little too fast."

His smile vanished. "Whaddya mean? You like me and I like you. What could be simpler than my

200

following you home and, well..." His smile returned. "You know what happens next, right?"

Great. He not only wants a kiss, he also wants sex.

This was not exactly what she'd had in mind. Roxie had a strict policy to never have sex with a man on the first or second date.

But she also knew she had to tread very carefully. A man's ego could be very fragile.

I've got to let him down gently...somehow...

"Like I just said, I think this is going a little too—"

She didn't get to finish her statement. Aaron leaned over and kissed her hard on the lips.

"Aaron!" She pulled away.

"What's wrong?" He sat back in shock. "It was just a kiss!"

"I know what it was."

"Then what's the problem?"

"Aaron, I think you're expecting a little too much."

"I really don't think I'm expecting too much at all..." His hand shot out, moving toward her right breast.

Before she had a chance to act shocked, he froze. Even in the darkness of the cab, she could see that his eyes had changed, turning from their bright chestnut color to an icy blue glow, with a strange sliver of light coming from the center of each eye. His face also changed, his features tightening, his nose wrinkling, his lips pulling back, baring his teeth. Froth gathered on his lower lip and covered

201

his chin. A strange foul smell filled the interior of the cab, and she gagged.

"*Aaron*?" Her heart thrashing, Roxie pulled back. Slivers of ice slid down her spine. Drops of hot froth pitted her shirt, making her nauseous. Unable to take her eyes from him, she reached behind her and blindly groped for the door handle. She quickly found that her hand had turned useless. All she could do was squeeze the padded arm rest.

A raspy, high-pitched groan had trickled out of Aaron's throat. His lower lip and chin were covered with slobber as he reached out for her. His hands no longer resembled hands. They'd turned into claws, and went right for her throat.

"*Aaron! Please!*"

The claws encircled her throat. They were sharp and as cold as metal, and would not yield even when she used all her strength to pound them with her fists. The claws pushed her down. The back of her head slammed against the side window and she nearly blacked out. The claws dug into her flesh, and she soon discovered that her head was cocked at an unnatural angle, cutting off her air. She struggled to breathe but couldn't move. She found herself helplessly wedged in her seat as if a giant boulder had dropped on top of her. The last image she saw was that of a salivating monster gazing at her.

A weak whimper trickled out of her throat as the blackness closed in.

***

Sitting behind the wheel of his restored emerald green classic '68 Camaro, Henry Bowen eyed the maroon Crown Vic parked less than a hundred feet away. He glanced at his watch and knew damned well that something bad was going on.

Rox should've gotten out by now.

He lowered the window all the way so he could hear better. Roxie just wasn't the type to sit in a guy's car and make out with him—especially if she was leery of him. Judging by what Sandy had told him, she was walking on eggshells with this guy. They could be talking, but the vibes he'd been picking up—those same vibes that had saved his butt more times in Afghanistan than he cared to remember—were telling him a different story. And what he'd picked up was the simple fact that if Sandy was right about Roxie being apprehensive about this guy, she wouldn't be sitting in his car with him at this time of night. Not voluntarily...

The tinted windows of the Crown Vic, as well as the darkness of the night, concealed whatever was going on inside the car. He'd followed the two of them to the Beef Handlers on Aloma and waited out in the parking lot to watch for anything suspicious. Roxie hadn't seemed nervous when they came back out, but he didn't want to take any chances. He knew full well that when a guy brought a chick home after an expensive date, he expected to get laid.

This guy looked and acted all right. He dressed well and held open the door for her. Even so, Henry had seen a lot of weird things in the last twenty years. Common sense dictated that you needed to go beyond someone's outward appearance and manners to evaluate him—especially if you

203

suspected he was dangerous. Many of the world's most vicious killers had been deceptively polite and proper. They knew how to act normal in public because they realized someone could be watching them. It was only when they were alone with their prey that their insanity took over, turning them into monsters.

From what Sandy had told him, this guy sounded like he might possibly have some sort of abnormality, but not in any conventional way. When she'd told him how Roxie had been acting, Henry couldn't help thinking that his good friend might be dealing with a psycho.

There was only one way to tell.

Just then, he heard Roxie yell. An instant later, the Crown Vic began rocking.

What choice did he have? Roxie's health and well-being were at stake. If he was right, she could really be in mortal danger.

If he didn't jump right in, there was no sure way of finding out what was going on. He couldn't help wondering if something out of the realm of logic might be involved. He knew this kind of thinking might be just his imagination. He'd been gun-shy since he'd come back from Afghanistan, seeing demons wherever he'd turned his head and dreaming of them when he'd closed his eyes. But this didn't mean a demon was actually involved, did it?

He hoped he was imagining the worst—that this wasn't a demon at all.

But if it wasn't, it meant something almost as bad. It meant that the guy with Roxie was someone she shouldn't be involved with at all.

So what was going on in that car? Was Roxie in trouble? Or was she having the time of her life?

Roxie was classy and reserved. She was the type of girl any guy would be proud to be with—the type any honorable man would bring home to his parents.

But she was *not* the type to put out in a parked car.

Henry grabbed his trusty metal sap from the glove box. Then, as silently as a cat, he slipped out of the Camaro.

205

CHAPTER TWENTY-THREE

When Roxie came to, she discovered that she was lying on the couch in her office.

A feeling of cold enveloped her. After some awkward investigating, she found that a damp wash towel covered her forehead as well as one on the front of her neck. The desk lamp was on, but the rest of the room was dark.

She heard a slight rustling on her left. Startled, she turned. The washrag slid off her forehead, landing on the leather cushion beside her.

Henry was standing beside the gurgling coffeepot. When he heard the crunching of the leather, he turned. "How's the neck?"

She carefully lowered the washcloth from her neck. The skin beneath it was sensitive, throbbing lightly, and she could feel some welts. There didn't seem to be any blood, and she could swallow without difficulty.

Confusion made her wonder if her senses had jumped ship. Was Henry really standing there? Or was she just imagining it? Last she remembered, she was arguing with Aaron. Then everything turned crazy, and she'd passed out.

So what happened? And why did her throat feel as if it had been placed in a vise? And why was Henry here? How did he know she was in trouble?

Something just wasn't making any sense.

And where was Aaron?

She cleared her throat and tried to speak. "I guess I'm all right..." Her throat was sore and burned a little, but she was happy it still worked. "Henry…what are you doing…how did you—"

"I talked with Sandy this morning. I wanted to talk to you, but you hadn't come in."

"But how did you…where were you when—"

"Sandy told me about this new guy you were seeing. When I asked her about him, she didn't say much, so I thought I'd check him out for myself."

"You were…following us?"

"You could say that. Good thing I was out there." He poured two cups and put the pot back.

"What happened?" She still couldn't make any sense out of this.

Henry placed a cup on the table in front of the couch and sat down in the chair beside the desk. "That guy you were with…he tried to kill you."

"What?" She couldn't believe what he'd just said.

"You don't remember?"

With effort, she sat up and reached for the coffee cup. She picked it up with a shaky hand and nearly spilled it. Steadying it with both hands, she brought it to her lips and carefully coaxed a sip of the hot brew into her mouth, wincing when it went down her throat. Sighing deeply, she placed the cup on the washcloth in her lap, leaned back and tried hard to remember.

Aaron had taken her to the Beef Handlers off Aloma. After a terrific meal, he brought her back to the bookstore and they sat in the parking lot out back, talking. Then, without warning, he kissed her. Then blackness.

But nothing else registered.

207

She tried reading Henry's expression but had no luck. He wouldn't make up something like that, would he? No. Of course not. Why would he? Still, it made no sense. "Aaron...tried to *kill* me?"

"He was on top of you when I got the door open. He would've strangled you if I'd been thirty seconds slower."

"He...actually tried to *kill* me?" Something was very wrong. This made no sense. Aaron wouldn't do something like that. "You're absolutely sure?"

Henry had a slug of coffee. "As I said, he was on top of you, and his hands were around your neck. Your face was turning blue, so..." He shrugged. "Do the math."

No. No sense at all. She closed her eyes and struggled to recall more details. After the kiss... Something had happened after the kiss. What was it?

What happened after he kissed me?
And why can't I--

"Oh my God..." A clutter of images flooded back in a violent wave, sending a cold surge shimmering through her. She had to grab her coffee cup with both hands so she wouldn't spill it.

Henry leaned forward. "Is any of it coming back?"

Aaron's eyes... They'd turned color and...and actually *glowed*... Hadn't they? Or was she just imagining it?

No. It really happened. It was sort of hazy at first, but as her mind cleared, so did the images.

"He...changed." Her voice came out as a tense whisper.

"What's that?"

"Aaron. He *changed*."

"How?"

"His eyes..."

"What about his eyes?"

"They...*glowed*..."

"They what?"

"His eyes glowed. My God... It was like...he wasn't Aaron anymore. He didn't even *look* like Aaron anymore. His eyes, his nose, his mouth... He was salivating, Henry. His chin was covered with the stuff. It was like...I had the strange feeling that...that he'd become...a *monster*."

Henry sat stiffly, watching her. She could tell that he was trying to process what she'd just told him. "What else?"

"His hands...they came right at me, but they didn't...they didn't look like *hands* anymore. They'd become *claws*—big, powerful *claws*..."

"Anything else?"

Anger burst unexpectedly from her. She couldn't believe Henry had just asked her such a stupid question. "He tried to *kill* me. His eyes *glowed*. His hands turned into *claws*. My God, Henry...isn't that enough?"

"Yes, if that's all there is. If there's more, then no, it isn't enough."

She closed her eyes again and told herself not to be angry. After all, Henry was only trying to help. And he had. He'd just saved her life. How could she have forgotten so quickly?

Then she realized there *was* something else— something she hadn't noticed until a moment ago.

"Something weird came out of his throat. It sounded like a growl, but it was really high-pitched."

"High-pitched how?"

"It was almost like...like it came from...a *woman*..."

***

Aaron opened his eyes.

He was sitting behind the wheel of the Crown Vic, and the back of his head throbbed mercilessly. When he tried to reach up to examine his skull, he discovered that his wrists were pinned together behind his back. He tried pulling them apart. They had a little play in them but held fast. He used his fingers to examine his bonds in the dark. In doing so, he shifted in the seat but soon found that he could barely move. This was when he realized he'd been strapped in tightly with his seat harness. Very little play there, so he shifted as much as he could. The moment he tilted his head, the back of his skull tapped the window. An explosion of white-hot pain made him cringe, and he jerked his head away. The throbbing made him grind his teeth. He sat quite still, his head forward, his jaw clenched as he rode out the pain.

After the throbbing had subsided, he shifted once again ever so slightly in the seat. Working by feel, he began examining his bonds a second time. Bungee cords. His wrists were fastened together with bungee cords.

Who had done such a thing? What happened? Why was he sitting alone in the Crown Vic, strapped in tightly by the seat harness, his wrists

210

tied together behind his back, when he and Roxie were sitting here only moments ago?

He gawked at the empty seat beside him.

Where was Roxie? What happened?

The back of his skull ached as if it had been pounded into pulp, but at least he could think clearly. He and Roxie had just been to the Beef Handlers and had a wonderful time together. Then he'd brought her back here, where they'd sat and talked...and after that—

I kissed her.

The image registered vividly in his head.

I kissed her, and then...

Nothing.

He'd blacked out.

No. He *hadn't* blacked out. Something happened first—something bad. And unpleasant. And totally unexpected.

What was it?

He struggled to remember, but as soon as he forced his mind to go back, his head swam with violent images. Something in the darkness had leaped out, lunging for Roxie. Something horrible and evil. Something with claws. Some loathsome creature that lived in a dark cave somewhere far away had jumped out of nowhere, going right for Roxie...

The Forbidden Place. Yes. That's what it was called. That's where the creature had come from.

More images drifted his way.

A woman lived in the Forbidden Place. A beautiful dark-haired woman with glowing, icy-blue eyes and a bone-chilling coldness deep within her soul. She emerged from the darkness whenever she pleased. Her name was Jessica and she lived in the cold darkness of the Forbidden Place.

And she collected things...

Aaron tried hard to remember what the woman had told him, but nothing would come. Just when he thought the memories would return, the throbbing in his head resumed, making all former thoughts dim in the darkness.

Once again, his head cleared.

The woman had taken something from him...

What was it? He knew it must be something valuable. He struggled to remember. The throbbing had subsided again, and his thoughts grew even clearer...

No. It *couldn't* be...

She's taken my soul!

What else could it be?

But how could she do it? Why would she do such a thing?

Why else had his mind been working so erratically? Why hadn't he been able to remember such simple things anymore? Why had his thoughts stopped the instant he began concentrating?

She's been manipulating me...

How long had she been doing this?

And why do I suddenly know about her right now?

His head began pounding again.

The blow to the back of his skull had dazed him. It had cleared his mind of the darkness, rebooting his memory. It brought back everything. Jessica. Her coldness. Her touch. *I want your soul.*

The trip to the Forbidden Place, where the nightmares were kept…

Nightmares. Yes. She collected nightmares…

There is a price…

He remembered everything now. There was a price for what she'd done, for what she'd given him. She'd given him everything he could ever want or hope for. The price was high—very high. It was too much for him to pay—for *anyone* to pay…

The price was everything he was, everything he'd ever be…

The price was his soul, his spirit…his very essence…

His head pounded even worse, and he heard her voice once again. It had come from the darkness of his mind and resonated from the very center of the excruciating pain filling his being.

It said, simply: *"Your debt has not yet been paid…"*

213

CHAPTER TWENTY-FOUR

After several tries, Roxie managed to sit up.

She experienced stiffness in her joints and limbs, and her shoulder blades throbbed. She felt as if she'd been run over by a semi. "I need to get up." Her head weighed a ton, and she sighed and let herself fall back against the back of the couch. "I...can't stay here. I've got to get up...get moving..."

"You'd better relax for a little while," Henry said. "Do you have any meds in your bag?"

"Just some Ibuprofen and a small bottle of Aspirin. Why?"

"You're gonna need something for the pain. And I think I'd better get you to a doctor to make sure you haven't popped a disk in your neck or back."

"Where's Aaron?" Once again, she couldn't help wondering what happened once Henry rescued her.

"Out in the Crown Vic."

She could tell by his dark expression that he'd done something terrible. Logic told her something violent had happened. Otherwise, Henry wouldn't have been able to get her away from Aaron and bring her in here.

But what had he done? He hadn't told her how he'd managed to pull Aaron off her. Henry was strong but was extremely civilized, and steered clear of physical violence. He'd been deployed in Afghanistan years ago but had come back in much better shape than most of the others she'd seen. Since he never mentioned what he'd done over there, she had no idea what he'd seen or been through. But since he hadn't changed much, she'd always assumed he hadn't been involved in the heaviest of the fighting.

But now she wasn't so sure. "What…did you do to him?"

"I hit him pretty hard."

She swallowed. "How hard?"

He pulled something out of his pocket and held it up. It was a small crescent of black metal about the size of his thumb, attached to a short chain about four inches long, with a dowel-shaped wooden handle screwed to the other end.

Her heat skipped a beat. "You didn't…*kill* him, did you?"

"He'll have a serious headache for a while, but he's still alive." He pocketed the weapon. "Since I had no idea how long he'd been choking you, I had to act quickly. Rox, I'm over forty, for God's sake. I didn't want to get into something that could've gotten you hurt even more, and I certainly didn't want to get into anything that might get me killed."

"We need to talk to him." She tried to get up again. She managed to lift her head this time, but another wave of heavy dizziness forced her back down.

"Take it easy. He won't be going anywhere." He patted his pocket. "I took his keys. Besides, I've got him strapped in and tied up. I always keep some bungee cords in the trunk of the Camaro for emergencies."

215

"My God…" She sank in her seat and rubbed her temples. This was getting worse by the second. "Did you…*have* to do that?"

"I didn't want him going anywhere."

She shook her head.

Henry shrugged. "Would you rather I'd dumped him in the trunk?"

She didn't reply.

"You know I'm right."

She sighed and finally nodded.

Henry got up. "You stay here and rest. I'll go check on him, see if he's up."

"Then what?"

"I'll come back and let you know what's going on."

She sat back and applied the washcloth gently to her neck. "I guess it'll have to do."

***

"*Your debt has not yet been paid…*"

Aaron cringed at the sound of her voice. It sounded very, very close… It was almost as if it had become a part of himself—as if it had entered his head and taken over his own thoughts…

Startled, he forced himself to twist around in the car seat to see if he was alone in the car but succeeded only in bumping his head again. Once again, the throbbing started up. He waited until it died down, then sat back and sighed. "You're…*Jessica…*"

"*I see you're beginning to remember a few things. It must have been that nasty blow to your head. This changes things a little—wouldn't you say?*"

216

"Where are you?" he muttered, trembling.

"I guess you don't remember a few very important things after all..."

"I remember the Forbidden Place. The cave. You. Your hair. But not—"

"Think, Aaron, think..."

"I don't know...I can't..."

"Think of what's happened to you in the last few days. The man in the alley. Remember him?"

Yes. Of course Aaron remembered him. That bastard nearly killed him. A man tended to remember something like that. But what did he have to do with this?

"I really don't know what you're..."

"He threatened you and said he'd kill you if you said anything. Then he slammed you to the pavement and you nearly died. While you were unconscious and hovering so close to death, I came into your life."

"He's dead. I saw his body in the morgue."

"Yes. He's dead, all right."

"He was shot by the police when they tried to arrest him. He can't hurt anyone anymore."

"It happened right after you wished him dead."

Wished him dead... I wished him dead... Her words slammed right home, turning this into a blood-chilling reality.

Had he really wished the man dead? Why couldn't he remember?

"Your emotions spoke for themselves."

Could something that strange have really happened? Or was it just coincidence?

217

"No. That can't be. No one can kill someone just by wishing it so. No one. If that was possible, most of the people in this world would be dead!"

"Do you happen to recall how easily you got your condo? Or that you didn't have to worry about making the last month's rent where you used to live?"

Once again, the reality thundered through him.

"What about the two thugs who tried mugging you the night you went to Visconti's?"

More chilling reality... They were both young and had accosted him outside the bar that night. They both carried switchblades, but it hadn't mattered. It wouldn't have mattered if they'd been carrying machetes—or even machineguns. "They somehow...forgot about me...and went at it all by themselves. I was standing off to the side, watching it. It was really very amusing...but really weird."

"Nothing can hurt you, Aaron. Nothing can ever affect you again. Doesn't that strike you as odd?"

"I thought... I thought—"

"You thought what?"

He didn't know what to think. He'd realized that his life had drastically changed course but had no idea why. Now that it was all coming back, he realized just how naïve he'd been...how stupid. "I thought things just started going well for me..."

"They did. They always will... Once you've paid the price, it will always turn out good for you."

"The price?"

"Your spirit, Aaron. That was our price. It now belongs to me."

218

"Y-You?"

"I own you now."

His heart sank. It couldn't be. How could he have made such a deal? His soul belonged to him—no one else. "It's my spirit. It belongs to me—me and me alone. It *can't* belong to anyone else…"

"You gave it to me, Aaron. We traded. You don't remember what happened when you came to the Forbidden Place?"

The Forbidden Place. He cringed at the name.

"Let me help you remember a few details."

The darkness rushed back, filling his being with a frightening coldness and a strong, unpleasant odor he recognized instantly. The cave. The horrible memories that had been plaguing him. It all came thundering back…

"For your soul, I took away your memory of all unpleasant events and gave you everlasting good luck. That was the price, Aaron. Your soul for unlimited prosperity."

"No. I can't *do* this anymore!"

"Sorry, Aaron. A deal's a deal."

"I didn't know what I was doing!"

"You knew exactly what was happening. The nightmares were destroying you. You wanted them gone. You didn't want them to come back. I took them away."

"I want my soul back!"

"It belongs to me, now."

"I want it back! I don't care about anything else!"

"You'll be sorry…"

"Like I just said, I don't care."

"You'll care—believe me."

"I *don't* believe you! You took my soul!"

"You sold it to me."

"You tricked me!"

"It was a fair trade. I took your nightmares away from you in exchange for incredible good luck."

"It *wasn't fair!*"

"Do you realize how many hundreds upon thousands of mortals would love to engage in a similar trade? How many of them who would gladly shed their sick, tortured souls for the unbelievable good luck you've been having?"

"I don't care!"

"As I just said, you'll be sorry. In fact, you'll be sorrier than you ever were in your entire life..."

"Leave me!"

"I own you..."

"Leave me! Get out of my head!"

"You cannot go back on a deal with me."

"Get out of my fucking head! And give me back my soul!"

A pause. Then: *"All right. As you wish. But before I go, I'll leave you with this..."*

"I don't care about anything you do or say anymore! Just get out of my head and leave me in peace!"

"You'll be really and truly sorry, Aaron..."

"Leave me. That's all I ask. Please!"

"Remember Lana?"

The mere mention of his ex-wife's name brought back a slew of memories. He cringed as the agonizing pain swept ruthlessly through him. Their

220

last argument...the new man in her life... Lana slammed against the wall, her head whacking the side of the table as she fell to the floor...the blood seeping down her cheek as she lay there, propped up by the table, her lips parted, her jaw resting on her collarbone as blood trickled out of her mouth and covered her chin and the top of her blouse, with droplets forming a dotted line in the center of her right breast...the long, numbing moments when he thought she was dead...that he'd actually killed her...

The ambulance, the hospital room...

The security guard ordering him to stay away...

He took a deep breath, shivering and gritting his teeth as the violent storm ravaged through him. The nightmares were back, but at least he had his soul back, too. Somehow, it seemed reasonable. The bourbon would take care of everything again. "I...I can handle that... I'll start drinking again..."

"No, Aaron... That's not all you'll remember..."

He swallowed and waited tensely.

"Here's the real article."

Just then, something else, something much worse, slammed into his consciousness with the force of a sledgehammer...

Lana lying across the front seat of her car, her face a deathly white, her bluish lips parted, her tongue sticking out as he pulled his hands away from her and stood beside her door, wiping off the glass slivers from his sleeve...

"No!"

"Yes, Aaron..."

"NO!"

"Here's another one for you. Have a nice life..."

A beautiful young blond woman lay on the pavement just a few feet from his car, her eyes bulging as he pulled his hands away and straightened. Her name was Brittany, and all she wanted was a ride home because her date had left Shannon's without her.

"No...no...NO!"

Just then, the driver's door yawned open beside him, startling him. A fairly tall, broad-shouldered man with dark hair and deep-set eyes stood there, looking down at him.

Aaron couldn't stop trembling as the pain raged through him. He found that he was barely able to open his mouth to get the words out.

"L-Lana...Brittany...they're both dead...I...*killed them both*!"

The man said something, but Aaron couldn't hear him. His mind had turned into chaos and he couldn't get the words out fast enough. "Lana...my ex-wife...I killed her at Winter Park Village...Brittany Michaels...a sweet young girl I met at Shannon's...Colonial Drive...I killed her...left her there...I'm a fiend...I...I lost my soul...I...gave it away...to a *monster*!"

Then, thankfully, he passed out.

CHAPTER TWENTY-FIVE

The short, stocky blonde in the paramedic uniform treated the bruises on Roxie's neck with a strong antiseptic and placed a small bandage over each of the four welts.

As soon as the girl finished with the bandages, Roxie jumped up from the stretcher, squeezed through the small group of cops standing between the ambulance and the squad car and hurried over to the rear wall of the bookstore, hoping she'd feel more secure there. Gripping her sides, she closed her eyes and tried to shut out the nightmare scene taking place so dangerously close to her personal space.

About thirty feet away, Henry was talking with one of the two cops who'd come over after the paramedics had strapped Aaron onto a gurney and pushed him into the back of the emergency unit.

The other cop came right over to Roxie. He had his notepad and pen out and immediately asked her what she knew.

She told him what she remembered and what Henry had told her when she'd followed him outside just fifteen minutes earlier.

"And you're sure of the two names he mentioned?" the cop asked.

She quickly found herself zoning out and no longer heard the cop's voice. She'd drifted off into a soft, warm swell of nothingness, and for several moments realized that she had no idea where she was or how she'd gotten there. The night had turned into a muddled collage of bright, blinking lights. Three police cars and two medical units had turned the front lot of the bookstore into a silent spectacle of fireworks. People had come out of the supermarket down the one-lane road just beyond the strip mall. Some walked around, being nosy, while others stood off to the side, taking in the activity. Several had their cell phones out and were taking pictures. Roxie wanted to snatch their phones away from them and toss them across the street.

All she could think about was what Henry had told her when he came back into the bookstore. Had Aaron killed two women? Was it possible Henry hadn't heard him correctly? Or was it more likely that Aaron had suffered a concussion from Henry's blow to the head and *imagined* everything?

Aaron? A killer? Was it true? She could hardly believe it. She'd been with him, shared meals with him. She'd even kissed him…

This couldn't be happening.

Her arm trembled as she brought it up and gently touched her neck. The skin was very tender. She felt a bandage and for a moment wondered what happened. Then reality set in and she suddenly remembered just how close to death she'd come. Aaron had tried to kill her—it was as simple as that. And if Henry hadn't shown up when he did, she would have probably died.

But why would Aaron want to kill her? Why would Aaron want to kill anyone?

"Miss Nash?"

A police officer was standing beside her, watching her closely. He had a notepad held out in front of him. Then she remembered that she'd zoned out with him standing right there.

"I'm sorry. I guess…actually, I'm really shaken up right now…"

"I understand. But we need to get the facts down while they're still fresh. You're sure the names Lana and Brittany were mentioned?"

"That's what Henry told me. Aaron had already passed out by the time I came outside. Can you please tell me what's happened?"

"A woman named Lana Grill Stedman was found dead in her vehicle in the Winter Park Village area at around one o'clock this afternoon."

"D-Dead?" She struggled to pull the word out of her throat.

"Strangled."

Roxie put her hand up to her mouth. Henry had already told her this, but hearing it from a police officer brought an edge of startling reality to the picture. "You said…Grill?"

"Apparently she was this man's ex-wife."

"Oh my God…" Then she remembered Aaron telling her he'd shopped at Winter Park Village that day. She had a startling image of Aaron strangling his ex-wife and then shopping for the outfit he'd worn. "This is so *horrible*!" She wanted to throw up.

The cop remained silent.

She took in some cool night air and tried to focus. Lana and Brittany. Henry had told her Aaron said he'd killed *two* women. "The other woman Aaron mentioned to Henry. Any idea who she was?"

"This happened a couple nights ago, outside Shannon's Irish Club on Colonial Drive. The woman was a paralegal secretary for some law firm in Orlando."

"And there were no clues?"

"Not until now." He pocketed his notepad. ". We'll be in touch. Thanks for your help. Try and rest. And take care of those welts." He tipped his hat, turned on his heel and marched back to the cruiser.

Henry came right over. "You *sure* you're all right?"

"Physically." This was going to hit her all at once. Hopefully, it wouldn't happen until she got back to her apartment and had a shot of something strong. She didn't want to humiliate herself right here in front of Henry, OPD, and the two dozen or so gawkers wandering around. After all, one or two of them might come in to the store one day and buy something.

"I guess we can both call it a night, then." Henry turned to walk back to his beloved Camaro, which was parked amongst the cluster of vehicles in the shopping center parking lot next door.

"Not so fast." She had a strange feeling Henry knew more than what he'd told her.

He turned back around.

"You haven't told me what happened."

He shrugged. "You know what happened."

"I don't mean what happened to *me*…"

"I told you what happened, and I told you what he said. That should be enough, shouldn't it?"

226

"Maybe...but I don't know what actually *happened*. Why it happened in the first place."

"I'm not sure about it, either. I'm just going by what he was babbling about when I opened the car door."

"But you must have *some* idea..."

"Why would you think I know more than what I already told you?"

"You were in the military. You know things."

"What does my military history have to do with—"

"I just think you're holding something back."

He didn't reply right off. He seemed lost in thought as he stared at her. "Maybe I think you've been through more than enough."

"Tell me. Please. I think I've earned the right to know."

"You have."

"Then tell me, okay?"

"Not yet."

"When?"

"When I know for sure."

She wanted him to stay with her but knew better. This was not the right time to be silly, or act clingy. Henry hated clingy and wouldn't tolerate it with her—not even in this situation.

"Need a ride home?"

"My car's right here."

"Need some company?"

She wanted to say yes, but decided it best if she kept to herself. She needed to think, so she just smiled and shook her head.

Henry nodded, turned and began walking away.

"Henry?"

"Yeah?"

"Thanks."

"For what?"

"Whaddya think, silly boy? For saving my life."

"That's what best friends do, Rox. You should know that by now." Then he turned and walked away.

CHAPTER TWENTY-SIX

Aaron was brought into a cold, dark building smelling strongly of antiseptic.

A large, muscular guy with his head shaved down to dark stubble wheeled him down a long corridor and took him into a small dimly lit room smelling of mint and more antiseptic. Two more burly attendants came in, picked him up easily and laid him down in a bed. Distant voices buzzed softly around him.

Once he was lowered onto the bed, his arms were placed at his sides and leather straps were used to secure his wrists. His ankles were then similarly secured. In seconds, the distant voices ebbed into silence, and he was alone.

It was cold in the room—much too cold for the single sheet they'd covered him with. He shivered, but soon found that he didn't mind. The peace and quiet had become very comforting.

About ten minutes later, a nurse came in and gave him an injection that relaxed him fairly quickly. He didn't seem to mind that, either. He discovered that he was no longer in that strange, cold room. Not long after he'd closed his eyes, he found that he'd drifted off to some faraway place.

He'd returned to the Forbidden Place. He remembered that he'd been here before but had forgotten much about it. But now he found that he could remember it quite clearly, perhaps because he'd come here of his own volition.

This was the place where his nightmares lived, and he'd returned because he had no choice. The nightmares had come back, sweeping violently through him and smothering him with gruesome images. He knew they would not stop because he'd betrayed the vicious creature Jessica. Because of his betrayal, she'd given them back to him, and he knew that if nothing changed, he'd go stark raving mad.

"You'll be sorrier than you ever were…"

Jessica had reopened the floodgates, and the horrors were unleashed. Every single nightmare that had ever plagued him before plummeted into him, shattering his consciousness, and blinding him with bone-chilling, gut-wrenching terrors.

But this time, there were even *more* nightmares coming at him…

The voices poured in…dozens of them, all at once, slithering into his head like hungry serpents and resonating deafeningly, drowning out all conscious thought…

He saw the vivid image of himself lying on his back in the middle of the street, trying to move even though his knees, shattered by the vehicle that had slammed into him, had become throbbing coals of blinding pain…

Another image filled his head, this one of Lana sitting on the floor, her eyes glazed as blood seeped down the side of her head and between her parted lips…

Standing behind him, the man in raggedy clothes brought up the dull blade of the filthy steak knife and sliced open his own throat, causing the blood to splash in a wide arc...

More voices flooded into his brain...

His own voice: *"I just got this new outfit because I'm meeting someone tonight. Her name is Roxie, and she's a great lady."*

Lana: *"Aaron,* please *let me drive away..."*

The next image showed Lana lying on her side on the seat, her eyes open, her blue tongue dangling out of her mouth...

Ice trickled down his spine as the dark memories thrashed past.

"The money, motherfucker..."

"Aaron, did you steal your father's cigarettes? You know he works hard...he shouldn't come home to find his cigarettes missing..."

His grandmother gazing at him with tears in her eyes...

"Aaron, were you the one who killed my roses? Someone was running around in my rose garden, and I know it wasn't the dog... Those were my favorite roses, and they're all dead... How could you do this to my roses?"

A high-pitched, long-forgotten voice from grade school...

"You peeked under my dress..."

"I didn't--"

"You did so!"

"Why have you come back?"

Her sharp voice wrenched him out of his frozen terror.

Jessica stepped out of the darkness. She wore a long black gown and stood with her hands on her

231

hips, glaring at him. Her thick dark hair spilled over her shoulders.

"I came…to see you."

"You didn't want to be here that first time—why would you come back?"

"The nightmares…" He rubbed his temples. "They're *killing* me!"

Jessica's harsh laugh echoed in the darkness. "Of course they're killing you, you idiot. That's why I took them from you in the first place."

"I can't *take* this anymore!"

"It's what you wanted, wasn't it?"

She was right—it *was* exactly what he wanted. But now that he'd gotten his spirit back and realized what it had cost, he realized that he couldn't possibly go through this anymore.

"Well? Wasn't it?"

"Yes…"

"You wanted the nightmares gone. I took them from you. And you liked it. You know you did."

He couldn't reply.

"Say it."

"I…liked it…"

Her icy blue eyes glistened. "Say it like you mean it!"

"I liked it."

"Say it louder."

"I *liked* it."

"Louder!"

"I *liked it, dammit*!"

"The moment I took them from you, your life improved. Nothing could hurt you anymore. Nothing could go wrong anymore. But that wasn't good enough, was it? Like all mortals, you became a blithering idiot. You couldn't handle it and got frightened. Then you changed your mind and backed out on our deal."

"Why did you make me a murderer?"

"It was necessary."

"Why was it necessary to kill Lana? Did Brittany *have* to die? She was a sweet kid—she didn't deserve to die. And because of you, I almost killed *Roxie*, for God's sake!"

"As I said before, you belonged to me. I gave you the gift of a life filled with success. A life free of failure, of worry, of anxiety. A life totally free of nightmares. For that, you sacrificed your soul. You were aware of this the moment we consummated our agreement."

"But why was I forced to kill?"

"I desired it."

"But *why*?"

"Figure it out."

Her statement wasn't clear. All he could do was shrug.

She sighed and looked disgusted. "When you gave me your spirit, you also gave me your body."

"My...*body*?"

"Your spirit belonged to me. I liked your body and decided that it belonged to me as well. And when I want something, I take it."

Then it registered. The times he woke naked, exhausted and rejuvenated at the same time. It was now painfully clear. Jessica had visited him during the night and taken advantage of him as he slept.

"Understand now?" she asked.

233

"My body wasn't part of our deal."

"It was to *me*..."

"In other words—"

"In other words, it's all over now. You wished it so."

He could only nod.

"So why did you come back? You want me to forget what you did? Take you back? Go back to our original deal and start over?"

If he did, the nightmares would stop. Things would go his way, and he'd have anything he'd ever wanted...

But he'd be a murderer. And he could never again have a relationship with another woman. He'd be owned and manipulated by Jessica for the rest of his days.

However, he wouldn't know. That was the way it was before. He'd been totally unaware of the horrors Jessica had been committing through him. The only reason he'd learned about it in the first place was because of the tap to his skull. If he hadn't suffered that blow, he would have never known what was going on.

Maybe it wouldn't be so painful to go back. The nightmares would be gone again, and the good things in his life would resume. Those two changes alone would make it all worthwhile.

But even if he wanted to go back, it would be impossible. They'd already arrested him, brought him to one of their mental wards, strapped him down and gave him periodic injections. He now belonged to them; they could do what they wanted. He'd stay in the ward until they'd finished their experiments, trying to make him suitable for society again. And when they'd finished, they'd send him off to prison to serve two life sentences for two senseless murders.

What was he to do? What *could* he do?

More importantly, what could Jessica do?

"Well?" She was waiting.

"Can you help me?"

She moved closer. The scowl remained on her face. "It depends."

"On what?"

"If I want to do this again."

"If you wanted to, how could you do it?"

"How do you think? The same way I did it the first time."

"But how would you get me out of there? I'm strapped down to a bed in one of their mental hospitals. They won't let me go anywhere. They'll even take me to the bathroom…"

Jessica shook her head. "Those are *mortal* problems. I am *im*mortal. I can't be bothered with such trivialities."

His heart pounded as fresh hope pulsated through him. "Then you'll do it?"

"I'll think about it. If I decide to go through with it again, you'll know. But if I do decide, there will be no backing out. Your soul will be mine for eternity, and nothing will help you out of this deal again."

"I don't know how much time I have."

"That doesn't matter. I have all sorts of time. As I just said, I am immortal."

"But I'm not."

"Your shortcomings don't matter to me. I don't work on a schedule down here. Time is irrelevant; it matters only to mortals. Do you understand?"

"I think so..."

"First off, you have to apologize to me."

"I'm sorry. I really and truly am."

She gazed at him in cold silence for nearly a minute. He could feel her in his head, looking around, making sure he wasn't keeping anything from her. Once she'd finished her search, she nodded. "I believe you."

He sighed in relief.

Jessica smiled. "Now...return to your psycho ward and wait. I'll let you know when I've decided."

He wanted to ask something else, but Jessica immediately vanished in the darkness.

Aaron blinked. The Forbidden Place was gone. He was back in his hospital bed. A heavyset middle-aged nurse with thick glasses and a strange purple birthmark on the side of her thick, jowly neck bent over him, giving him another injection.

This time, the darkness became a soft layer of gray...

236

CHAPTER TWENTY-SEVEN

The doctor was large, broad and imposing.

His nametag said *DR. ARTHUR HILL*, and as he listened to Henry, his impassive expression mirrored what one would expect from a stone statue. He stood with his arms crossed, his clipboard pressed against his massive chest, gazing at Henry as if he was staring at the plaster wall behind Henry's head.

Henry couldn't help wondering if the man was sneaking in a quick nap with his eyes open. Henry made sure he'd spoken clearly but realized almost at once how little difference that made. He'd dealt with doctors before and knew how little attention they paid to people with serious problems. It reminded him of a couple of the psychiatrists he'd dealt with when he was sent to the Army clinic in Germany, after he'd seen two of his friends blown up by mortar rounds.

"My hands are tied," the big man said flatly after Henry had finished making his request.

"Can't you just let me see him for a moment?" Henry asked.

Hill shook his head.

"Two minutes, tops?"

"From what I've been told by the Orlando Police Department, the patient you're referring to is a major suspect in a double homicide, and also the attempted murder of a third woman. I'm bound by law—as well as professional ethics—to abide by their orders, as well as what I've been told by the

237

Justice Department. And the orders have specifically stated that this man should have no visitors."

Terrific, Henry thought. He understood where the man was coming from, but he also knew that this guy could bend the rules if he really wanted to—especially if it might clear up a few things concerning a double murder.

He didn't know how much clearer he could be without giving away crucial details. He also knew that if he was any more persistent, this man would consider him a certified nutcase. He might even call Security and have Henry escorted out of the building. But he needed to know if he was right about any of this. Grill clearly exhibited the classic signs of a man possessed. However, Henry couldn't possibly tell for sure until he talked to Grill. "I really can't emphasize how extremely important this is," he told the doctor.

"I'm sure it is. But as I said, my hands are tied."

Henry realized how dangerous it would be to tell this man or anyone else his suspicions. But if he was right, Grill would eventually find a way to escape, and everyone in the hospital would be at risk. "You can come with me and stand right there beside me when I talk to him."

The big man frowned and uncrossed his arms. He regarded his clipboard for a moment. "Like I said, I'm very sorry. What exactly did you say your interest in this case was?"

Henry glanced behind him to make sure no one had snuck up to him in the corridor to listen. He'd passed two reporters when he'd come in the building. Both were talking on cell phones and watched him curiously when he'd passed. He knew how little it would take to get them started on a blood scent. This wasn't something the tabloids needed to get wind of. The media just couldn't be trusted these days. "The third woman Aaron Grill attacked survived but was seriously hurt. She's also a very close friend of mine."

"I'm very sorry to hear that, but as I just said…"

"Yeah, I know. You're bound by ethics."

"And, of course, the law."

"Right. Let's not forget the law."

"If you can find an attorney and a judge to provide you with the necessary papers, I'd be more than eager to let you see Mr. Grill."

"Thanks. I would've never thought of that."

***

Roxie was finishing up her last transaction at the register when Henry came in just a few minutes before one.

She was both surprised and glad to see him. It had been three days since her attack, and she hadn't heard much about it since. There were, of course, local stories about it on the TV news stations, but she'd avoided watching them. She knew how the media circus loved fudging stories—especially potentially big ones—long before they were able to collect enough information to cover it fairly. She refused to listen to anything until Aaron had been examined by professionals and was properly diagnosed.

Henry promised her he'd find out what he could, but she was skeptical. Everyone knew how the police dealt with murder suspects. Since Aaron was responsible for the deaths of two women and also an attempt on her life, she was afraid they'd treat him as a serial killer. He'd be taken somewhere secret and held without bail. He'd be strictly guarded and would not be allowed visitors. A staff of doctors and psychiatrists would be brought in. If it was determined that Aaron was telling the truth, the police would take over and begin their investigation. Henry wouldn't have a prayer of finding out what was going on.

He came over to where she was and glanced at the receipts dangling from her hand. "I guess I came at the wrong time."

"Just doing my morning tallies." She could clearly see the exhaustion on his face. "You look tired. I take it you didn't find out anything."

"You're not far from wrong." He studied the fresh bandages on her neck. "How are you feeling?"

"Much better."

"Aside from the bandages, you look pretty damned good. Your color's back and you're just about your sensational self once again." Before she could respond or blush, he said, "Can we talk somewhere?"

"Certainly." She led him into the office.

Sandy was closing the tiny cash box and shoving it back into the desk drawer when they came in. "I'll be out of your hair in a second," she said, smiling. "Hi, Henry."

He smiled back. "Sandy…"

Sandy turned serious. "I didn't thank you."

"For what?"

"For saving my friend's life—what else?"

He grinned. "No biggie. I didn't have anything better to do. Besides, I just happened to be in the area anyway…"

"No biggie?" Roxie tilted her head. "Nothing better to do?"

He shrugged a shoulder. "Figure of speech."

"It had better be…"

Sandy laughed.

"It really *was* no biggie," Roxie said. "I believe Henry was actually stalking me."

"Good thing," Sandy said.

Henry grinned. "Like I just said, I didn't have much to do that day, so…"

"Oh, stop." Roxie wanted to swat him. "The Clint Eastwood bit just ain't working."

He went over and sat in the chair. "Best I can do. You wouldn't like my Charles Bronson *at all*."

"*I* might." Sandy was still smiling.

"Don't encourage him," Roxie said. "We both know what he's like when he's full of himself."

Laughing, Sandy hurried out of the office.

Roxie pointed to the coffeepot. Henry nodded. She poured him a cup and placed it on the edge of the desk. Then she fell into the chair and took a deep breath. "Well? What's been going on? As I said, you look exhausted—*and*, I might add, frustrated."

"No one would let me near him. I got as far as the reception area. I did get to talk to one of the doctors—in a way. I've never had any luck with

241

doctors. Every single one I've ever known has been a genuine asshole. They all seem to have the irritating habit of getting nauseated whenever they're forced to talk to people who aren't other doctors."

"I'm surprised you even got that far."

"Everyone's freaking out over this legalese shit. The District Attorney's got everyone's panties wound super tight. He's got everyone in the place walking on eggshells. It's a double homicide, so I can see why everyone's nervous. But since you're involved, it makes this even more complicated."

"How?"

"You're a surviving victim. I'm surprised they haven't been in touch with you by now."

"A few people called yesterday, but I let all the calls go to voicemail."

"Well, be prepared. It won't be long before they start sending people here. Once they find out about this place, they'll show up in droves. If Grill's confession is proven legit, that's when the lawyers will start circling. I've already been subpoenaed to give my statement, so it won't take long for them to get to you. They'll send them out, one by one at first. Then you'll get two or three at a time."

"I can't wait." She sunk in her seat.

"It'll be loads of fun. The Assistant DA, most likely, will start up the show. And if Grill gets representation, his defense lawyer will be after you to get you to change your story, or at least say anything that'll shed reasonable doubt on the case. Then you'll be forced to hire your own attorney, and it'll turn into the battle of the shysters, with you being their prize."

"I wonder what the odds are that Aaron was lying to you..."

"Judging by his mental state and how he was rambling, I'd say he told me the truth—at least what he honestly believed was the truth." He had a sip of coffee. "I'm no professional, of course, but I can tell when someone's telling me the truth. He wasn't lying, but that doesn't explain what actually happened."

Roxie's thoughts returned to that dreadful night. "Even after all that's happened, I can't help thinking Aaron really is a nice guy. He was always polite and considerate with me. I know a gentleman when I see one. My God...what would make him act like that? He never showed me any signs whatsoever of being a psychopath."

"That's probably because he isn't one."

"But he killed two people. At least, he said he did."

"I know. I was there."

"It makes no sense, does it?"

"Not really..."

"But you seem to have an idea. I can tell."

"I also told you I wouldn't say anything until I knew for sure."

"Right. You did. But since they won't let you talk to him, when will you really know?"

"Good point." Henry stared at his coffee cup. She could tell he was deciding what he should say. "This is going to sound fantastic, and I could be totally wrong, but..."

243

"Just tell me, okay?"

"You probably won't believe me…"

"Try me."

"But you might think—"

"If you really want to know what I think, I believe Aaron might be possessed."

Henry stiffened in his seat. "What makes you say that?"

She shrugged. "Just a feeling I have…and going by what I've read in school, and in books."

Henry didn't speak.

"I could be right—is that what you're thinking?"

After a long pause, he said, "That's exactly what I'm thinking."

Roxie felt her blood turn cold. "Then we're actually on the same page." She couldn't believe she'd been right in her thinking. "We're talking *demonic* possession, aren't we?"

Henry rubbed his temples. "Well, we can't possibly be a hundred percent certain. There are several different types of possession, of course. But something's obviously taken him over. Nothing else could be responsible for what he's been doing or the way he's been acting. Nothing, that is, unless it's some sort of mental illness. And since everything I've learned about him so far tells me he was pretty much normal and okay until fairly recently, I have to go with the distinct possibility that something took him over."

"What about something other than possession?"

"Such as…?"

"An accident, maybe? Or traumatic event?"

244

"Unless he hit his head or suffered a severe accident recently, I'd say we're not looking at mental illness."

"If he hit his head recently, there would be swelling, or perhaps a gash." She shrugged. "I haven't seen either."

"Then it's definitely something else."

She went back to the time she and Aaron met, struggling to remember every single detail. "When I first met him, he told me he didn't have to work anymore. I believe he mentioned an investment paying off—something like that."

"Then he's rich?"

"At Beef Handlers, he handed the waitress a hundred and told her to keep the change."

"That doesn't necessarily mean he's rich, but it does say he might be pretty well fixed. That outfit he was wearing on your date was pricey." He shrugged. "Unfortunately, it doesn't tell us anything about his mental state."

"So where does this leave us?"

"I wish I knew, but I'm still going with my demonic possession theory. Call it gut instinct—or call it my only idea, since there's nothing else I can pin this on that makes any sense."

Roxie thought about this for a moment. "Then you're telling me you honestly think some negative force has somehow taken possession of him and has been forcing him to kill people?"

"I think so, yes."

"Have you seen anything like this before?"

He was silent for a while. Then he nodded.

She could tell by the way he kept fidgeting that this was difficult for him. Because of this, she didn't want to ask him the next question. But she had to know. "Has this…ever happened to someone you knew?"

The darkness filling his eyes told her the worst. It most likely had something to do with his deployment in Afghanistan. She decided to stop the questions. She didn't want to be responsible for bringing back the memories.

Seconds later, the dark moment passed. Henry was still watching her, but she was pleased that the darkness filling his eyes moments earlier had disappeared.

"What was he doing before he tried strangling you?" he asked suddenly.

"*Just* before?"

"The instant before."

"He'd just…kissed me…"

Henry said nothing, but she could tell by the way he closed his eyes that he hadn't liked hearing that.

"Does that tell you anything?"

"Other than the fact that the man has very good taste, it tells me that if Grill is possessed by a demon, it could be a jealous one. This also suggests it could be a female. A succubus."

"How can you tell?"

"He's killing women, isn't he?"

"That would explain a succubus?"

"Succubae are many things, but they all seem to possess similar characteristics. The one trait I'm talking about—at least in this case—is jealousy.

246

Those who've been unfortunate enough to be possessed by one have found out the hard way."

The hard way. Murder. Yes, that was pretty harsh.

So how could they help him? How could they possibly free someone of the control of a jealous female demon?

"You're thinking Aaron needs to be exorcised, aren't you?" she asked.

"Demons usually don't leave of their own accord. Once they've found a suitable host, they'll stick with it."

"Forever?"

Henry shrugged. "Until the host dies."

247

CHAPTER TWENTY-EIGHT

As Aaron drifted in and out of consciousness, he found that he'd lost all conception of time.

He was aware that he'd been given two more injections, and what seemed like just a few hours later, he sensed someone loosening his straps. Two large men dressed in baggy green scrubs were standing beside his bed. Although his vision was somewhat blurred, he could tell neither was looking directly at him as they bent over him and began removing the straps from his ankles, then his wrists.

They both took a firm grip on his wrists and shoulders, and he let them pull him into a sitting position. One of them pushed a wheelchair closer to the bed while the other came over to assist. They both picked him up as if he were a child and lowered him carefully into the chair. One of them pushed him across the room, to the bathroom, while a large, uniformed guard with scary dark eyes and one bushy black eyebrow stood close by, watching. The aide pushed him into the small brightly lit room, helped him out of the wheelchair and let him stagger into the stall. He barely managed; coupled with his blurred vision, his legs were weak, and he was forced to support himself by gripping the thick horizontal rails bolted to the sides of the stall.

It was while he was sitting on the commode that something strange happened, and for a moment he thought he'd blacked out. When he opened his eyes, his vision had cleared, but he had no idea where he was. He could tell he was in a bathroom. It was brightly lit and cold, smelling strongly of Lysol and a minty antiseptic. A public restroom? He looked down at himself and discovered that he was wearing one of those godawful one-piece hospital gowns. He tried to remember what happened, but his mind had gone blank. All he knew was that he was dizzy and slightly nauseated, and his stomach was growling. He tried to remember the last time he'd eaten. This brought about another blank. All he could think of was that he had a strong craving for steak and some good bourbon.

He regarded the gown for a few moments and wondered if he'd been in an accident. He struggled once again to remember. More blackness filled his head, but this time, the fog cleared a little, and he saw Roxie's image sitting across from him at a candlelit table in a restaurant. Logs from a fireplace popped and crackled just a few feet from their table. Chamber music serenaded them romantically from a speaker. The dinner was terrific. Afterward he took her to a block building across the street from a strip mall. Then he remembered—it was her bookstore. He'd dropped her off so she could pick up her car. Then he'd left her there.

He must have been in an accident once he'd started the drive back home. Yes. That might have been what happened. He was involved in an accident and was taken to the hospital.

But why the straps? The guards? The injections?

He struggled to remember. Once again, his mind had gone blank. He wondered if Roxie was all right. He suddenly felt guilty for leaving her—for not making sure she'd gotten home safely.

Then he wondered if he was right about the order of the events. Could he have been wrong? Had the accident taken place *after* he'd left her? Had they even reached the bookstore? Or had all this happened *before* he'd dropped her off?

Damn… Roxie might have been injured—or worse.

He'd had wine during their dinner. Could this have caused the accident? Had he sucked down more wine than he remembered? Was he sober when they'd left the restaurant? Had he been charged with a DUI? Was Roxie all right? Or had something horrible happened?

My God… I was driving drunk.

I must have wrecked the car!

Oh my God…Roxie's dead!

It could explain the straps, the guards. The injections. The hospital gown.

His heart pounded violently, and he trembled. He had to know what happened. He had to know about Roxie. The guard was probably standing close to the stall, making sure Aaron didn't try to escape. He strongly suspected the big ape was close enough to hear him.

"Guard?"

No response.

He didn't need this—not now, while he was dangerously close to the panic mode.

"Can you hear me?"

No reply.

"Can't you talk?"

Silence.

His pulse hastened. Why wasn't anyone talking to him? Was it because he'd actually killed Roxie? Was it because he'd killed other people? *Damn. What have I done?*

"Please...I need to talk to someone!"

Someone standing on the other side of the stall divider tapped the door lightly. "Are you all right in there?"

"No. I'm *not* all right. I need to talk to someone." He flushed the toilet and pushed himself into a standing position. "Get me out of here. I need to see a doctor!"

***

"I seem to remember you telling me a while ago that you studied a number of religions in college." Roxie poured more coffee from the pot.

"Why do you ask?"

Roxie replaced the coffeepot. She'd scanned the store a minute earlier, but saw only two browsers checking out the bargain bin. Sandy was at the register, finishing a transaction with a paying customer. Roxie sat down at her desk and crossed her legs. "I was just wondering. The Catholics—"

"I think I know where you're going with this, but I'm not sure it would help us much. I did study exorcism for about a semester and learned some disturbing things."

"Such as...?"

"For one thing, the Catholic clergy take this problem seriously—maybe too seriously."

"*Too* seriously?"

251

"Seriously enough to put up a solid wall of silence whenever the subject is brought up by the non-clergy."

"But they have been known to perform exorcisms, right?"

"Of course they have. It's actually an important part of their religion."

"Then wouldn't they at least take the time to look into something like this?"

"First of all, we'd have to find a local priest and present the problem to him in detail. Then, if we managed to convince him that this was a matter worth taking on, he'd have to approach it using their standard protocol. The Catholics have got a regular chain of command very similar to the military. It would take weeks before a case like this reached the top of their pecking order. They'd sit on it for a while before getting to it, and once it was finally addressed, the meetings and discussions would start up, and who knows when or even if they'd be able to make a decision whether to go ahead with it? They might just put it aside and forget about it for the next few months—which they've been known to do, by the way."

Roxie felt her spirits sinking. "By that time, Aaron's trial would be over, and he'd be serving two life sentences."

"Exactly."

"So not only will he face prison for life, but he'll still be also possessed. And who knows what'll happen to him in prison?"

"He probably won't last long at all. Serial killers usually have to be segregated for their own personal safety."

"This means we've got to work this from a different angle."

Henry sat in silence, staring at her. "I take it that you really want to pursue this?"

She found herself weighing the odds once again. Despite everything that had happened, she was convinced Aaron was a helpless victim, and if she didn't try to defend him, no one else would. "I think Aaron deserves all the help he can get."

Henry didn't reply.

"You don't agree?"

"You actually want to help him after what he did to you?"

"If we're both right about this, it wasn't his idea to strangle me. And it certainly wasn't his idea to strangle the other two women."

"Since we really don't know what's going on, we can't say for sure."

"I definitely want to help him. Are you with me on this?"

She could tell that he saw the sincerity—as well as the urgency—on her face. But would he want to help her? Even if he did, they had no plan or procedure to follow. She couldn't blame him if he didn't want to get involved.

After about a minute, he put his coffee cup down on the desk. "I'll help you. It won't be easy, but we can at least try."

"Where do you suggest we start?"

"I'd like to try the hospital one last time. Even if they don't want to help us, maybe they can refer us to someone who can."

"When you were there, did the doctor tell you anything at all?"

"Just that Grill had undergone some preliminary tests and that they had him under close watch."

"What does that mean, exactly?"

"They'll keep him heavily sedated and restrained until the experts are brought in to study him. Why do you ask?"

"I'm just wondering about his demon. If you're right about it being a female, I'm wondering what she'll do while all this is going on."

"No one can really know, actually. My guess is that she's waiting."

"For what?"

"An opportunity."

"For what?"

"To cause some really *serious* shit…."

CHAPTER TWENTY-NINE

Once he was returned to his hospital bed, Aaron tensed up in fear and frustration as the two attendants strapped him down again.

"Are these really necessary?"

They didn't respond. Aaron was getting even more suspicious about what had happened and why he'd been brought here. He tried once again to recall past events, but all he could remember was the dinner with Roxie and the trip back to her bookstore. If something else happened, he had no clue what it was. However, the straps and the cold, indifferent attitude of the guards suggested that something else was going on and that it must be very bad.

Had he really killed someone on the road that night? Had Roxie been injured? Had she died because of her injuries? Or were they treating him like this because they were afraid he was going to hurt himself?

"I really need to see a doctor," he said.

They finished tightening the straps but said nothing.

"I have something very important to tell him."

"He's on his way," one of them said flatly.

Without another word, they both turned and walked away.

He sighed in relief and forced himself to relax. Then, closing his eyes, he tried once again to determine why his memory refused to cooperate. It didn't take him long to realize that he was fighting a losing battle. As before, the vast blackness in his mind would not clear.

About twenty minutes later, a large figure blocked the doorway. It stood there for nearly a minute before coming in. When it finally entered the room, the haze of the lamp at the other end of the room cast a cloudy golden beam, revealing certain features. A long white coat appeared. A few steps later, a clipboard held in the crook of one arm and a stethoscope hanging from the figure's thick neck became more vivid. The figure was a doctor. Aaron was certain he'd seen him before. The man was very large and broad, his small blinking eyes revealing both nervousness and anger. He came in cautiously, approaching the bed and stopping about three feet away. He didn't say anything right off, just gazed at Aaron with the same intensity one might use to study a strange microscopic creature swimming around in a test tube.

Aaron began growing even more uncomfortable and wanted to ask what all this was about, why everyone was treating him like some dangerous animal. However, something inside him told him to just lie there and relax, and the man would eventually give him an explanation.

In the very next moment, he sensed a way to get out of this predicament. He couldn't understand why he felt this way; it seemed highly unlikely that he was going anywhere. He was strapped down, closely guarded and given frequent injections. Freeing himself and getting out of this bed seemed downright impossible.

Yet he couldn't shake this feeling, and despite the doctor's cold, impassive expression, Aaron found himself growing more and more confident that he'd soon be free again.

"You wanted to see me?"

"I did…"

"I'm here, now. What is it you wish to say?"

Aaron glanced at the others in the room. Two of them were watching him in the same cold manner. The third man was staring at the plaster wall directly above Aaron's head.

But that wasn't the issue, and Aaron soon found that he was no longer concerned about any of them. He focused his attention on the big man standing beside his bed. "I'd feel better if we talked in private."

The big man watched Aaron in silence, regarding him with both disdain and suspicion. "Whatever you have to say to me," he replied tensely, "you can say in front of these people. They work here and have been instructed to stay close to you until this matter has been resolved—"

I really think we could talk in private. Aaron focused on the man's broad forehead. He felt that he might be able to get his point across if he directed his request in some other way. *I'd feel much more comfortable if you cleared the room.*

The man began coughing and gasping. He cleared his throat and continued hacking away. His eyes glistening, he snatched a handkerchief out of his coat pocket and used it to wipe his eyes.

Understand? Aaron thought, watching the man closely.

257

The big man managed an awkward nod between hacks.

You'll feel much better once we're all alone...

Still coughing, the doctor cleared his throat and turned around. "Mr. Grill and I...we're to be...left alone..."

Two of the men started to protest, but he waved them down. Glaring at Aaron, they backed up slowly and reluctantly left the room. His coughing gradually subsiding, the doctor watched them leave.

Once they were alone, the doctor cleared his throat, took a deep breath, coughed once more and pocketed his handkerchief.

"I told you you'd feel better," Aaron said.

Shaking a little, the doctor stared. "How did you...what the hell—"

"Don't question it. Just stand there and listen."

The man continued staring.

"Did you hear me?"

The man cleared his throat. "Y-Yes..."

Aaron focused on the man's fleshy face and felt even more confident about the situation. He lowered his voice. "First of all, I'd like it very much if you loosened these straps. They're cutting off my circulation. Once you've finished with that, I'd like to have my clothes back. Then you can do one last teensy favor for me, and I'll let you off the hook."

***

As Henry drove Roxie to the hospital that evening, she found that she couldn't think of anything but the problems they both faced.

How could they possibly find someone to talk to about Aaron when everyone had been told to keep quiet about the case? Even if they were lucky enough to find someone who wasn't afraid to discuss it with them, they'd be asking for trouble once they even hinted at demonic possession.

But she didn't care. She couldn't let anything stop them. Aaron needed help, and he wouldn't get it by conventional means.

They reached the hospital at around eight-fifteen. As soon as they stepped into the well-lit reception area, Henry stopped cold.

"What's wrong?" she asked.

He was silent as he slowly scanned the large, busy area like a predatory animal sniffing the air and smelling imminent danger.

"Henry?"

He settled his gaze on the two women sitting at the reception desk. "Something just doesn't feel right."

Off to their right, men in white jackets scurried past while women in green scrubs dodged fast-moving gurneys. Just another day in the tombs, she thought, wondering why something seemed off. Could they both be feeling just a little paranoid about all this? After all, this was a hospital. The people working here saw life's worst possible moments within these walls every single day. Death was commonplace; so were mental meltdowns and every other crisis imaginable.

Even so, she couldn't help wondering if something particularly bad was going on, and that it might involve Aaron. She reminded herself that hundreds of other things were happening in this building, none of which involved Aaron. There were, after all, several hundred others in this hospital. For all she knew, a highway fatality could have just brought in several new trauma patients. Just because something felt off didn't necessarily mean Aaron was involved.

The receptionist glanced in their direction. "Help you?"

"Is Doctor Hill working tonight?"

She froze. Her face turned pale.

Henry glanced at Roxie. She knew right then that something was indeed very wrong.

"Well? Is he or isn't he?"

The receptionist stared at him. "And you are…?"

"I saw him earlier," he said. "He'll remember me."

Two police officers passed them quickly and disappeared down the corridor. Their grim expressions made Roxie's heart skip a beat.

"This is urgent." Henry had lowered his voice. "It involves a patient. His name is Aaron Grill."

Her expression tightened. However, she said nothing.

"Something obviously happened." Henry leaned over the counter. "What was it?"

Two more cops came in, crossed the area and disappeared down the corridor. They also looked tense. Roxie told herself not to be frightened; all cops had that same expression when they were on the job. They couldn't very well walk around with stupid grins on their faces, could they? No one would take them seriously.

Another cop came in, talking to his radio. He gave the reception desk a quick glance before disappearing down the corridor.

"Tell us what happened," Henry said.

"*Please* tell us," Roxie said. "It's very important."

The receptionist glanced at the woman sitting behind her, who was handling a call. Then she turned back to Henry and Roxie. "Doctor Hill...it seems that...he was in an accident..."

"What sort of accident?" he asked.

No reply.

"Ma'am..." Henry continued leaning over the counter. "This is extremely urgent. The patient Aaron Grill...we need to talk with Doctor Hill as soon as possible about this man. We don't know anything about an accident, but as I just said, this is urgent, and—"

"You *can't* talk to him," she whispered, her lower lip trembling. "Doctor Hill...he's...he's *dead*..."

CHAPTER THIRTY

Waking up in the back of a van, Aaron had no idea where he was or how he'd gotten there.

Suddenly frightened, he pushed aside the curtain covering the side window and saw that the vehicle was parked in the rear lot of a large, well-lit, eight-story building, and that it was fairly late at night.

What was he doing here?

He struggled to remember, but his thoughts turned hazy and muddled. Jagged images of a cold, dark hospital room played havoc with the chaos filling his mind, making everything foggy. He looked down at himself. He was wearing the clothes he'd worn on his date with Roxie.

His date. Those images showed clearly.

What was he doing in the back of a van? And what was it about that hospital room that moments ago seemed vaguely familiar, yet now had become a distant memory?

About a hundred yards away, blinking lights lit up the hazy darkness as ambulances and police cruisers gathered in a jumbled cluster in the side lot of the building. The flurried activity suggested that something had just happened, but he was much too far away to see anything specific. He sensed that he might have known what happened. He wanted to take a few moments to think about it, but some other inner sense warned him of imminent danger if he stayed here. A nagging fear that someone might be looking for him nipped at his senses.

He climbed over the back seat and squirmed his way up to the front of the van. No keys, of course. He had to get out of here and find Roxie. He had to find out if she was okay—if something had happened after their date. He should be with her now. He'd just brought her back to the bookstore after their elegant dinner and was going to ask her to invite him to her condo. But something obviously happened before he had the chance to ask.

Using the driver's window, he watched the activity outside the building, waiting until the last of the cruisers and the other units had left the area. When he decided the coast was clear, he pushed open the door and climbed down.

It was a cool, clear night. The lot was about half-filled, and nearly all the vehicles were sleeping peacefully beneath the hazy white lights emanating from the lampposts. There were a few people moving about—some walking toward the building while others came outside and approached the sidewalk leading to the parking lot. Hopefully, he might get lucky.

For the next fifteen minutes, he tiptoed down the endless rows of parked vehicles in the rear lot, until he heard an engine starting up about two rows down from him. He sprinted down the aisle, slipping between two parked SUVs. Straight ahead, the hazy golden shadow lit up the darkness of the next aisle.

He ran over and tapped on the driver's window just as the Audi began backing out of its spot.

The car stopped abruptly; the window rolled down. The driver, a young blond woman in hospital

263

scrubs, turned toward him and gave him a nervous smile. "Yes?"

Aaron smiled pleasantly. "I'm very late for an important appointment and was wondering if I could possibly borrow your car..."

***

A tall, slender man dressed in a white jacket appeared in the archway.

He was about forty years old and stared curiously at Roxie and Henry behind a large pair of thick bifocals. A stethoscope hung around his neck. Obviously nervous, he stood stiffly, and was reluctant to approach them.

Wasting no time, Henry marched right over. "Doc? Got a minute?"

The man glanced briefly in Roxie's direction. "You're the folks inquiring about Doctor Hill?"

"Yes."

He regarded them both in silence. A moment later, he motioned for them to follow him over to the corner, where the coffee machines sat on a metal table, spewing out black puffs of burnt java. He introduced himself as Doctor Austin. "May I ask the nature of your inquiry?"

Henry kept his voice low. "It's a long story. We've got valuable information about the patient Aaron Grill who was recently brought in by the police—"

"In case you haven't yet been told, there was a terrible accident a short while ago, and we've been trying our best to deal with it..." He stopped talking and turned to Roxie. "And who are you?" he asked, noticing the bandages on her neck.

264

"I'm Roxie Nash. I'm—"

"She's the woman Aaron Grill tried to strangle," Henry said quickly. "So...you were saying?"

Austin continued gazing at Roxie. She could tell he was uneasy, and thinking of some way of walking away from this gracefully. He glanced at his watch, then at the clock on the wall behind the reception desk. "This really isn't a good time..."

"For what?" Henry asked flatly.

Austin didn't reply.

Henry took a moment to calm himself. Roxie could tell he was struggling to keep his frustration in check. "Something bad happened, Doc," he said in a much softer tone. "I know it, Roxie knows it, and so do you. It isn't every day that a doctor dies in a hospital. So please tell us what's going on."

Austin blinked. "H-How do you...know about this? Who told you?"

"That isn't important. Not now, anyway. Just tell us what happened. How did Doctor Hill die?"

Austin regarded the people passing them and waited until they were alone again. He lowered his voice. "Please...follow me."

Henry and Roxie followed him down the hall, to the first door on the right, marked *Administrative*. He eased the door open and stuck his head through the slim opening. After a few moments, he slipped inside and gestured for them to follow. He then closed the door behind them and pointed to the two chairs facing the metal desk at the far end of the big room, near a long row of filing cabinets. As they took their seats, he sat down heavily behind the

265

desk and massaged the back of his neck. He looked like he was having a rough day. "This has been a really horrible..."

"We can tell," Roxie said.

"You just have no idea—"

"You wanna tell us what happened, Doc?" Henry was getting impatient. "Our day hasn't exactly been what you could call red letter material, either."

Austin sat forward and thumped his elbows on the top of the desk. He rubbed his eyes and took a breath. "About an hour ago, Doctor Hill...he apparently climbed the stairs to the roof of the building..." Then he went silent.

Henry leaned forward. "What happened after that?"

Austin swallowed. His face had gone pale, and he remained silent.

"Doc?" Henry had lowered his voice. "Please. Tell us."

After a pause, Doctor Austin shivered and took a deep breath. Then, in a strained whisper, he said, "He...jumped off the roof..."

CHAPTER THIRTY-ONE

Aaron parked in the small, paved lot behind Roxie's bookstore and sat there for the next few minutes, wondering where his car had gone.

He had no recollection of the drive over, nor could he remember why he was driving this car. Everything felt very strange. To make things worse, he couldn't even remember where he'd come from.

For the next few minutes, he examined the interior of the car. He soon discovered that it held no memories—not a flash of familiarity. It even smelled strange. A pine-smelling freshener hung from one of the knobs on the dash, and the sweet scent of perfume lingered faintly. This car obviously belonged to a woman.

So how and where did he get it?

Why couldn't he remember anything? It was becoming painfully obvious that something terrible had happened to his brain and that he should see a doctor.

He closed his eyes and tried again. After a few moments, the image of a dark hospital room flickered briefly before fading. This was followed by a flash of two large faceless figures strapping him down to a bed. Neither said anything, and once they'd finished, they both turned and walked away, leaving him all alone.

He wondered why such insane images had filled his brain. His last clear memories were of Roxie—driving her here after their dinner, kissing her, then driving away and heading home.

Sitting here in this unfamiliar car strongly suggested that the evening hadn't ended that way. He was wearing the same clothes he'd worn on their date, but he wasn't driving his own car.

Where had he left the Crown Vic?

This made no sense. Somewhere along the line, he'd switched cars. And Roxie's Honda was gone.

He struggled to make sense of all this, but he just couldn't see the logic of dropping her off, driving away, switching cars somewhere along the way and then driving back.

Had he stolen it? It was an Audi—an expensive, top-of-the-line vehicle. He just wouldn't be able to pull it out of thin air, would he? And he certainly wouldn't be able to find such a classy vehicle abandoned alongside the road.

If I stole this car, why can't I remember doing it?

He had to call Roxie and find out what was going on. All he remembered was that he'd dropped her off. Since her Honda wasn't here, she'd probably used it to drive home. But if she'd driven home, how would she know what was happening to him?

Somehow, none of that mattered. If he could call her, he could ask her if she knew what was going on.

He checked his pockets. His cell phone was gone.

He'd probably left it in the Crown Vic. But since he didn't know where he'd left the car...

He suddenly remembered that she'd given him the number of the bookstore.

Why were certain things coming to him while others remained in total blackness?

Stop worrying about that. You've got more important matters to address.

He had to get inside the bookstore and find her home number. It had to be somewhere in the office—possibly on the table, where she used her laptop. He hated breaking into her place, but this was an emergency, and he didn't know what else to do.

He crept up to the door. He knew it was probably locked. He tried the heavy metal handle. As he'd expected, it didn't give. He figured it was dead bolted. Briefly he wondered if he should search the Audi for a crowbar. There might be one in the trunk. It would take only a second or two to find the button for the trunk, open it and have a look.

He hated that idea right off and scolded himself for considering it. He couldn't commit vandalism to Roxie's store. That would be despicable, and he'd loathe himself for it.

But what choice did he have? He had to get inside and find her number…

The panic growing inside him made him tremble. Then he decided to give the door another try.

This time, the handle clicked loudly as the deadbolt slid back into its shaft.

He stared numbly at it for nearly a minute.

What the hell? The damned door just…*opened*? Roxie probably didn't lock it properly. No. It wasn't Roxie; it was the blonde, who hadn't double-checked the deadbolt before she left. Since Roxie had gone with him to the restaurant, the blonde had no doubt stayed here until closing time.

Shut up and do what needs to be done!

Forcing his mind off these irritating distractions, he pulled the heavy door open and slipped inside.

***

"He just *jumped*? Off the *roof*?" Roxie whispered.

She couldn't believe what Doctor Austin had just told them. "Are you saying Doctor Hill committed suicide? Just like that?"

Austin sighed deeply.

"Did the man have problems?" Henry was just as shocked as Roxie. "Was he delusional?"

Austin's expression turned solemn. "Doc Hill was the sanest, most sensible man I knew. He was my mentor. I'd known him the last fifteen years, for God's sake. He helped me with my residency once I'd finished med school and then my internship and even pushed the right buttons to enable me to pay off my school loans." He shook his head. "This is so...so *incredible*... I can't even begin to understand why this happened."

"I think we might," Roxie said before realizing it.

"Pardon me?"

Henry tapped her ankle lightly with the tip of his shoe before she could continue. "I think she means we might have an idea."

Austin gazed at Henry. "Go on..."

270

Roxie caught something in Henry's eyes that told her he wanted to do the talking. She trusted him completely and let him have the floor.

"What we're trying to say," he said, "is that we both suspect this might have something to do with Aaron Grill, the patient who was brought in a couple of days ago."

"You're sure about this?"

"Reasonably."

Austin went silent. His face immediately wrinkled up. "Then this raises another question."

"What's that?"

"It involves Grill himself."

"What about him?" Roxie asked.

Austin's gaze settled on her, then on Henry. "The patient's not in his room."

Neither Henry nor Roxie could reply.

"The moment Doctor Hill's body was found, his rounds were checked extensively. The attendants who'd been with him all stated the same thing—Grill was the last patient he'd seen. Grill's room was immediately checked, but the bed was empty."

"Wasn't he restrained?" Henry asked.

Austin nodded. "Standard procedure for a violent criminal case. All four harnesses had been unfastened."

"Interesting," Henry said. "What did the attendants have to say about that?"

"That's the most bizarre aspect of all this. Once he went into the room to talk with Grill, Doctor Hill ordered all the attendants to leave."

"That sounds very strange," Roxie said.

"The aides thought the same thing. But they all said Doctor Hill was very insistent."

"And that was that?" Henry asked. "The Doc and Grill were alone?"

"Not for very long, it seems. Less than ten minutes later, Doc Hill was observed leaving the room and entering the stairwell that went up to the roof."

"And no one went back into the room once the doc left?"

"Apparently two of the guards did."

"Was Grill in his bed?"

"They both said it was empty."

"And no one saw him leave?"

"Not one of them saw anything."

"How could that have happened?"

"No one knows."

"The aides and the guards were questioned?" Henry asked.

"Thoroughly. According to every one of them, no one saw Grill leave the room."

Henry turned to Roxie. She could tell he was thinking the same thing she was—that the demon manipulating Aaron had eluded everyone in the building.

Austin sat back and rubbed his eyes. He looked even more exhausted than moments earlier. "We've had every security guard and assistant in the building as well as half a dozen police officers looking for him for the last hour and a half."

"You didn't find *anything*?" Henry asked.

"The only thing they all seem to agree on is that Aaron Grill has vanished."

Aaron flicked on the small desk light in Roxie's office and sat down.

For the next ten minutes, he studied the hastily scrawled messages and phone numbers on the dozens of yellow post-it tabs stuck to the bottom of her laptop and desk blotter, when he suddenly had the strong feeling Roxie could be in grave danger. A brief image of a man with dark hair and dark eyes penetrated his thoughts. Aaron's initial reaction was that he might have seen this man before, but the image vanished the moment he tried to remember.

He wants to hurt her, his inner voice told him. *He's a very bad man, but he's gained her trust, and when she least expects it, he will hurt her.*

How do I know this? he asked himself. *Where are these dark thoughts coming from?*

You must not question the source of these thoughts, the inner voice replied. *You must concentrate only on finding Roxie. You have to get this man away from her.*

Yes. He had to find Roxie. Then he could concentrate on finding out why his brain had been betraying him so much lately.

Turning back to the task at hand, he studied each and every post-it he could find, discarding numbers that belonged to other people. He had no idea how he knew; he only knew that Roxie wouldn't have her personal number out in the open.

But where? Her laptop?

He hated going through her personal information but didn't know what else he could do. It was a definite violation of her privacy, and he felt

273

like a lowlife for even thinking of it. But how else could he find her number?

Try her desk...

He immediately checked the top drawer and found it unlocked. A little black book sat there amongst the checkbooks and scatter of envelopes, many of them opened. The word ADDRESSES was scrawled in black ink on a small white window in the center of its dark leather cover. He felt his heart skip a beat the moment he'd grabbed it.

Before opening it, he noticed a small pile of envelopes lying in the drawer. There were about eight in the pile, all bound together with a rubber band. They'd all been opened and were apparently bills or personal correspondence. He decided it didn't matter. What mattered was the address printed on the front.

It was Roxie's home address.

He pulled a slip of paper from the envelope on top, which turned out to be a bill from her cell phone carrier. The invoice provided her name, address and personal cell phone number—all of which were printed at the top of the page.

He couldn't stop his heart from thumping wildly as he carefully wrote down the number and address on a fresh post-it from the pad on her blotter.

274

CHAPTER THIRTY-TWO

Roxie and Henry left the hospital shortly before ten that evening.

Her thoughts looped wildly as they wandered out into the cool night. Henry was also deep in thought as they went down the walk and crossed the road that led to the front lot, where his Camaro was parked.

Roxie could tell Henry was just as troubled as she was. She figured she should probably be more perplexed than Henry since she'd been involved in this firsthand. But that didn't make this any easier. If anything, it made the situation even more hopeless.

How could they possibly deal with a creature capable of manipulating people's minds? How could they cope with someone totally controlled by a demon? And lastly, how could they battle such a demon, whose powers had drastically increased during the last couple of days?

For some terrifying reason, the demon controlling Aaron had progressed from mind manipulation to murder in a very short period of time. It had caused him to strangle two women and would have succeeded in strangling Roxie if Henry hadn't intervened.

But this reign of terror hadn't ended. It had gotten worse. The demon manipulating Aaron had just forced him to send a sane, mature doctor plummeting to his death from the roof of the hospital.

The demon's powers were obviously much stronger than either of them could understand. Its powers had not only caused a suicide, but it had also enabled Aaron to walk out of a crowded hospital even though he'd been placed in restraints and had been closely guarded by a team of armed security guards.

For Aaron, the demon had made the situation simple. It had given him *carte blanche* regarding his comings and goings. Convenient for Aaron, of course, but not so much for the hospital staff or anyone else unfortunate enough to cross Aaron's path.

What frightened Roxie most of all was the increased viciousness of these attacks. The mind manipulation thing was frightening enough. The nausea, dizziness and shortness of breath that came with it were far from pleasant, but not life-threatening.

Murder, however, was much more serious.

Aaron had obviously been forced into dangerous waters and was unable to come back. His demon had grown tired of mind games and now craved bigger and better things. Nausea was boring. So was dizziness and shortness of breath. Coughing could be amusing in the right circumstances but would quickly become dull. Something more serious, such as a blackout, or even a mild heart attack, would be just the thing to overcome the monotony.

Murder was inevitable. Strangulation could serve as a temporary respite. However, even that would pall after a while. Something much more exciting would be needed to challenge the boredom of a hungry demon.

Suicide would provide the perfect escape. Coaxing someone to do away with himself would really hit the spot. It would be the ultimate high. *Just walk up to the roof and do it, Doc. Take that swan dive you've always thought so much about. Fly like the wind. There you go. No fuss, no muss.*

What was next on the agenda? Where would the demon go from there?

Wherever it was, it meant certain death for Aaron.

Roxie slid into the seat next to Henry and sat in tense silence as he started up the engine, flicked on his lights and eased out of the spot.

"What exactly do you know about demonic possession?" she asked after some thought.

He remained silent as he took the sleek car up to the turnoff and pulled onto the two-lane road leading to the main highway. "What exactly did you want to know?"

"I think we need to talk about this. Since we have no idea what we're dealing with…"

"You've been running a bookstore for years, Rox. Haven't you read anything about it?"

"Mostly fiction. Blatty, Poe, Blackwood… The actual scientific stuff is confusing and contradictory. I dabbled briefly with the religious aspect of it, which more or less clings closely to the standard Dante's Inferno line of reasoning. But what I discovered mostly was that there were entirely too many different theories for my little brain to wrap around."

Henry pulled out onto the main highway and joined the heavy flow. "From what I've learned, most cultures believe in possession. The oldest, of course, is the Sumerians, and various Shamanic cultures have dealt with it for centuries. It's called different things in different religions. Most modern doctors don't believe in it. Doctors are scientists; they refer to such things in terms you can find in medical textbooks, such as hysteria, or mania. They also pigeonhole it in categories like psychosis, Tourette's syndrome, epilepsy and various forms of schizophrenia. This way, they don't look so stupid or clueless when they're asked specific questions."

"Would any of that explain how Aaron influenced Doctor Hill to take his own life?"

"If she influenced Grill to strangle two women and nearly did you in, I'm sure a suicide wouldn't be that much of a challenge."

"Are there any actual symptoms of possession? The only thing I remember from my college studies is a kind of personality disorder."

"There are four separate symptoms. The most common is erased memories. Then there are the personality disorders, convulsions, and fainting spells—which could also include blackouts."

"Erased memories?" That one seemed to stand out more than the others. "I don't know why, but that one hit me the hardest."

Henry nodded. "It'll make itself clear, eventually. The most important thing about all this is that there are no clear answers, and each individual case will be different. I believe each case depends on the individual demon. But we can't make light of any of this, and we sure as hell can't treat it as if it doesn't exist. Whatever is living inside Grill has been destroying people. We've already seen three separate examples of it. The demon has taken complete control, and I've got this eerie feeling that it's just getting started."

"What do you think it wants?"

"Right now, it wants him."

"And when it's finished?"

"It'll dump him and find someone else. Demons get bored easily. That's probably why it's been getting more active."

Roxie couldn't help wondering what was going through Henry's mind. "You're beginning to sound like you've actually been through this before…"

Henry said nothing.

"Henry?"

No reply.

She knew right then that she might have ventured a little too close to the limits of his comfort zone. But she had to know. "Don't you think we'd be much better off if we shared what we know? Just in case something really bad happens, and one of us ends up having to go at this alone?"

"I saw some things in Afghanistan that literally scared the shit out of me," he said finally, in a soft voice.

She knew better than ask him anything else. She could see the agony inside him taking over by how he gripped the wheel.

"Well, judging by what happened to me in his car that night, I can truthfully say I know first-hand what it means to be literally scared half to death."

"You never did tell me any of the gory details," he said. "I didn't want to ask, but now that we're being so open about everything…"

"When he was strangling me, I sensed that he'd disappeared. I already told you that his eyes changed, and that he looked like a monster in a horror flick—the smell, the slobbering. I honestly don't think he was in control."

"He wasn't."

"I also think he has no recollection of what happened."

Henry was silent for a little while. "If his demon has actually done the erased memory job on him, I'll bet Grill doesn't even know the doctor is dead."

Roxie nodded. "I know it sounds incredible, but you could actually be right."

Henry didn't reply. At first, Roxie thought he was thinking it over, but then she couldn't help wondering if he was remembering something that happened in Afghanistan.

"Manipulation works in many ways," he said finally. "Once the demon takes over, it blanks out whatever it wants its host to forget. It's got more control that way. Less clutter to bother with."

"That makes this even trickier, doesn't it?" she asked.

"Sure—especially if Grill has no idea what's actually going on. And she'll make it where he doesn't. She'll want him to only when it's convenient."

"For her?"

"Of course. Whenever she senses danger, she'll switch him off and take over."

"This will make finding him even more difficult."

"I just hope no one does. If a cop approaches him and ID's him, he'll draw his weapon and Grill will be shot dead."

"But there's *got* to be a way we can find him."

He glanced at her. "Going by what we both know right now, do you really want to?"

She knew exactly what he meant. But she also knew she couldn't live with herself if she didn't try helping Aaron. "Henry, we might possibly be the only two people in this town who can actually help him."

"Maybe…but who's gonna help *us*?"

CHAPTER THIRTY-THREE

A few minutes later, just as Henry took the Camaro onto the road that led to Roxie's Casselberry apartment, her cell buzzed.

The number registering on the display was the phone in the bookstore office, and it made her wonder what Sandy was doing there at this time of night. That didn't make sense. Sandy never stayed in the office this late. She was much too paranoid about being by herself.

So what was going on?

"Who is it?" Henry asked.

"It's...the bookstore..."

"What's Sandy doing there this late?"

"She shouldn't be there at all."

"Better answer it, anyway."

She nodded. Henry was right; she had to find out what was going on. "This is Roxie..."

"Roxie? This is Aaron. Where are you and what are you doing right now?"

Her mind immediately went blank. It took her several moments to collect herself, to come back from the sudden shock and start putting this together. This was Aaron calling her, and he was calling from the bookstore. She had no idea what was going on, but it was definitely him.

This just didn't add up.

"Aaron? Is that...is it really you?"

Henry swerved, bumping the curb.

"Roxie, I need to see you, talk to you..."

Everything leaped out at her at once. This man had strangled two women and nearly strangled her. He'd also been responsible for the suicide of a doctor, had escaped a heavily guarded wing of a hospital and walked out of the building without anyone seeing him. He was a wanted fugitive and was hiding in her bookstore.

Then it dawned on her. If she and Henry had been right, Aaron wouldn't know anyone was after him in the first place. He wouldn't know that he'd persuaded Doctor Hill to commit suicide or that he'd escaped a hospital. He probably wouldn't even remember that he'd been staying in a hospital in the first place.

Still, something didn't quite add up. Something that made her blood chill to the bone...

How did he get inside?

"Roxie? Are you still there?"

She knew to tread carefully. Otherwise, this could blow up quickly. "Aaron...where are you right now?"

Silence.

"Aaron?"

Henry had slowed down and kept glancing at her as he drove.

She took a breath. "I didn't give you my cell phone number. How did you get it?"

His silence told her something had happened that he didn't want her to know about.

She took another breath. Above all else, she needed to stay calm. Under the circumstances, it would be nearly impossible, but she had to do it. She also had to stay focused and couldn't let on that

283

she was frightened or upset. Aaron was very vulnerable right now. He might not have any recollection of what had happened during the last few days but probably knew *some*thing was going on, and this uncertainty would surely frighten him. Anything she said could set him off.

The demon living inside him was no doubt listening to every word.

"Aaron, where are you?"

"Roxie, I did a bad thing…"

Her heart was pounding, but she forced herself to stay strong. If Aaron knew he did something bad, then maybe he wasn't totally possessed. The demon might have left him temporarily. She had to use this opportunity to somehow coax him back. She couldn't stand idly by and let him hurt anyone else, and she surely couldn't stand by while the demon destroyed him.

"What…did you do, Aaron?"

"I…broke into your bookstore…"

She sighed in relief. At least he knew what he'd done. And he hadn't told her that he'd killed anyone else.

"What's going on?" Henry whispered.

She waved him down. "Why did you break into my store?"

A pause. "I had to, Roxie. I'm sorry, but I needed to. I didn't have your number, and I had to talk to you…"

Her heart crawled up her throat when she said, "Is that…*all* you did, Aaron?"

Another pause. "I didn't mess anything up, if that's what you mean. Your number was right there,

284

in your desk drawer. When I saw it, I wrote it down. I had to call you and let you know that I want to see you again…"

"It's all right, Aaron. It really is." Thank God Sandy hadn't been there…

"What did he do?" Henry whispered.

She put a hand over her cell. "He broke in, but he said he didn't do anything else."

"Keep him on the line. We've got to think of something."

"You're not…angry?" Aaron asked her.

"I'm not angry, Aaron."

"I really need to see you."

She glanced at Henry. "Aaron…"

"I know it's late and all, but I really need to see you. We had a nice time at the restaurant tonight, didn't we?"

She swallowed. "The restaurant?"

"The Beef Handlers. We were just there a few hours ago. Please tell me you had a good time…"

She began getting angry. The demon had done a terrific job of erasing his memory. "Yes, Aaron. I had a lovely time."

"It was just a few hours ago, wasn't it?"

"Yes. We were at the restaurant just a few hours ago."

Henry's eyes grew as he gazed at her.

"I'm glad you enjoyed yourself," Aaron said.

"Yes, Aaron. It was a terrific evening, and I really enjoyed myself. Why do you want to see me?"

"I need to talk to you and chat. There are some things I have to find out."

285

"Like what?"

"I have to find out why my mind is so messed up—why I can't remember certain things."

"Aaron, listen to me…"

"Roxie, I have to see you. I think we might have something good together. I'd like to talk to you about it and find out what you like, what we have in common. Maybe we can go out for drinks…"

"Drinks?" She shot a glance at Henry. "No, Aaron. I don't want to go out for drinks. It's late."

Henry whispered, "Invite him to your place."

She gawked at him.

He nodded.

"Roxie? Still there?"

She didn't reply. She was watching Henry, who was gesturing for her to wrap this up.

"Roxie?"

"Aaron…why don't you come over to my place?"

"I'd love that. When would you like me to—"

"Why not right now?"

"Right now?"

"Why not?"

"But I don't…I have no idea where you live…"

"I'll give you directions."

Silence.

"Aaron?"

"I'm still here. I've got a pen."

CHAPTER THIRTY-FOUR

It was nearly a quarter to eleven when Henry parked the Camaro in one of the six visitor parking spots across the street from Roxie's building.

"I don't want him to think you've got company," he said.

"Are you sure about this?" she asked uneasily. "I really don't want him knowing where I live."

"It's the only way I know of to get him back to the hospital, where he belongs."

"But what if we both can't handle him? If the demon manipulating him—"

"I'm gonna have to take him by surprise," he said grimly. "I don't know any other way of doing it. We both know he won't come with us voluntarily if he's not in control of himself."

"Do you really…need *that*?" She pointed to the Taser he'd shoved down the inside pocket of his windbreaker before he got out of the Camaro.

"Under the circumstances, it's exactly what I'll need." His expression remained solemn. "I'd use the sap again if I could get near him, but I don't want to take the chance of not getting him on the first try—not with you right there, just a couple of feet away. The Taser's got a range of about fifteen feet and will keep him under control until we can get the cops here."

"Why not call them now?"

"I don't think we should get them in on this until he's actually in the condo with us. Since we don't know exactly when he'll get here, they could

287

scare him off. He's a wanted fugitive, so they won't be coming in quietly. There could be five or six cruisers sitting out here by the time he shows. This way, once I zap him, you can make the call and tell them what's going on. Hopefully, they'll get here quickly."

She felt her pulse hammering again. This was so overwhelming. "This could go terribly wrong, you know."

"I won't let anything happen to you, Rox."

She wanted to ask him how he could make that promise, but the sincerity in his eyes told her he meant it. "I hope you're right."

They went up the walk. Roxie unlocked the front door and Henry followed her inside. She closed the door and flicked on the light in the hall. Then she wondered if she should turn on the living room light as well as the light in the kitchen. She wanted all the lights on but knew that would be impractical. The call from Aaron had unnerved her, leaving her clueless and frightened. She reminded herself that Henry was here with her and would need a dark place to hide.

"Would you like a drink while we wait?"

"I think I'd better hold off on that. I have to be a hundred percent focused while we do this."

Roxie nodded. "If you don't mind, I think I'll go upstairs and put on my sweats and slippers. Make yourself comfortable. I'll only be a minute."

As Henry slipped into the darkness of the living room, she turned and began ascending the steps.

"I think we just ran out of time," Henry said only moments later. "There's a car pulling in beside

288

your Honda. It looks like an Audi. I think it could be him."

She froze; her heart fluttered wildly. She could barely breathe. "If that's Aaron, where'd he get an *Audi*?"

"Now isn't exactly the right time to worry about something like that."

"I can't help it..." She began trembling. "I...I can't...this is so...so overwhelming..."

Henry hurried right over. "I'm right here," he said softly. "And as I just said, I won't let anything happen to you."

She watched her hand reaching out for his. He immediately covered it with his own. His touch was warm and strong. She looked into his eyes and saw something she'd never seen before. At first she thought it was warmth but realized it was more than that. It was something she couldn't explain, something she hadn't experienced before with another human being—not even with Trent during their brief marriage. But just as she was about to wonder what it might be, Henry whispered, "I'll be in the living room, hiding behind the armchair. I'll be right there, and I can get to you in just a few seconds." He winked. "I may be over forty, but I can still move pretty fast."

She took a deep breath and nodded.

He remained standing there, still smiling. "I can't do it until you let go of my hand..."

Suddenly embarrassed, she let go of him. "Oh! Sorry..." As she watched him move away into the darkness of the living room, she could still feel his warmth in the palm of her hand.

Aaron parked beside Roxie's Honda and sat there a minute, staring at the two-story, white stucco building just twenty feet or so beyond the windshield.

Then he began wondering if Roxie was alone in her condo.

Was the man who was about to harm her also in the condo?

The outside lights were on; so was the light showing in the small opaque window of the front door. However, the living room window was completely dark. Did this mean that if the man was there, he was downstairs with her? Or was he somewhere else?

It doesn't matter, that strange inner voice told him. *You'll know what to do as soon as she invites you in...*

That sounded reasonable, didn't it? If this man *was* there, Aaron would simply send him away. Once Aaron and Roxie were alone, they could finish what they'd started. Their date, for some reason he simply could not remember, had ended abruptly. He considered it his duty to make things right. It wasn't every day a guy met someone like Roxie. Anyone with any common sense would do whatever it took to make things right with her.

But if someone else was there, Aaron had to get rid of him. It was now well past eleven—Roxie should be alone at this hour. If the man was in Roxie's condo, he'd probably invited himself in. Why else had Roxie let him in at such a late hour? Was he an intruder? Aaron didn't think so. Roxie hadn't sounded stressed on the phone. If something bad *was* going on, he would have been able to hear it in her voice. And if someone had forced his way in and was threatening her, she would have been told to hang up quickly and certainly wouldn't have been permitted to invite anyone else over.

Who was he, then? A friend? A relative? If so, this matter would have to be handled much differently. A pleasant conversation would be necessary. Aaron would have to make sure he didn't upset Roxie while he did what was necessary to get rid of—

No. He didn't have to go through the aggravation of pleasant conversation, and he certainly didn't have to worry about upsetting Roxie when he got rid of the intruder. His new gift made all these irritating informalities unnecessary.

His face broke out in a grin and he nearly laughed out loud.

People can no longer argue with me. They have to go along with whatever I say. Otherwise...

All he had to do was tell this man to go away and that would be the extent of it. Aaron would be alone with Roxie again. But he had to do it at the right moment, before anything could go wrong...

I can't let him do anything to her.

You won't, the strange inner voice said. *You'll do everything right.*

I wish I could believe that.

Believe it, because it's true.

Suddenly relieved, Aaron got out of the car.

CHAPTER THIRTY-FIVE

Roxie moved unsteadily to the front door.

Each time she told herself everything would turn out all right, other things slipped into her head to tell her otherwise. Aaron was coming in, and he was possessed by a demon. He'd strangled two women and was directly responsible for a doctor jumping off a hospital roof.

And he tried to strangle me...

The message tore mercilessly into her.

My God... I'm inviting a demon into my home...

Stop this. She had to pull herself together. Henry was in the next room and would come to her aid—just as he'd done before. His Taser would incapacitate Aaron but wouldn't hurt him—not seriously, anyway. This way, the police wouldn't be forced to shoot him. They'd safely arrest him and take him back to the hospital.

This has to turn out all right, she promised herself. It didn't seem possible that it could, but she had to believe it anyway. *It has to. It just has to...*

The doorbell buzzed, and her heart leaped up her throat. She froze, staring at the small pane of glass in the center of the door as if expecting it to explode in her face.

You can do this... You can... You have to...

Trembling, Roxie reached out to pull the door open.

***

Roxie appeared in the doorway.

292

She'd changed her clothes. Aaron guessed that at this hour, she should be wearing her bedclothes. Perhaps she'd changed after his call. Their date had been just a few hours ago; she'd no doubt come home, undressed, taken a bath or shower, and gotten into her bedclothes. She might have put on this casual outfit because she wanted to be more presentable for his visit. The idea made him feel better, and he smiled.

But he reminded himself not to let down his guard. He still clung to the strong suspicion that a man who wanted to hurt Roxie was somewhere in the condo with her.

"Hi, Aaron..." Her voice was soft, trembling a little. She looked nervous, in fact. He clearly saw fear in her eyes. She was probably just uneasy for having a visitor at such a late hour. Single women had to be careful nowadays. There were too many predators wandering around, hunting for victims.

"Would you like to come in?"

"Could I?"

"Of course."

He closed the door behind him. Roxie didn't turn around; she'd backed up a few steps and watched him closely.

Something was wrong. He'd felt it the moment he saw the fear in her eyes. He decided that her trembling didn't have anything to do with him, but something else.

It's the man with her. He's hiding and might even have a gun. You need to act nonchalant. He can't know you suspect anything.

293

"Is everything okay?" he asked softly. He knew to trust the inner voice but decided to see what he could find out anyway.

"Fine. Would you like a drink?"

"Yes. Please."

She hurried down the hall, to the kitchen. He followed. By the time he slipped through the kitchen archway, she'd already opened the freezer door. She pulled out a tray of cubes and dropped two in a glass sitting on the island in the center of the room. She poured from the bottle in front of her and went back to the fridge to replace the cubes.

He sat on a stool and watched her. She pushed the glass toward him. He picked it up and sipped. It fired up his mouth and heated him up on its way down. It made him feel a little better, but the strong suspicion remained. He noticed that she hadn't moved, hadn't even fixed a drink for herself. "You're not having one?"

She shrugged. "I think I had enough...at the restaurant."

"You had a glass of wine." He found it strange that one glass of wine would be enough for anyone.

"Two glasses, actually."

"It was a table wine, Roxie. Not very potent at all."

"We didn't want to get drunk at the restaurant, did we? You were driving."

"No, we sure didn't." The image of them sitting in the Crown Vic flashed immediately. That kiss... He could never forget that kiss. He stared at her lips and realized right then how much he wanted to kiss her again. He wanted to take her in his arms and kiss her more passionately than he'd ever kissed anyone—even Lana. He also wanted to push her down on the bed and--

Lana popped into his head—Lana and her thick red hair, her bold blue eyes... Lana really knew how to wrap her arms around him when they kissed, when they made love... Suddenly he wondered what happened to their relationship, why they weren't still together...

The inner voice intervened, making him remember. *It's over. Lana's gone. She walked right out the door and into the arms of someone else. It destroyed you, but you gradually mended and got back on your feet. Now you've got your chance to start all over again, this time with Roxie, who's right there, just a couple of feet away, waiting for you to take her in your arms--*

"Aaron? You all right?"

"I'm fine..."

"You...don't look fine..."

Why was she looking at him like that? What did she see?

"I said I'm fine..."

The other man is hiding in the living room...

The inner voice rang loud and clear, warning him of the imminent danger.

"Aaron...why did you come here tonight?"

"I told you on the phone, I wanted..." His thought processes stopped abruptly, and his mind went dark. He suddenly couldn't remember why he was here. For some reason, all he could think of was that the other man had come here to hurt Roxie.

"What did you want, Aaron?"

He's got a gun, and he's going to kill you...

The inner voice grew louder, more insistent...

"Who else...is here, Roxie?"

Her face instantly paled. "Wh-What?"

"You heard me." He got up from the stool. "Someone else is here. Who else is here, Roxie?"

"N-No one's here, Aaron. It's just you...you and me."

He moved over to the corner of the island. "Someone's here with you." He shot a quick glance at the kitchen archway. He saw only the empty hall leading to the front door, but that didn't mean anything. Even if the man wasn't hiding in the living room, the condo had two floors; there were plenty of other hiding places. "Someone's here to kill us...both of us."

"No, Aaron." Roxie backed up a couple of steps. "No one else is here."

He took two more steps toward her. "Who's here, Roxie?"

She backed up until she'd reached the kitchen counter. When her back pressed against the cabinet, she cringed...and froze.

He took two more steps, until they were just five feet apart. The fear in her eyes had grown, making her eyelids twitch. Her skin had turned a chalky white. She trembled, her hair hopping across her shoulders as her eyes darted. She was obviously looking for an escape.

"Roxie," he said, keeping his voice barely above a whisper, "you don't have to tell me anything. I'll take care of this..."

Darkness consumed him.

CHAPTER THIRTY-SIX

Sharp slivers of ice raked heavily down Roxie's back, and she trembled.

Aaron's eyes had glazed over and were beginning to change.

She couldn't believe this was happening again. This was just like the other night... If she was right, it would only be seconds before his eyes changed color. He'd be at the mercy of the demon again. And the demon would attack her viciously again.

Hopefully, Henry had heard everything and would soon be out in the hall. Roxie cursed herself for letting him turn off the living room light. If he tripped on something, this could turn out very badly. The demon obviously sensed someone else in the condo.

"Where is he hiding, Roxie?" Aaron asked suddenly, in a strange voice.

How on earth could she possibly fight a demon? How could she battle the fiend's cunning? How could she outwit the instinct of the perfect predator? It obviously possessed six senses, perhaps more. How else could the demon manipulate Aaron into killing people and succeed in letting him walk out of a closely guard mental facility? How could Roxie and Henry fight a demon when it knew everything that was going on? How could they possibly survive this at all?

You're going to have to turn this around somehow...

But how? she asked herself.

Find a way. Use Aaron as a go-between. Gain time while Henry gets in position.

The realization slammed into her, and suddenly she knew what had to be done. "It's...not hiding...at all," she whispered uneasily.

He blinked. "What?"

"It's right there, living inside you, and it's been destroying you ever since."

"What are you talking about?"

"Aaron, please listen to me, and listen carefully. You've got a demon inside you. It's living inside your head, your body, and it's been controlling you."

"Who's in this condo with us?" Aaron's voice no longer sounded like his own. It had become that of a stranger, suggesting Aaron was no longer in control. "There's someone hiding in the living room, isn't there?"

She struggled to keep her composure. She had to somehow get through to him. "Aaron, *listen* to me..."

"There's someone else here, and you're trying to trick me..."

"No, Aaron. The demon is tricking you. I'm not."

"Tell me who's here with you, Roxie..."

"What's its name, Aaron? Tell me the demon's name."

"Roxie, you can't trick me..."

"Tell me its name, Aaron!"

"You can't do this!"

"It's inside you, Aaron. I just heard it. It's hiding inside you, and it's making you do horrible things."

"Why are you doing this to me?" His voice began changing back. "I thought you *liked* me…"

"I do, Aaron. But we've got to get rid of the demon. It's turned you into a murderer. You've killed three people!"

His eyes quickly returned to their natural color. "Wh-*what*?"

"You killed a young woman who worked as a paralegal secretary. Her name was Brittany, and you strangled her in the parking lot of Shannon's—"

"No!"

"You killed Lana, Aaron. You strangled your ex-wife."

He began to shake. "Why are you lying to me? Why are you telling me these horrible things?"

"It's the truth. You strangled Lana at Winter Park Village just a few days ago…"

"*No*! I *didn't*! I *couldn't*!"

"You killed a doctor at the hospital earlier today. His name was Doctor Hill. You were staying in the hospital until just a few hours ago. They took you there the night you tried to kill me. The demon inside you ordered the doctor to walk up to the roof—"

"I wouldn't *ever* try to kill you, Roxie. I'd *never* do that!"

"You did, Aaron." She raised her head and pulled back her hair to expose the welts on her neck, which hadn't yet healed.

Trembling, he gawked at them, his lips trying to form words. "N-No! I *wouldn't...*I *couldn't...*"

"The doctor went up to the roof and jumped off—"

"Why are you *saying* these things?"

"It's all true, Aaron. You don't remember any of it because the demon won't let you. It's been manipulating you ever since it took over."

"Things have been great for me. People do things for me. They give me things. They let me do anything I wish."

"The demon took away something very valuable from you in exchange for—"

"People can't resist me anymore. It's my destiny. It's karma. It's—"

"It's the demon, Aaron. Nothing else. It's killing you."

Out of the corner of her eye, Roxie caught movement at the end of the hall. Henry had snuck out of the living room and was tiptoeing silently toward them.

"No. You're wrong—dead wrong. I won't let you lie to me. I won't let you trick me!"

"It's taken over, Aaron. You don't hear me anymore, do you?"

"I hear you. This is me—Aaron Grill. No one can do something like that to me. No one."

"The demon's already done it. And it's so good at its job that you don't even know it's in your head, or what it's doing."

"You're lying to me. I won't let you lie to me!" He took another step toward her.

"Aaron, *please...*"

Just then, he stopped moving. His eyes changed color again and his facial features turned taut. In one swift movement, his right arm lashed out, toward the kitchen counter, where the glass salt and pepper shakers stood next to the large white porcelain jar marked SUGAR. His hand closed over the salt shaker. In the next instant, he spun around and tossed it down the hall, where Henry stood in front of the door, just three feet from the living room archway.

The shaker slammed him directly in the center of his forehead with a loud, sickening *thump*!

Henry dropped heavily to the floor and lay still. The Taser fell from his grip and clattered on the tile three feet from his outstretched arm.

CHAPTER THIRTY-SEVEN

The moment the hard object slammed into Henry's forehead, bright lights flashed across his vision.

Blackness followed, and he had the sensation of falling. When he opened his eyes again, he found that he was staring at a solid wall of darkness. The strong stench of cordite assaulted his nostrils. He'd somehow returned to the deserted concrete building outside Afghanistan, where he'd just been shot and was waiting for his unit to come back for him.

But in the next instant everything changed, and he was no longer lying on the filthy dirt floor in the concrete building. He was now clinging to an overhead canvas strap in an Army chopper as he and a group of men he'd never seen before dropped from the sky and slammed onto the hard ground.

The moment the chopper crashed, the locals pounced on them. Everything went berserk. The sounds of gunshots reverberated dangerously close to his ears. Blood splashed in front of him, soaking his sleeve. A series of ear-splitting screams ringing close behind him caused his skin to stand out in gooseflesh. Something hard pounded him in the kidneys, and he was then viciously yanked out of the chopper and slammed to the ground. He tried holding on to his weapon, but it was ripped from his grasp when someone's boot stomped on his hands. More bloodcurdling screams echoed around him. The sounds of more gunshots thundered in the air, and hot blood singed the flesh of his forehead and

302

cheek. He tried crawling away, but something slammed him in the lower back, and waves of red-hot pain sliced up and down his back.

Moments later, something broad and hard crushed him in the back of the skull, and he was knocked unconscious. When the blackness thinned sometime later, he had the vague sensation that he'd been tossed in the back of an old truck.

A few miles later, the truck stopped abruptly, rocking on ancient springs. He was then dragged out of the back, dragged somewhere else then dropped in a damp hole in the ground. He lay there, surrounded by darkness. Aside from the labored beating of his own heart, he heard only a heavy silence. Compared to what he'd just been through, he welcomed the quiet as if it had actually been a warm wave of euphoria. However, as he lay there, he wondered what was going on, why his nightmare had changed.

His thoughts clouded again, and he lay on the hard ground, struggling to calm himself. When he was calm, he could think better. All he could remember was that something wasn't right, and the more he tried to analyze the situation, the more confusing everything became. He caught a brief image of Roxie calling to him but knew that didn't make any sense. The only thing that made sense was that he was somehow trapped in a nightmare he'd never experienced before.

He relaxed once again and let the darkness take hold, but just when the silence began to caress him, the thumping of heavy footsteps made his heart sputter. A moment later, he was yanked out of the hole by two pairs of hands, stripped naked, bound tightly with wire, dragged to another truck, tossed in the back and taken away.

After another painful bumpy ride, he was pulled out of the truck and made to stand. An old foul-smelling horse blanket soaked in kerosene was wrapped around him and bound tightly with more wire, and a blood-caked wooden yoke was fastened around his neck. He was then paraded through the streets of a small village. A crowd of dark-haired civilians had gathered, anxiously awaiting his arrival. One by one, they stepped up to him and punched him, slapped him, spat at him, and kicked him. Each time he stumbled or was knocked down, he was yanked to his feet by the yoke and forced to continue walking.

Once the procession reached the other end of the town, he was led to a deserted stone building. The yoke was removed. He was pushed inside, slammed in the lower back with the butt of a rifle and pushed down a short flight of wooden stairs.

He lay on the dirt floor in that dark, damp cellar, unable to move, the wire wrapped around his body keeping the kerosene-soaked blanket mashed tightly against his skin. He lay very still, listening to the frenzied scratching noises the rats made as they scurried across the dirt floor, anxious to feast on his flesh.

Just then, he heard a strange voice. It sounded very close.

"I've come to help you." It was a low-pitched female voice, and as his vision acclimated itself to the dark, he could see the vague image of a tall, slender figure with long black hair emerging.

"Who…are you?" Henry's whisper was a weak, raspy croak. It was then that he realized he'd been whacked brutally in the forehead—probably by a rock or something else tossed by one of the locals when he was paraded through the village.

Her image became more distinct as she moved closer. He could see fine features and large, penetrating deep-blue eyes. "I'm the one who can help you. Is that not enough?"

"What's your name?"

"I am called Jessica."

"What do you want?"

"Your spirit."

Your spirit. He was obviously hallucinating. He was talking to an apparition. Only an apparition would say such a thing.

"I'm only imagining you."

"I am real, and I can help you."

"Get out of here."

"Your spirit for your freedom. Is that not fair?"

"You're in my head. Get the hell out of there. Get out now!"

Just then, a pale hand with long, elegant fingers emerged from the darkness. It moved toward his face and gently touched his left cheek. The touch was cold and made his skin tingle. He shivered; his heart sputtered.

She pulled her hand away, but the spot on his cheek remained cold. "If I wasn't real, would you be able to feel my touch?"

He didn't reply. She was real, all right. But her icy touch had frightened him. It told him she was evil. Cold wouldn't come from a benevolent spirit.

"Well? Would you?"

"N-No…"

She smiled, but her deep-blue eyes remained cold as ice. "Now… where were we? Oh yes…I was telling you how I could get you out of this."

"You want my spirit?"

"Yes."

"Why?"

"It is what I do."

"I don't believe you."

"I will make it happen."

"How?"

"Want a small sample? Close your eyes."

"Get away from me."

"Close your eyes. I will help change your mind."

Despite his efforts, Henry felt his eyes closing. Something cold—her hand again, no doubt—touched the top of his head, and the darkness filling his being changed at that same moment, turning gray, then a hazy yellow.

"Now open your eyes."

The blinding light of the blistery afternoon made him turn away. A kerosene-soaked horse blanket lay in a burning heap twenty yards away, in front of the crumbling stone building that looked frighteningly familiar. He was standing on the sandy ground in his Army uniform, gripping his service revolver in his right hand. Several choppers flew over the deserted village. The sharp sounds of

306

machinegun fire close by sounded like echoing thunder. The bodies of six slain Iraqis lay in a bloody heap just ten feet in front of him.

What the hell?

He gazed numbly at the .45 in his hand. Then he slowly raised his trembling arm and sniffed the barrel. The cordite stench was overwhelming. With his left hand he gingerly touched the slab barrel. It was hot.

He scanned the area. There was no one else around, so...

But how did this happen? How did he get here? Why couldn't he remember anything?

"What the hell happened?" he asked no one in particular.

"I am here," a voice said just a few feet away.

He couldn't see anyone. The voice was familiar, but he couldn't remember anything else. He was curious why he saw no body attached to the voice.

"Well? Is it a deal? Is your soul mine now?"

The flicker of a tall, slender figure appeared briefly, and his mind caught a fleeting flash of what had happened only moments ago in the cellar of the building behind him.

The woman with long black hair and deep-blue eyes had somehow done this. Henry struggled to remember what had transpired, but his mind had gone blank. He turned away from the pile of bloodied corpses. "What happened? What did I do? Why can't I remember any of this?"

"I told you I'd give you back your freedom."

"Why would you do this?"

"Your soul is what I desire. I will give you whatever you wish for your soul."

This was so terribly wrong. Although his thoughts were muddled, a few things began drifting into his head, and some very important details rose readily to the surface. The first one, of course, was that he was only in an Army chopper twice. Neither trip had resulted in a crash. And he was never captured. He certainly would have remembered that.

This isn't even Afghanistan, for God's sake!

This bitch was making him hallucinate. He didn't know how, but it was the only thing that made any sense. She was a demon—nothing else could explain any of this.

"Well? Do we have a deal?"

"No. I will never deal with you. Not ever."

"But I told you—"

"I don't care what you told me. I don't believe anything you say."

"Are you sure you want to go this route?"

"I'm positive."

"You don't believe what you see? You don't believe you've just escaped the damp cellar? The darkness? The rats? The wire? The horse blanket? The agony of what the locals did to you?"

"There's only one minor detail that concerns me about all this."

"And what is that?"

"This nightmare…it isn't mine."

Silence.

"Did you hear me? This isn't my nightmare, you stupid bitch."

The silence continued.

308

"You stuck me in someone else's nightmare. This isn't even Afghanistan. This is Iraq! Don't you know the difference?"

The silence became heavy, and he could no longer hear the choppers or the machinegun fire. In the next few seconds, the blinding light of the afternoon faded into darkness, and he let himself surrender to the peace and quiet of complete nothingness.

Just then, he heard Roxie calling for him, and she sounded frightened. The nothingness gradually drifted away, and he suddenly realized that he no longer could just lie there. He had to wake up.

Roxie needed him.

CHAPTER THIRTY-EIGHT

Numb with fear, Roxie prayed for some sign of movement from the motionless figure lying in the hall.

Henry did not stir.

Get up, Henry! Please! I need you!

Had Aaron killed him? *No.* She refused to believe it. Henry was simply unconscious. He was badly hurt, but he'd come to—he *had* to.

A sudden coldness enveloped her, and a feeling of weakness took hold. She wanted to collapse, to fall into a quivering mess on the floor. The thought of Henry dying—of his lying there, just a few feet away—brought about a feeling of chilly despair she'd never experienced before.

No. This can't be happening.

*Henry...if you can hear my thoughts...*please *come back...*please*!*

The despair vanished and was immediately replaced by anger. It brought her right back, and she realized almost at once that there were other things to worry about. Aaron hadn't been the one who'd actually tossed the shaker. The monster lurking inside Aaron was the one responsible. And it was standing just a few feet away, getting ready to murder her.

Her heart pounded wildly, but she told herself she had to hold it together a little while longer. She just had to keep Aaron distracted until she found some way of getting to Henry's Taser.

"Why...Why'd you do it, Aaron?" It took her three tries to find her voice. "Why'd you sell your soul?"

Aaron stood there silently, his eyes giving off their icy glow. "He had no choice," the creature said in its strange voice. "We made a deal. He gave me his soul and I gave him a life of incredibly good luck."

Roxie's pulse skipped a beat. The demon had been responsible for everything that had gone wrong and right in Aaron's life. Henry had been right all along; the succubus living in Aaron had been manipulating him all along. "You've been using him for your own selfish purposes."

"It is of no importance," the creature said. "He is just another worthless mortal I chose for my own personal amusement."

A seething anger began building up within her, and she knew that if Aaron hadn't been caught in the middle of all this, she would have reached out and tried clawing the filthy creature's face. But it wasn't the demon's face, it was Aaron's. She had to keep reminding herself of that. "You're disgusting!" It was the worst thing she could think of to say, and it came out of her throat hotly, like the foulness she felt in her gut.

"It doesn't matter to me what you think. In fact, nothing should matter to you anymore." The creature took another step in her direction. Its arms slowly came up. Its fingers had turned into claws.

"It does matter," she said, struggling to stay focused. "It matters a lot. I like Aaron, and I hate what you've done to him." Henry still hadn't

311

budged, but she couldn't think of that right now. She forced herself to believe she could survive this. Henry's Taser lay on the tile not much more than ten feet away from her. She couldn't possibly circle the kitchen island fast enough and get to it before the creature grabbed her, but that wasn't the point. Right now, she had to stay in control until she thought of some way she *could* get to it. Without giving herself away, she began concentrating on the toaster sitting at the far end of the counter. If she could grab it, toss it and hit the creature in the head, it might give her the few precious seconds she'd need to get to the Taser. She knew she'd really be hitting Aaron, but that couldn't be helped. She'd deal with the consequences of all this once she could subdue Aaron and call the police and the paramedics.

"What I've done is what we both agreed on," the creature said.

"You tricked him. You're a demon. Demons trick people."

"As I've already said, he was just another worthless mortal plodding aimlessly through life, trying his best to avoid all possible brain activity. I found him during one of my frequent rounds through my favorite section of town. His nightmares were strong and quite distinctive, so I tuned in to them and decided to make several necessary improvements to the situation. Ever since, I've been using him the way I see fit."

"At what price?"

"The price I decided on, of course."

"Then I was right after all. You *did* trick him."

312

"For that, as well as *all* things in life, there *is* a price…"

As soon as the words were uttered, Aaron shook himself and gazed at her as if seeing her for the first time. His eyes had returned to their chestnut color. "R-Roxie?"

"Aaron? Is it you?"

"R-Roxie? Is it true? I heard…does she really have my soul?"

"I'm afraid so, Aaron."

He began trembling. "Roxie, I'm so—" Then he stopped moving.

"Aaron?"

His eyes closed, and when they opened, they'd changed once again. Glaring, the creature took another step in her direction.

"Aaron?"

No response.

"Aaron? Can you hear me?"

The creature took another step.

"Aaron, *please* listen to me!"

The creature took one more step and reached out for her. Just as its claws began closing around her neck, Roxie screamed.

The creature froze; its eyes instantly changed back. Aaron quickly pulled away, twisted toward the kitchen counter, and lunged at the wooden knife block sitting beside the coffeepot. He snatched one of the steak knives from the rack and brought it toward his unprotected throat.

"*No, Aaron!*"

Time slowed…then stopped. Aaron stopped moving. His eyes changed again, and his

313

outstretched arm froze the knife in mid-arc. He glanced at the knife and focused on it as if he hadn't even been aware that he was holding it. Then he turned to Roxie. His face tensed up, and Roxie whimpered when she saw the rage in his glazed, steel-blue eyes.

The creature brought the knife up and aimed the glistening blade in her direction. Then it moved toward her.

Roxie noticed movement behind the creature. Henry had finally regained consciousness. He groped for the Taser and forced himself up on one knee. Swaying a little, he extended his left arm and pulled the trigger.

The creature was zapped in the center of its back. It immediately turned back into Aaron and went into convulsions. His right arm dropped to his side. His fist relaxed then opened, and the steak knife slipped from him, clattering on the tile. Jerking and twitching, Aaron followed the knife, dropping to his knees and collapsing to the floor.

Snapping out of her panic mode, Roxie dove for the knife. Grabbing it, she rolled away from Aaron, who lay on the floor, gasping and writhing as the convulsions took over.

Henry remained kneeling another few moments. His arm dropped but he kept a tight grip on the Taser. His eyes stayed on Roxie, but she could tell by his dazed expression that he was staring at empty space. His forehead was a mess. Blood had clotted darkly over his right eyebrow, and a purplish knot the size of a golf ball showed prominently in the center of his forehead. Blood pitted his cheeks, and two thick streams of blood had traveled down his forehead, settling in his eyebrows. He lowered his head and, for a split second, seemed to be gazing at the tile. Then he collapsed and lay on his side.

Roxie rushed over and knelt over him. "Henry...*please* stay with me!" She took the Taser from him and squeezed his hand. There was a response, but it was weak. "Henry? *Please* don't leave me..."

His eyes were barely open, but she could see the beginnings of a smile. "I never will," he whispered.

She took a breath and struggled to keep it together. She continued holding his hand with both of her own. "Promise?"

"You owe me...a date...maybe two...after this..." His eyes closed, and he lay still.

She heard moaning behind her. She turned. Aaron was recovering. *The Taser. Get it*! She snatched it up and squeezed the trigger. Aaron gasped and went back into convulsions.

While her nerves began settling, she grabbed her cell with her free hand and dialed 911.

CHAPTER THIRTY-NINE

Three days later, Roxie came into the hospital room wearing a cream-colored crepe blouse, brown skirt a couple of inches below the knee, and open-toed white sandals. Her hair, recently washed, was brushed straight back. It shined magnificently in the afternoon light.

Henry watched her from his hospital bed and realized once again how lucky he was. His head still throbbed but was no longer a major issue. When he'd awoken an hour earlier and reached up to feel the bandage, he could tell that it had been changed again. The swelling in his forehead remained and was still tender to the touch, but not nearly as severe as it was the day before.

But that wasn't why he felt so lucky. It didn't take a genius to figure that one out. Each time he found himself gazing into Roxie's beautiful green eyes, he realized once again how stupid he'd been for not taking advantage of the situation and marrying her. After all, she'd been an important part of his life for the last ten years. It was funny that it took the shock of nearly losing her to realize it.

My career was always more important.

He wanted to curse himself for even going that route.

But at least now there was time to correct this enormous blunder…

That is, if he could somehow coax Roxie back.

"Feeling better?" Roxie came over and stood next to the chair beside the bed. The strong scent of her lavender perfume made him feel even better than moments ago, when she first came in.

"Much." He didn't need to take any time at all to realize that her visits were the main reason for his quick recovery. In fact, they'd become the highlight of his hospital stay.

She smiled as she sat down. "I'm *so* glad. So how's the pain in your head?"

"Actually, it hasn't been really bad since yesterday. It's still throbbing, but not so much."

"That's good. They said you'll probably be ready to leave by tomorrow morning. They're no longer worried about that concussion and said that you're healing much faster than they thought."

"I can't wait to get out of here. By the way, any word on Grill?"

"Actually, I still haven't seen or heard anything since the police took him away. Do you remember anything I told you the day before yesterday, when you finally came out of it and they let me talk to you for a few minutes?"

He shrugged. "They had me doped up. I was feeling pretty damned spaced out, so I really don't remember too much."

"Well, two of them stayed for a little while at my place that night and asked me a bunch of questions. I was more concerned about you, so I was kind of short with them. I was in too much of a hurry to find out what they were doing with you. By the time I was able to leave, the paramedics had already put you on a gurney and taken you away. One of the cops told me they were taking you to Winter Park Hospital, so I drove right over. I was

317

worried about Aaron, of course, but you were my main concern…"

"We did just about all we could do for him."

She sighed. "I know…"

"But you still feel bad."

"I can only imagine what he's going through right now."

"No. You can't."

She straightened. "You know more about this than you're telling me, don't you?"

"I can only tell you what I *think* he's going through."

"I'll take that, then."

"Well, we're both pretty sure Grill was manipulated by a demon and had no idea what he was doing. Actually, he's probably not conscious of anything that's going on right now."

"You think she's still in control?"

"I've been doing a lot of thinking since I came to. I should've seen this long before we went to your place. The demon that took control of him appeared as a dark angel. It took possession of both his spirit *and* his body."

"Henry…how do you know this?"

He stared at the ceiling before replying. "I saw her."

"You *what*?"

"When I was whacked in the head, I went out like a light, and when I woke up, I had this strange nightmare about being captured in Iraq. It was so vivid that I thought it was really happening, and she appeared right in the middle of it. She told me she could get rid of my nightmare if I gave her my soul, but I knew right off that it was just a trick."

"How did you know that?"

"For one thing, I was never in Iraq. I was in Afghanistan for six months, but I was never captured. I caught some shrapnel in the back of the left thigh and was sent to an Army hospital in Germany to recover."

Roxie's eyes grew. "You never told me you'd been wounded."

"It was no biggie, actually."

Her eyes remained large. "You caught shrapnel. It was no biggie?"

He shrugged. "Not really. Just a few shards got me, but none of them nicked the femoral, or anything important. Anyway, they got them all out then kept me there, talking with their shrinks for a couple of weeks before they shipped me back home."

"Did you suffer mental trauma?"

"Hardly, but whenever you're wounded, they automatically send you to talk with their shrinks before you're sent home. I was near the end of my tour anyway, so they decided to send me home a few weeks early."

"Tell me more about this demon."

"As I said, nothing in that nightmare happened to me at all. When she knocked me out in your kitchen, she obviously saw something in my memory and decided to work with that, but since my nightmares about the shrapnel event hadn't taken over, she decided to fabricate something she could use to bargain with."

Roxie didn't say anything for the longest time.

"What's wrong?"

She looked down at her lap. "I...had this nightmare several days ago. It was vivid, but something about it just wasn't right. When I was sixteen, I was joyriding one Saturday afternoon, when a very large dog appeared from out of nowhere and stood right there, in the middle of the road. It was all I could do to swerve out of its path and avoid it without killing myself or totaling my parents' car."

"And you dreamed it?"

"Yes, but when I dreamed about it the other day, I'd actually hit the dog."

Henry frowned. "You think she got into your head while you were asleep?"

"I really don't know why I had that dream. However, there was a woman in it. She had dark hair, and she threatened me to stay away from someone. She kept telling me that he belonged to her."

Dark hair. The shocking familiarity of the situation made him want to grind his teeth. "Other than the dark hair, what did this woman look like?"

"Tall, slender, and beautiful."

Henry didn't reply. He found that he was having some difficulty controlling the heat climbing up his spine.

"Does this ring a bell?"

After a few moments, he sensed his focus coming back. "It sounds like her. I take it you had this nightmare not long after you met Grill?"

"It happened after our first date."

320

"She was obviously warning you off, and when you didn't do as she said, she tried to kill you using Grill."

"My God... This demon deals in nightmares."

"She uses them to get what she wants. She senses weakness in mortals just as a predatory animal, like the wolf, senses fear—or sickness—in its prey."

"When I was facing her in my kitchen, she told me she focused on Aaron because his nightmares appealed to her and stood out..."

"You said he told you he'd gone through a painful divorce, didn't you?"

"When I first met him..."

"Well, the fact that he strangled his ex-wife tells me he'd been hurting for quite a while. If the demon was able to pick up on his nightmares, she obviously had to be close by. Since nightmares are apparently her forte, she'd be highly sensitive to them. Nightmares would be extremely valuable for her. If you think about it, nightmares are an important part of our lives. They help us appreciate life and its many battles. For others, however, they keep the fear and the panic a little too close. The bad thing about all this is that if the nightmares are taken away, a lot of other things go away right along with them. Memories—some good, some bad—are gone, and the heavy emptiness filling one's mind in the end serves as clear evidence that a large part of the spirit—as well as the human heart—has been wrenched away forever."

"This could be academic right now. Aaron was arrested and put away again, so she might not be controlling him anymore."

"Maybe, maybe not. She might consider this another challenge and manipulate him into killing someone else."

"Maybe she'll just help him walk out of the hospital again."

"That's another maybe."

"Should I be worried about him coming after me again?" she asked uneasily.

"I honestly don't think that'll be a major issue anymore."

"You don't?"

"Not really."

"What *do* you think will happen?" she asked.

"In my opinion, one of two things could happen. She might stick with him and get him to do more killings, or she'll just leave him. Personally, I'm leaning more toward the second possibility."

"Why?"

"Grill pissed her off. I really don't think she'll forgive him for that."

"By trying to save me?"

"That would do it."

"Then if she leaves him, Aaron might not be suffering anymore."

"Actually, I think he's most likely not conscious of what's going on anymore."

She blinked. "Then...you think he really *is* suffering?"

Henry didn't reply right off.

"Henry?"

"No. He's not. At least, not in the world of the living…"

CHAPTER FORTY

The cave was pitch-black, the stench coming from inside horribly rancid as Aaron climbed the grassy slope leading to it.

When he was just ten feet from the mouth of the cave, a tall, slender figure appeared, blocking the entrance. She wore a long dark robe, and her thick black hair covered her shoulders. She stood watching him, her beautiful face grim. Something cold and frightening oozed from her deep-blue eyes.

"Why have you come here?" she asked.

"Something very strange has happened to me." He struggled to remember the last few days. Despite his efforts, he could manage only partial, disjointed images. Roxie's face flashed briefly, followed by a fleeting image of her in her kitchen. The fear in her glistening green eyes was unmistakable. As he approached her, her fear grew, and she slowly backed away.

She was afraid of me. Roxie was really and truly afraid of me...

The kitchen dimmed, the fear in Roxie's face flared again, and then something hot and tingly slammed into his back.

The darkness returned, along with brief flashes of brightness. In the brightness, men in blue uniforms were bending over him, picking him up and placing him on a gurney. Just as they pushed the gurney toward an awaiting van, the images faded, and the darkness returned.

What seemed like only moments later, the darkness lifted, and he discovered that he was climbing the grassy hill that approached the oddly familiar cave, and as he neared the cave opening, he couldn't help wondering where Roxie had gone, how he'd gotten away from the men in uniforms and why he'd come here.

And now, as he faced this woman, his inner senses told him that he'd seen her before.

"Why have you come here?" she'd asked, and he could clearly feel the venomous hatred emanating from her.

"My head," he muttered thickly. "Things aren't making sense anymore..."

"You are no longer welcome here," the woman said.

"What's happening to me? Where am I? Who are you? Why am I here? Where did Roxie go? Her condo? The man with her? How did I get here? What the hell happened?"

"It is no longer of any consequence."

"Please...tell me..." He couldn't understand why she hated him so much. He tried remembering where he'd met her but could no longer recall that, either. He began wondering if she'd just appeared at some random point in his life, but when he tried focusing on specifics, he could see only the heavy darkness smothering his thoughts.

"To me, you no longer exist. I don't ever want to see you again."

"But you must know what's happening to me, don't you?" The fact that he'd come here suggested that she knew, yet he couldn't remember how.

"I've already released you from our arrangement."

An arrangement? What did she mean by that? He dimly recalled something that happened long ago—something that had turned his life around, shifting certain events...but again, the darkness swallowed up the details.

What did all this have to do with Roxie?

"What...arrangement?"

"You remember, don't you?" the woman asked.

"Everything's so...so *fuzzy*..."

"It'll come back. Once it does, you'll wish you'd never brought it back. But you've made it so, and it'll come back despite your wishes. I took your spirit in exchange for the perfect life. You were granted opportunities very few others can even imagine. You enjoyed this arrangement and benefited immensely from it. You could have used it to make yourself incredibly rich. You could have lived in a mansion and had a fleet of servants tending to your every need. Nothing would have been out of reach for you. You could have made yourself Governor of the state...or a Senator...or even the President of the United States. Yes, you truly enjoyed this arrangement, just like many others have, yet you ultimately wished to have it rendered null and void."

"*I* did that?" He couldn't imagine turning away from such a wonderful arrangement.

"Yes. And when you wanted out, you angered me. As I said, our arrangement has become null and void."

"What exactly does that mean?"

326

"It's very simple. I've given you back your soul and never want to deal with you again."

Images began trickling back, but he couldn't piece them together. He remembered walking out of stores without paying for his purchases. This, of course, led to many more questions. Who was this frightening woman and how did she enter his life in the first place? And what was this dark, foul-smelling place?

He suddenly realized that he'd ventured into forbidden territory. *I've given you back your soul.* This sort of thing didn't happen in the real world. This would happen only in that dark, vile place everyone referred to as Hell.

Did that mean he was dead? Did it mean Roxie was also dead?

Why had he sold his soul in the first place?

That wasn't the point, was it? The important thing was that this woman said she'd returned it to him.

"Why did you give it back?" he asked.

"You wanted it back."

It sounded too easy. Maybe she wasn't a demon after all. Demons didn't work like that, did they?

"My life…it'll be as it once was?"

"You've got your soul back, and with it, everything else."

"Everything…*else*?"

"Everything that was part of you before I entered your life is now part of you again."

For some reason, that sounded ominous…and frightening. "What…does *that* mean?"

327

"Everything that once belonged to you is yours again. Your memories. Your guilt. Most of all, your nightmares. Everything that has ever happened to you, that you've seen and done, has come back. Most important, once you leave, everything about this place will be erased from your memory forever. You won't remember any of it. And, of course, you won't remember me."

It had suddenly become frighteningly clear. He began trembling.

"Goodbye, Aaron Grill."

"Can you do one small favor for me...before I...before you—"

"No. You've angered me for the very last time. I don't do favors unless they serve my purpose. You no longer serve my purpose."

"All I'm asking is that you erase a few things from my memory. You can do that, can't you?"

"Of course I can do that, you idiot. I can do whatever I wish with your memory. I can do whatever I wish, any time I choose."

"Then all you have to do is—"

"I know what you want me to do. You want me to make you forget every bad thing collected in your memory, but you want me to do this without giving me your spirit."

He couldn't reply.

"I will not do it. You no longer belong to me."

"But—"

"I said no."

"All I ask is—"

"*NO!*" The blood-curdling sound exploding from her throat echoed sharply through the trees and the mouth of the cave behind her. The black robe suddenly dropped from her shoulders, and her appearance changed completely. Her long black hair became thick snakes slithering up and down her arms and breasts. Her sharp features turned a translucent white. Her skin peeled away, dropping to the rocky ground at her feet and revealing a skeletal mask with holes where the eyes had once been, a triangular-shaped jagged hole in the center of her skull, and long, sharp teeth protruding from her gaping mouth. Oozing sores and bloody scabs clung stubbornly to bone and whatever soft tissue remained.

A horrible foulness filled the area.

Aaron found it difficult to breathe. Coughing, he backed up and turned around. He couldn't look at the creature anymore. The sight of it made him want to puke. He bent over and tried breathing through his mouth and soon found that the foulness had eased up. After a few deep breaths, he began breathing normally again. He straightened and took in some fresh air. The foulness had mysteriously disappeared. After some hesitation, he gathered the courage to turn around.

Both the vile creature and the cave had vanished.

He stared into the darkness, expecting the cave to return. It did not. A heavy, numbing silence was all that remained. That and his desperation.

"Please," he muttered at the darkness, hoping with all his heart that the situation was not hopeless. "You can take my spirit back. Just take my nightmares away…please…I'll give you my spirit, this time forever…"

Silence.

"Please?" His voice had become a broken whisper.

The vast darkness sneered at him. He rubbed his eyes, hoping he might be able to see more clearly. His heart thumped wildly as he waited for them to clear.

When he opened them again, he discovered he was strapped down in a hospital bed. Strange figures in white and a pale blue moved quietly around his bed and past the doorway out in the hall.

Darkness filled his head as well as his vision. Moments later, it dimmed, turning gray, then silver, then vividly clear. The instant it cleared, his entire world spun with disgusting images. He couldn't turn them off, so he closed his eyes again. But this time, the images showed even in the darkness.

He was lying in the middle of the street, his heart thrashing as he watched three punks covered with tattoos, earrings and facial studs approach him. He tried getting up but found that he couldn't move. He had no feeling at all in his lower body and was forced to lie there while they bent over him. All three were glossy-eyed and had silly expressions on their young faces. The two boys watched him curiously while the girl reached for his pockets.

"Man, you fucked up my old man's ride!"

He closed his eyes and prayed for everything to disappear. When he opened his eyes, Lana and a strange man stood over him, kissing and groping one another.

"*No!*" He tried twisting, turning over so he couldn't see, but only succeeded in making everything dark again. He was crawling on his stomach in the darkness, ghastly images flying past his vision at a frantic pace. Loud, unpleasant voices ricocheted in his brain, shattering his nerves.

What's his name, Lana?

I no longer want you.

Lana, please…

What are you gonna do, Aaron? Keep me here against my will? It's over. Can't you understand that?

He buried his face in his arms, but the images would not stop. Even in his head he could see his arms reaching out for her…reaching out as Lana pulled away, her face red, her wet, blood-stained eyes filling the sockets.

Grabbing me won't change things, Aaron!

I won't let you go!

He covered his ears, but the voices would not stop. Neither would the images. Lana moved closer, her face flushed, her eyes straining the sockets. Closer, closer…until he could actually feel the intense anger oozing from every pore in her body, the seething hatred…

He watched numbly as his hands thrust forward, pushing her into the wall. The back of her head slammed into the wall with a sickening crunch, causing the plaster to crack in every direction as she gasped and passed out. She stayed in that position only for a second or two before her knees gave out, and then she slid slowly to the floor. On her way down, the side of her head whacked the corner of

331

the table, and she collapsed silently to the floor. She sat slumped forward, her eyes closed, blood seeping down the side of her head and covering her neck and the front of her blouse.

"*No!*"

He covered his eyes and saw Lana sitting behind the wheel of her car, screaming and gasping, her blood-soaked eyes bulging as his hands closed around her throat.

Blackness filled his mind, and the images changed once again.

Lana lay on her side on the car seat, her face white, her bluish tongue dangling out between her parted lips.

More blackness…

Brittany Michaels lay on her back on the cold pavement, struggling and gasping beneath him. He watched in utter terror as his hands closed around her neck, choking the life out of her.

A big, broad man in a long white jacket stood trembling on a roof, gazing in horror at the parking lot eight stories below. *Jump, Doc. Do the plunge. Free yourself!* His eyes bulged and his face turned deathly white an instant before he lurched forward and jumped, his skull splitting open and splashing the hard pavement ten feet around him.

Blood. Brain tissue. Skull fragments.

Lana's head split open, her throat swollen and blue.

Brittany's eyes bulging in their sockets.

Roxie's face turning blue.

The nightmares had become a rollercoaster gone berserk. His screams burned like large chunks of broken glass as they tore out of his throat.

In the midst of the bloody chaos, two long-haired figures dressed in white approached him. One of them held a syringe in her hand.

The following blackness was comforting but couldn't match the terror overwhelming him as the cave suddenly reappeared, swallowing him up one last time.

CHAPTER FORTY-ONE

Two days later, as Roxie stood behind the cash register, handling a transaction, the cowbell above the front door clanged a few minutes before eleven.

It was Henry. The sight of him made her forget what she was doing. She immediately struggled to pull herself back to the present. Her surroundings—the store, the register, the customer facing her—had dimmed into the background.

Money in my hands. The register. A customer. Snap out of it...

"Miss?" Her customer, a short, elderly lady with platinum hair and blue tinted glasses, looked worried. "Anything wrong?"

"Everything's just fine." She smiled in embarrassment. "I just had a brain blip."

The woman chuckled. "I get those all the time. Wait till you're older."

Roxie forced herself to concentrate on what she was doing. It was tough, and she knew things would stay that way—at least for a while. The memories of the previous week would remain with her. The nightmare she'd faced with Aaron was bad enough...but what happened with Henry was something else entirely.

Was it love? She had no idea. She and Henry had been very close for years. Although they'd discussed marriage at one time, neither considered a permanent arrangement more important than their individual careers. It was much easier to distance oneself by concentrating on business rather than make a commitment that would most definitely change everything.

However, the last few days had turned everything around. For all she knew, the gratitude she'd felt for Henry for saving her life—not once, but twice—had metamorphosed into something else—something she'd never seen coming.

She knew it wasn't gratitude she'd felt when she visited Henry at the hospital. When she gazed into his beautiful dark-brown eyes, she saw something she'd never seen before. She thought she'd seen it during her short, ill-fated marriage right after college, but this was different. She was convinced this was the real deal—the necessary ingredient for a lasting relationship. She sensed that what she saw in Henry's eyes was something you see only when you've fallen in love.

But that wasn't the only issue she had to face. What happened the week before would quite possibly stay with her the rest of her life. She'd survived a terrible ordeal. But since it hadn't killed her, she decided that, according to Nietzsche, it had made her stronger. It would probably give her nightmares for years to come, but it certainly wouldn't kill her. As Henry told her, nightmares were necessary. Without them, there could be no past, no memories, and no balance. Nightmares gave you stability; they made you aware that you were a survivor.

I am *a survivor,* she told herself. *I* am *much stronger than I once was. And the nightmare Henry and I endured will forever be an important part of my life. But it will be all right because it was shared. A shared nightmare miraculously turns into something else...something not quite so bad...something that, over the years, transforms into an event that book-marks a special time in one's past.*

She hoped that, in time, she could look back on it with not quite as much dread as she felt now. Time would work its magic to turn the experience into something that appeared to have happened in another life.

Besides, she couldn't dwell on such setbacks. She had things to do—a business to run, a life to live. And she intended to do it with all the gusto and courage she could find within herself.

Henry was leafing through an old hardbound copy of *Pickwick Papers* at one of the bargain bins next to the large, tinted window.

"How's the head?" She tried not to frown at the sizeable bump beneath the small square bandage hiding the gash in the center of his forehead.

"It's still there," he said.

She smiled and found herself reliving the moment. But she caught herself. *Focus,* she told herself, *and move on. Concentrate on the here and now. You'll never forget what happened, but also don't forget that you survived it all.* "I never thought you were a Dickens fan."

He closed the book and regarded it for a moment or two before replacing it carefully on the shelf. "I've read half a dozen of his books, as a matter of fact. It was years ago, but I managed to plow through them. I even enjoyed most of them..."

"What brings you here?"

336

Henry didn't reply right off. She could tell by the sudden grimness on his face that he was about to give her some bad news. "Aaron Grill slipped into a coma last night. He's been unresponsive ever since. They don't expect him to pull out of it."

"My God..."

"You okay?"

"Let's go into the office."

She led the way and collapsed in the chair behind her desk. She sat in silence, rubbing her temples while struggling to keep the tears from coming. She hadn't known Aaron very long and didn't understand why such news should hit her so hard. Maybe it was because she felt sorry for him and knew that despite everything, Aaron really was a decent guy.

"Need something?" he asked.

"I could use a shot of something really strong, but since I'm at work, I'll have to settle for a cup of strong coffee."

He went over to the pot. "Is this stuff fresh?"

"Sandy made it about twenty minutes ago."

He poured two cups and brought them over.

Roxie blew on the hot brew and had a tiny sip. "Can you tell me what happened? Doesn't something like that usually follow a head injury? Or severe trauma? Or organ failure?"

He sat and put his cup on the edge of the desk. "Normally, it does. But as we both know, this situation has been far from normal. From what Austin told me, Grill was severely agitated since he'd regained consciousness. They said he was fighting the restraints for three hours after they

337

brought him in. He was crying and whimpering and kept calling out his ex-wife's name, as well as the name of that young woman he strangled outside Shannon's nightclub. He was babbling non-stop, was incoherent and didn't respond to their efforts to pull him out of it. They had no choice but give him strong sedatives to calm him down and help him sleep."

"Did he have any ill effects from your shooting him with your Taser gun?"

"Definitely, but not the way you're probably thinking."

"What do you mean?"

"When I zapped him in your kitchen, I also zapped his demon. I'm sure it didn't hurt or affect her, but I'm also sure she didn't take kindly to it."

"What do you think she did?"

"We can't be certain, of course, but my guess is that she left him."

"That's a good thing, isn't it?"

Henry turned grim and didn't speak right off. "If she left his body, she also left her damage in her wake. As a result, everything would revert back to how it was before she'd taken control."

"In other words, Aaron went right back to how he originally was."

"Yes, but with a few drastic changes. While she was manipulating him, she had total control of his mind, which included his memory. He could only remember what she wanted him to. And now that she's gone..."

"His memory's back. That can't be *that* bad, can it?"

338

He sighed. "When his memory returned, so did every damned thing she ever did to him. Unfortunately, Grill won't realize a demon was in control when all that mayhem happened. He won't even know a demon was responsible for all that damage. He'll see himself committing the murders, and that's what'll eventually destroy him."

"Then he's trapped in his own mind?"

Henry's nod was slight.

"Poor Aaron…"

"We've done all we could possibly do," he said. "But we *were* facing a demon. Remember that."

"She isn't the only one, is she?"

He frowned. "Of course not. They're all over the damned place. Why do you think the world is in such a horrible mess?"

"I guess it doesn't help that not very many people even believe in them."

"That works in the demons' favor. It makes it much easier for them to get away with their evil crap when no one's paying attention."

As she watched him, she suddenly realized that he'd been through so much more than she originally suspected. "Henry, how do you know so much about demons?"

He shrugged. "I saw combat. Anyone who's seen combat has seen evil in all its forms. Everyone knows that where there's evil, there are demons."

She didn't reply. She found that she was very grateful he was able to come back relatively unaffected.

"Just be glad you were able to live to tell about it," he said after a short silence. "You were very fortunate you weren't as unlucky as his ex-wife…or Brittany…or Doc Hill."

Henry was right. She *was* glad. And fortunate. And she knew that from now on, she'd never take anything for granted.

"I have you to thank for that," she said.

"You've already thanked me."

"Henry…" She realized right then that he just couldn't grasp how much this meant to her.

"Friends help one another," he said softly. "They even save one another's life—if it comes to that."

"But—"

"You would've done the same for me, right?"

"Of course."

As they stared at one another, Roxie she saw the same thing in Henry's eyes she'd seen before. But this time, she sensed that he might be seeing the same thing in her eyes.

"What are you doing for lunch?" he asked suddenly, very softly.

"Actually, I haven't thought much of it. Why do you ask?"

"What would you say about some Italian cuisine?"

She glanced at the wall clock. It said 11:15. "It's a little early, but…"

"I can come back."

She didn't want him to come back. That meant that he had to leave, and she didn't want him to leave. She suddenly realized that she didn't want

340

him to leave her ever again. "Why don't we just skip out right now, if you'd like?"

"That sounds good."

"I *am* kind of hungry. I didn't have much of a breakfast."

"Then let's go. Sandy won't mind, will she?"

She smiled. "I'm sure she won't."

"Good. If she did, I'd feel guilty."

"Really?"

He laughed. "No, but I didn't want to come across sounding like a selfish asshole."

"You're not selfish," she teased.

He laughed but didn't reply.

They continued gazing at one another. Once again, she saw the same thing in Henry's eyes. Did this mean he felt the same thing? Or was she just imagining it?

"I'll be right back." As Roxie got up and left the room, she realized she was grinning just as stupidly as she did in high school, when a popular boy flashed a smile in her direction. It made no sense. Here she was, a thirty-four-year-old divorcee and business owner and acting just as silly as she was when she was fifteen.

Was this the beginning of genuine love? That transition period when a solid friendship, coaxed along and strengthened by a shared trauma, suddenly blossomed into something bordering on the unexplainable?

As she went out into the store to tell Sandy her plans for lunch, she hoped with all her heart that she was right, and that time would soon become their best friend.

OTHER WORKS BY DAVID BERARDELLI

THE APPRENTICE
THE WAGON DRIVER
DEMONCHASER
DEMONCHASER II
STEPPING OUT OF MY GRAVE
ESCAPE CLAUSE
FATAL INNOCENCE
THE FUNNY DETECTIVE
JUST A SIMPLE ERRAND
COLORS
WORKING FOR A MOB BOSS
AND DARKNESS FELL
AFTER DARKNESS FELL
DEMONCHASER III
IN ANOTHER REALM
BEYOND RECOGNITION
LOOKING FOR A DEAD GUY
HUNTING THE TALL BLONDE
FAVOR FOR A FRIEND
A RIPPLE IN TIME
YESTERDAY'S JOURNEY
AWAKENED

Titles available through:
www.fiction4all.com